Libby felt self-conscious each time she thought about having been cared for so intimately by a complete stranger.

She was disturbed by the warmth that twisted in her belly each time Jack touched her, clinical and professional as those encounters had been.

"I really appreciate all you've done for me," she told him. "Now, if you'll just tell me where my clothes are, I'll get dressed. Then you can take me home."

Jack stared at her, then shook his head as he swallowed. He leaned toward Libby, and his green eyes held hers as he spoke.

"I can't do that, Libby. For all intents and purposes, you were killed last night. And for the time being, you're going to have to stay dead."

Dear Reader,

We're back with another fabulous month's worth of books, starting with the second of our Intimate Moments Extra titles. *Night of the Jaguar* by Merline Lovelace is the first of a new miniseries, Code Name: Danger. It's also a fabulously sexy, romantic and suspenseful tale of two people who never should have met but are clearly made for each other. And keep your eyes on two of the secondary characters, Maggie and Adam, because you're going to be seeing a lot more of them as this series continues.

Award-winner Justine Davis presents one of her irresistible tormented-but-oh-so-sexy heroes in *Out of the Dark*, another of her page-turning titles. And two miniseries continue: Kathleen Creighton's Into the Heartland, with *One Good Man,* and Beverly Bird's Wounded Warriors, with *A Man Without a Haven.* Welcome bestseller Linda Randall Wisdom back to Silhouette with her Intimate Moments debut, *No More Secrets.* And try out new-to-contemporaries author Elane Osborn, who offers *Shelter in His Arms.*

As promised, it's a great month—don't miss a single book.

Enjoy!

Leslie Wainger
Senior Editor and Editorial Coordinator

Please address questions and book requests to:
Silhouette Reader Service
U.S.: 3010 Walden Ave., P.O. Box 1325, Buffalo, NY 14269
Canadian: P.O. Box 609, Fort Erie, Ont. L2A 5X3

SHELTER IN HIS ARMS

ELANE OSBORN

Published by Silhouette Books

America's Publisher of Contemporary Romance

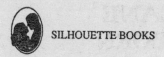

SILHOUETTE BOOKS

ISBN 0-373-07642-8

SHELTER IN HIS ARMS

ELANE OSBORN

is a daydream believer whose active imagination tends to intrude on her life at the most inopportune moments. Her penchant for slipping into "alternate reality" severely hampered her work life, leading to a gamut of jobs that included, but was not limited to airline reservation agent, waitress, salesgirl and seamstress in the wardrobe department of a casino showroom. In writing she has discovered a career that not only does not punish flights of fancy, it demands them. Drawing on her daydreams, she has published three historical romances and is now using the experiences she has collected in her many and varied jobs in the "real world" to fuel contemporary stories that blend romance and suspense.

To Skip, Jenny and Travis. For loving me, even when dinner wasn't on the table or the clothes weren't folded, and for not letting me give up.

Chapter 1

Play dead.

The whispered order was a haunting melody, echoing through Libby Stratton's mind in the silence between each throbbing pain.

Play dead.

She had no choice. She had to obey the whispered words. Her backward tumble into the shallow culvert had ended when her head struck something hard and unyielding, leaving her too stunned to do anything but stare up at the black leaves silhouetted against the night sky.

A ray of light reached out from the darkness. Heavy footsteps followed the filtered beam, announcing the approach of Libby's abductors. Every aching muscle in her body tensed, urging her to leap to her feet, to flee or to fight, but only her eyes were capable of motion.

The whisper, *play dead,* warned her not to blink against the onslaught of light.

Libby had years of practice at holding her eyelids still. Pretending that she was staring through her camera's viewfinder, she drew a quick gasp of air while the footsteps came closer, then held her breath and widened her eyes as if she were waiting for the perfect moment to press the shutter release. When a gloved finger probed the side of her neck, Libby remained motionless, unflinching, even when a harsh whisper rasped loudly in the silence.

"If she has a pulse, I can't find it." The chilling touch slid from her flesh. The next words echoed farther above her. "Well, I'm glad that Nick recommended you, Minetti. Next time we meet, I just might have a more lucrative assignment. In the meantime, I suggest we get out of here."

The light shifted. Libby continued to act the corpse as she listened to the footsteps recede. Not until the flashlight's glow disappeared completely did she allow herself to close her eyes and to drink deeply of the faintly salt-scented air.

She was alive. Alive, despite the three shadowy forms that had only an hour earlier come up behind her as she focused her lens on the moon hanging above the Golden Gate Bridge. Alive, in spite of her fierce but futile struggle with the monster who had grabbed her and bound her hands behind her back. Alive, even though she'd been gagged and thrown into the back seat of a car before she'd had the opportunity to tell these men she had no way of identifying any of them, so it wasn't necessary to kill her.

The sudden rumble of an engine roaring to life made Libby jerk. Her eyes flew open to blackness as she listened to the engine's growl fade slowly into the night. Her muscles relaxed one by one. They were gone. She had won the game. They actually believed she was dead.

Play dead.

The deep-toned whisper seemed to ring out in the silence. She had obeyed the order blindly, self-preservation crowding out all other considerations. But now, with the men gone and her bound hands and bruised body leaving her with little to do but think, all of Libby's unasked questions clamored for attention.

Who *were* those men? And why had at least one of them been convinced she should die? What about the brute who had grabbed and bound her, tossed her in the back seat of the car, only to pull her out on a deserted spot where the sea whispered below? And what puzzled her the most, why, after towing her up a sharp rise, had her captor issued that barely audible order?

As Libby's aching head began to spin, to pound with brutal force, she shut her eyes. There was no doubt his words had saved her life. Against her closed lids she recalled the glitter of moonlight on the gun in his hand just before a loud "pop" had made her jump, sending her into a wild backward somersault as a second shot rang out.

The hard object that now pillowed her head so harshly, rock or tree stump she wasn't sure, had dealt such a sharp blow to her head that she was sure the only thing that kept it from splitting in two was the gag tied around it. The pain was so severe that she could barely feel past it, other than to sense a vague ache in various muscles. For all she knew, one of those bullets had found their mark.

But what did it matter, after all?

Even if her hands weren't bound, the slightest movement made her head swim, rendering the darkness before her even deeper. The moist night air was already condensing on her body, chilling the flesh beneath her thin blouse as a malignant lethargy seeped into her limbs. If someone didn't come to her rescue soon, she was certain to die where she was, bullet wound or no bullet wound.

Someone.

Libby's mind played with the word. Her thoughts were fuzzy, as if she'd had one too many margaritas while waiting for dinner to be served. *What* someone? Did she actually expect anyone to know that she was hidden above a lonely road, listening to the ocean roar far below?

A hero would know, she supposed. An omniscient, all-powerful hero.

The silliness of this notion made the corners of Libby's lips attempt a smile. The gag stilled the motion, so she frowned as she sternly reminded herself that there were no such things as heroes, at least not in *her* life.

Certainly not the man who had run off twenty-seven years earlier, heedless of the child he'd fathered. Nor her grandfather, who had anchored her world for the first seven years of her life. She'd once cast him in the role of hero, but he'd left, too, slipping out of life quietly in a way that no respectable warrior would consider.

Then there had been her husband, Dan. Handsome, charming—everything a hero should be, until life refused to give him what he wanted, turning Dan from white knight to black villain.

Memories of those dark days combined with the frigid moisture blanketing her body to make Libby shudder violently. Through the mental fog formed of disappointment and pain, she told herself yet again that there were no such thing as heroes. And anyway, she didn't need one. She was more than capable of going to her death alone. Alone and unafraid.

If only she weren't so cold. And so very thirsty.

Libby was suddenly, sharply aware of the sound of water trickling softly somewhere nearby. She was equally conscious that she lacked the strength to move toward it so she could moisten the fabric that held her mouth open to the drying air. Her blood was barely pumping through her frozen limbs now, her breathing had become slow and shallow. The bravado that had momentarily lit a flame within her breast had flickered then died. Suddenly, she no longer felt like being alone.

Unbidden, an image appeared on her closed eyelids, a face set into an oval picture frame, a strong, masculine face possessing eyes that held wisdom and courage, a mouth that spoke of humor and passion.

Libby concentrated on the image until the frame disappeared and the features took on a lifelike animation. As she watched firm lips curve and dark eyes crinkle at the outer corners, a surge of warmth flowed through her veins. Willing the vision closer, she imagined strong arms around her, felt heat and strength melting into her form, then let the illusion lull her into oblivion.

The northern tower of the Golden Gate Bridge formed an orange H in the sky above the fog. Night was graying into dawn as Jack McDermott downshifted to take the last exit before the highway moved onto the bridge, encouraging the vintage VW bus up the hill and around the first curve.

He was fully awake now, no longer drugged with sleep as he'd been when he scrambled for the pealing phone, then tried to make sense of the clipped orders hissing in his ear. Even now, those words made him scowl as he peered through the mist, searching for a specific turnout, one he hadn't taken in years.

His heart raced with a sense of anticipation he hadn't tasted in months. The taste was bittersweet as adrenaline raced through his veins. The once-familiar sharpening of his senses sketched a taut smile beneath his dark mustache, a grimace that mocked all who had hinted that his career might be dead.

Dead.

The word recalled the urgent note in Matt's voice, *I don't think she's dead, but she might be hurt. At any rate, you've got to get to her as quickly as possible.*

The curve loomed up sooner than Jack had remembered, making him jerk on the wheel with his left hand and scowl as the fingers of his right hand were slower to respond. Even so, he made it into the turnout cleanly, leaving plenty of room for other cars to get by.

Not that too many people drove Conzleman Road during the week. On weekends, the artery winding along the edge of the headlands north of San Francisco Bay drew swarms of tourists to hike the towering cliffs and gaze past the bridge at the glitter of San Francisco. But in the middle of the week, especially in the chilly hours before dawn, it was a deserted spot.

The van shuddered to a stop in front of a wide tunnel leading into the hill. A wealth of memories lay on the other side of that dark passageway, but today Jack's mission lay elsewhere. Kicking open the door of his vehicle, Jack crossed the dirt turnout to climb the short, steep rise to the left of the tunnel. He stood on the crest, staring down into the gently sloping hollow that he and Matt had discovered in their preteen rambles, during simpler days when they'd played cops and robbers on the other side of the hill, dodging between the concrete bunkers that had once housed Nike missiles.

There was nothing simple about Jack's life now, a fact that struck home when he tightened the fingers of his right hand around the flashlight and tried to push the button with his thumb. For one agonizing moment, he thought his damaged nerves would once again refuse to obey. When the muscles finally responded, his lips twitched with bitter pleasure.

The strong beam flowed downward, filtering through the low branches to reveal the body Matt had described. Jack began moving, even as his focus sharpened on the crumpled shape. A tight smile rode his lips as his left leg took his weight with little protest. The therapy sessions had met with success there, at least.

The hill drew him down quickly. Two steps later, his left foot slipped on a rock, waking a dull ache in his nearly healed knee. Scowling at his body's betrayal, Jack bent forward to search for signs of life in the motionless female at his feet. Nothing moved. She was curled in fetal position, facing down the hill. Jack reached out to touch her arm and found the pale blue sleeve gritty with dirt, the fabric thin and damp. Sliding the material up her arm, he encountered smooth flesh that was as cold as porcelain. With eyebrows knit in concern, he pressed his fingers to the side of her neck, relaxing slightly when he found the slow, thready beat.

Hunkering down, Jack studied the inert form, his mind churning with a dozen unanswered questions as to how this woman might be connected to Matt's case, the case that had once been Jack's. Her appearance told him little. She was very slender. Her mud-dampened jeans hugged slim legs that displayed the well-defined musculature of a dancer or a runner. Dark, shoulder-length hair fell in wavy tangles that clung to pale flesh and prevented him from seeing her face.

And at the moment, Jack reminded himself, what the young woman looked like and how she'd come to be here were beside the point. He needed to assess her injuries, then figure out how to get her to safety. Leaning forward, he brushed soft curls from her face to stare at the small oval bruises that marked the ivory skin of her cheek above and below the gag tied at her mouth.

Noting that his touch hadn't aroused so much as a flicker from her thick, black lashes, Jack drew his hand away. Indecision brought his eyebrows together in a scowl. If he moved her, he risked causing her further harm, yet he couldn't let her lie here in the misty air and go into shock. Staring at the helpless individual he'd been called upon to rescue, Jack's eyes were once more drawn to the gag around her mouth, then to what appeared to be a necktie binding her hands.

In that instant, years of training kicked in, galvanizing him into action. After forcing the handle of the flashlight into the hillside so that the beam illuminated her body, Jack loosened the knotted fabric at her wrists. Stuffing the binding into his back pocket, he then attacked the rolled handkerchief that had been wedged in her mouth and tied behind her head.

The feel of something warm and wet made him draw his hand back. He knew the smell of blood. He stared at the dark stain on his fingertips for a moment, then bent forward again to tug at the tight knot and the strands of hair trapped within the cloth.

At the very moment that the twisted mass finally came loose beneath his prying fingers, a muffled moan escaped the young woman, a moan that became frantic muttering as the head that had been so still moments before began to toss wildly from side to side. Cupping his hand gently over the curls atop her head, Jack leaned close.

"Hush, now," he crooned in her ear. "Take it easy. You're going to be all right."

Wide, dark eyes opened, then blinked against the light. In the brace of seconds it took Jack to swivel and lower the angle of the flashlight's beam, she moved. A quick, jerking effort flipped her around and pulled her into a crouched position before Jack had time to react. When she put her hands on the ground as if preparing to leap to her feet, he placed a firm hand on her shoulder.

"Hey, not so fast."

The wide eyes lifted to him again, shining like the darkest of sapphires in that pale, pale face. Ebony waves fell in a knotted mass to her shoulders, framing delicately sculpted features that seemed frozen, emotionless, except for the terror in those large eyes.

She reminded him of his youngest sister, Kate. Not that they looked alike. Kate's hair was the brightest of reds, her face longer, more narrow than the soft oval features lifted to his. It was the bravado that attempted to hide this woman's fear that made him think of his sister, reminding Jack of the times he'd soothed Kate when she'd woken from a bad dream. Reaching slowly across the narrow space between him and the wide-eyed waif opposite, he touched her cheek.

"Hi there, Princess." His sister's nickname seemed to fit. The young woman's eyes widened, almost as if she were accustomed to being called that, encouraging Jack to go on, "You're safe now. I've come to get you out of here. You can trust me."

As those unblinking eyes gazed at him, Jack tried to gauge her strength. The fact that she'd managed to move so quickly told him that she hadn't sustained any serious injuries to her back or neck. But that didn't mean she was capable of climbing back up that rise then scrambling down seven feet of loose dirt.

Trust me, he'd said.

Jack's lips twisted in a self-mocking smile. Three months ago he would have simply lifted this slender thing in his arms, then carried her to his waiting vehicle. And that was what he'd do now, if he didn't have to worry that his left leg might give out in the middle of the operation, very likely causing him to stumble and drop her.

Self-pity, Jack?

He frowned the question away and concentrated on the way those thickly lashed eyelids were beginning to droop. Her body's slight sway gave further warning of fading energy. All right, he told himself, so the days for heroic moves are gone for the moment. You'll just have to come up with some other form of action.

Jack placed both hands on her shoulders. When questioning eyes lifted to him, he asked, "Do you think you can stand?"

She blinked, then stared up at him for a moment before nodding slowly. Very slowly.

Jack reached for the flashlight with his left hand, clicked it off and stuffed the handle in his back pocket. Enough morning light spilled down the hill for him to see that her eyes were beginning to close again even as he curved the fingers of his good hand firmly around one slim arm just below the shoulder. He tried to do the same with his right hand. When the fingers were slow to obey, he barely wasted time for a scowl before wedging his hand beneath her armpit.

He stood, gently urging her to her feet, as well. A moan escaped the woman's lips. As Jack drew her forward, bracing her body against his, soft breasts pressed against his chest. Slim arms slid trustingly around his waist, bringing long legs in contact with his in a way that made his pulse leap, then race. Jack swallowed and frowned away his body's reaction. If nothing else, it was highly inappropriate, given the circumstances.

"You need to put your arms around my neck," he said in a voice that was far more gruff than he'd planned.

He felt her body stiffen, then her hands lifted to his shoulders and slipped around his neck. The sensation sent a warm chill down his back, and again Jack frowned. "Hold on," he ordered. When she complied, Jack leaned forward and adjusted his hold on her waist. Drawing her up, he clasped her against his chest, letting her feet dangle above his as he made his way up the gentle slope, figuring that if his knee gave out, this position would allow him to lower her to the ground without harming her.

At the top of the rise, he found he was nearly out of breath so he did just that, letting her slender form slide down his until she was bearing her own weight. She leaned into him, though, her hands still clasped lightly behind his neck, half buried in the hair that curled onto the back of his neck.

Something about her gentle touch made Jack's already pounding heart race. His breathing became more ragged. Forcing himself to take long, slow breaths, he trained his attention on the sight of the Golden Gate Bridge above the pink-tinted fog. From this spot on the hill, he could look down on the wide span as it moved across the opening to San Francisco Bay. Across the water and to his left, the city rose from the morning mist, tall structures climbing the hills like clusters of white crystals tinged pink by the rising sun.

Lovely imagery, Jack, but this is hardly the time or place, Matt's voice chided. Irritating, how his cousin's voice intruded. Even more aggravating was the fact that it spoke the truth. All these months off the job had definitely taken the edge off his street-sense.

And the moments spent gazing at the scenery was sapping what little strength the young lady in his arms had left. Already the hands behind his neck had unclasped and slipped onto his shoulders.

"Hey! Princess," he whispered.

Jack felt her jerk. He looked down just as she tipped her head back to look up at him from beneath a puckered forehead. Her dark eyes had a less than focused gaze, as if she were staring through, rather than at him. Then slowly her lips curved.

"Yes?"

The word was a raspy whisper, a husky note that caressed Jack's senses. Tightening his jaw, he spoke quickly.

"We still have a ways to go. You have to hold on tight, so that I can get you out of here and somewhere safe."

Thick lashes fluttered. The dark eyes gazing into his widened with an expression that spoke of dawning wonder. Her full lips eased into a soft smile, then parted to breathe a word that sounded like "hero" just before she lifted her warm mouth to his.

It was a very brief kiss. Only the barest touch of flesh against flesh before Jack felt the form in his arms go limp. Her hold on his neck slackened and the sudden dead weight made him stagger. Vaguely surprised at the heat lingering on his lips, Jack struggled to remain standing as he wondered just how he was going to get this unconscious woman to safety without at least the slight cooperation she'd offered before.

With her sagging body pulling against his grasp, Jack did the only thing he could. Propping her up with his good hand, he bent forward and balanced her midsection on his shoulder. As he stood, she stiffened and squirmed as she released one pitifully small cry of protest. Then, even as he said, "Relax, Princess," her body went slack once more.

Jack struggled down the steep hill to the VW bus waiting in the mist. By the time he'd managed to settle her limp body on the bed that took up the back half of the vehicle, his knee was throbbing and he was sweating. Neither was a good sign. After months of strenuous rehabilitation, he shouldn't be left feeling like a freshly cooked noodle after such a minor search-and-rescue mission.

Clenching his jaw against the signs of weakness, Jack turned the key in the ignition, and the elderly engine coughed to life. This was only a minor setback, he told himself as he made a U-turn and started back toward Highway 101 North. It was only a matter of time before he would return to work, disproving the diagnosis of possible permanent nerve damage to his hand. It would be his greatest pleasure to make a mockery of the doubt he'd heard beneath the jolly cries of, "Hey, when're you going to get off your fat butt and get back on the job?" each time he'd dropped into the station. He was *not* going to allow his career to end just because a single mistake had put him in the path of a couple of well-aimed bullets.

Libby heard the word, "Princess," again. A deep, pleasant-sounding voice pleaded, then demanded that she wake. A frown tightened her forehead. She didn't want to wake up. She was warm and she wanted to go back to her dream, where the father she'd never known cradled her in his arms and crooned soft apologies for the past and sweet promises for the future.

It was such a nice dream, especially after that horrible nightmare in which huge shadows had whispered threats of death, where a black dungeon had swallowed her up, a giant had hit her on the head and the knight who'd come to save her had rudely tossed her over his shoulder like a sack of flour.

"Come on, you *have* to wake up."

The voice held a note of urgency as a firm hand closed over her shoulder and shook her twice. Libby took a deep breath, then forced her eyes open. She found herself in a room filled with pale sunlight. Two faces, blurred twin images, floated before her. As her eyes slowly focused, the features solidified into one wide, strong face, a face that seemed vaguely familiar.

"Princess," the man repeated. A scowl shadowed the dark green eyes gazing into hers as he went on. "Talk to me. Tell me how you feel."

Worry edged his words. Libby wanted to give the man a breezy reply to ease his concern, something along the lines of, *I feel like I've been forced to eat balls of cotton, then placed into a burlap bag and beaten to a near pulp. Other than that, I'm fine.* But her tongue felt so thick that all that came out when she opened her mouth was, "Thirsty."

The word was a croaking whisper. The effort to speak it left her throat raw and made the dull pounding in her head flare to a piercing throb.

The bed rocked, and the face moved away. As Libby tried to follow the man with her eyes, she realized that she wasn't on a bed, after all, but on a couch upholstered in faded rust-colored corduroy. She noticed that maple paneling covered the walls and that an afghan crocheted in orange, yellow and brown squares blanketed her inert form, before she once more focused her attention on the man across the room.

He turned from what appeared to be a kitchenette and began walking toward her, carrying a glass. Libby didn't need his gruff voice urging her to, "Try and sit up," to make her take action. The memory of water trickling a tantalizing tune mere feet from her gagged, parched mouth pulled Libby into a quick sitting position.

Too quick.

As soon as she became vertical, her vision blackened and a merry-go-round motion joined the throbbing in her head. She felt herself sway. Then a strong arm encircled her shoulders, offering support and stability, and for one moment she basked in the sensation of total safety, of complete warmth. A warmth that was shattered when something cold and wet splashed onto her chest.

Libby gasped. The sound was followed by a deep-voiced, "Damn!" from the man who held her.

As he eased her onto the pillows, Libby squeezed her eyes shut, only to open them when the man said, "I'm sorry. The blasted glass slipped out of my hand."

He was glaring at the fingers of his right hand as if they had committed some unforgivable crime. Libby wanted to tell him that the water hadn't hurt her, but the dry ache in her throat stilled the words.

She heard the man say, "Let's get you situated better before we try this again." He then drew her forward, and strong arms once again held her against that wonderfully firm chest as pillows were plumped behind her. Each time she took a breath, she drew in a heady scent that combined salt and musk, as soothing as it was stimulating to her senses. Warmth flowed through her veins, softening the tension in her aching muscles as she was once more eased back against the cushions, this time at a more upright angle.

"There. Is that better?"

His husky voice made Libby blink. The green eyes gazing into hers were once again shadowed by a frown, but their expression spoke of concern, not anger. Above them, a shock of medium brown hair, glinting with red highlights, fell in thick waves onto the man's broad forehead.

She blinked again, suddenly struck by a strong sense of familiarity, by a memory of this face that seemed older than the misty hours since he'd come to her rescue. The impression was lost, though, as she recalled his question and managed a nod in reply.

The man's scowl eased as he rose and turned. Libby watched him cross the room again, this time noting long, strong-looking legs encased in well-worn jeans, and a lean torso enshrouded in a nubby ivory sweater. When he pivoted back to her, she took in the impressive width of the man's shoulders before her attention was once more captured by the glass he held in his hand.

Libby stared at the tumbler as he came toward her, saw the surface of the liquid rise and fall as the man worked his way past a brown chair and lowered himself to the edge of the couch. She watched the water tilt toward her as the rim of the glass moved closer to her lips.

Heaven. The pure taste, the soothing chill, the wonderful moisture that brought liquid soothing to raw membranes. Such a simple thing, water was, until you had to go without it.

"Slow now," the deep voice cautioned. Libby gave a scant nod as she fought her desire to swallow the contents in one breathless gulp. Placing her hands around his fingers, Libby urged the glass to tip up completely so she could catch every blessed drop.

By the time she had drained the last trickle, her eyelids had fallen shut. She slid the tumbler from her lips, then slowly lowered it to her chest, holding it there as she savored her release from torture.

"Hey, Princess. You can't sleep. Not yet."

Princess. Her grandfather used to call her that. Libby smiled, then opened her eyes to stare at the mouth that had revived the memory of nearly forgotten moments in time, those days of innocence when she had taken for granted this feeling of being looked after, cared for.

Set beneath a thick brown mustache, this man's mouth was wide, well shaped and framed by deep, curving lines that might have been dimples in a younger man. Not that this one was old. Somewhere in his early- to mid-thirties, she guessed.

And once again, he seemed to be familiar. His features teased her memory in a way that sent warm, slow pleasure flowing through her. Moving her eyebrows together, Libby recalled gazing into this rugged face, barely lit by the gray dawn. A thrill of recognition had raced through her then, too, as if she'd been waiting for just this man to come to her aid.

But when Libby began searching her mind for the source of this feeling, she found that her thoughts were a place full of dark shadows and threatening whispers that banished all sense of warmth. The man's features slipped out of focus as Libby's head again began the merry-go-round spinning that urged her to give up the attempt to think, to let her eyelids drop shut.

"Hey!" The word was a sharp command, followed by, "Wake up."

Libby's eyes popped open as the man went on, "You have to stay alert. Talk to me. Tell me your name."

Orders. Libby had learned the hard way how important it was to respond quickly to such sharply issued commands. Old conditioning instantly tightened her muscles and made her blink as she mentally reached past the pain behind her eyes for an answer.

"Libby," she said at last. "Libby Stratton."

"How old are you?"

Libby lay very still for several seconds until the answer formed. "Twenty-six."

"How many fingers am I holding up?"

A blur of flesh appeared before her eyes. She squinted before she replied, "Two."

"Good." A pause, then, "Can you tell me what happened last night?"

Libby gazed into the man's dark green eyes, drawing on the strength she saw there to keep herself from slipping back into the horrifying dream that his question conjured up.

"Yes," she said softly. "Someone tried to kill me."

"I gathered that." His tone was dry. "Do you have any idea who or why?"

Libby shook her head, winced in pain, then replied, "There were three of them, but I never really saw their faces. One wore a hat. He kept whispering that I might be an undercover cop, insisting I was trying to take pictures of them with infrared film, or some such nonsense. I...I tried to explain that I was only there to photograph the moon, but one of the others held his hand over my mouth and wouldn't let me speak.''

Libby found herself breathing harder as she recalled the suffocating pressure of that huge hand, the fingertips digging into her cheek as she tried futilely to break his hold long enough to make use of her self-defense skills.

''Where did this happen?''

The sudden query pulled Libby back from the remembered horror. She blinked and answered, ''The dock at the Sausilito Yacht Club, just below the bridge.''

The eyes boring into hers were once again shadowed by a frown as the man nodded slowly. Libby felt a frown of her own form as it occurred to her that he was not the only one in the room with questions. She had several of her own.

In the first place, how had this man found her at that deserted spot? Surely he hadn't just happened to stumble upon her, tucked up off the road as she had been. And why did he seem so very interested in how she'd come to be on that hill? For that matter, where was she and—

''Who are *you?*''

The room echoed with the suspicion in her words. The man's eyes widened in surprise. Then he smiled, a generous smile that etched deep creases at the corners of his eyes, that revealed even, white teeth beneath his dark mustache. Despite her doubts about who this man was and why he'd brought an obviously injured woman to this place instead of taking her to a hospital, his smile made Libby feel warm all over, as if the sun had suddenly come out from behind a cloud to shine on her with all its might.

''My name is Jack McDermott,'' he replied.

McDermott.

Libby stiffened as a harsh voice rose from the dregs of her nightmare to whisper that name, pulling her back to those heart-stopping moments when she had stood on that dark pier, trapped in an iron embrace, listening to three men plan her death.

Chapter 2

The sudden pressure of Libby's fingers on Jack's was his first clue that something was wrong. The second was the terror in her dark blue eyes.

"What's the matter?" he asked.

When she jumped and drew back against the nest of pillows, Jack realized just how sharply he'd spoken. Reminding himself that he was talking to an injured woman, not one of the thieves or murderers he was accustomed to questioning, he repeated his query in a softer tone.

"Libby, tell me what's wrong."

Confusion tightened her features. "Your name. They—" She broke off, then shook her head. "He—" She stopped again. Another shake of her head sent a dark tendril twisting down the side of her face as she took a deep breath and started again.

"Someone mentioned your name last night. It was the man who always whispered, the man in the hat, the one who said I had to die."

Libby's words made Jack's pulse race. Years of training urged him to interrogate her more closely about this man. But as he opened his mouth to do so, he noted the way Libby shivered beneath the afghan. She had answered his primary questions about who she was and how she'd happened to be with Matt last night. Before he asked her any more, he had to calm her fears.

"Listen to me, Libby," he said softly. "You're safe here. One of those men last night was an undercover police detective going by the name Tony Minetti. His real name is Matthew Sullivan. I..." He paused, and his lips tightened as he went on, "I'm also a cop. Matt's working on the case I was pursuing before I was shot."

Jack watched Libby's eyes narrow. He lifted his eyebrows and said, "I can show you my badge, if you'd like."

The pressure of Libby's fingers on his relaxed slowly. Her shoulders rose and fell in a sigh before she replied, "That won't be necessary. I remember now. The man in the hat who mentioned you said that they wouldn't have been forced to meet in the dark if you had died like you were supposed to."

A gnawing bitterness lifted Jack's lips in a caricature of a smile. He'd been told by more than one person that he was too stubborn to die, had heard it said over and over as he languished in his hospital bed. But he *had* lived, a rather ironic situation, since he now faced the very real possibility that he might never again be fit to perform the very work that gave his life meaning.

"I'm glad to know that my being alive inconveniences them," he said quietly.

"Who?"

Libby's question brought Jack's thoughts back from the months of pain and the doubts that still surrounded his full recovery. He looked into her eyes and softened the smile he was sure must be acid-tight.

"That's far too long a story to go into now. For the time being, just know that you showed up at the wrong place at the wrong time last night. You're just lucky Matt was there to keep you from being killed, that he managed to call me so I could find you.''

Jack watched Libby nod slowly, as if she was mentally digesting his words. Her nods grew slower, and her eyelids began to droop. When her hands slid from his, Jack turned to place the empty glass on the old steamer trunk that served as a coffee table, then looked back to see that her eyes had closed once more.

''Libby!''

Her head jerked up. Her eyes flew open to gaze into his as he bent toward her, searching their sapphire depths.

''Too damn dark,'' he muttered finally.

''What?'' she asked.

Jack lifted one corner of his mouth. ''Your eyes. I'm supposed to study your pupils, to see if they're the same size.''

Again Libby seemed to be turning his words over in her mind. Her eyes were wide, unfocused. Taking advantage of the way she gazed past him, Jack leaned forward. He stared into those midnight depths for a very long moment, a moment in which his breath seemed to mingle with hers. Jack's attention dropped to Libby's mouth. Full and softly parted, her lips called to mind that feather-light kiss she'd pressed to his lips in the gray light of dawn, made him feel once more the warmth that had remained on his flesh even after her mouth had slipped from his.

A frown tightened Jack's forehead. This was hardly a professional way to examine a victim. Forcing his attention from those tempting lips, he studied the tiny freckles that dotted Libby's slender nose and peppered her high cheekbones, only to realize that he couldn't for the life of him remember just what it was he was supposed to be looking for.

A blush blossomed beneath those sparse freckles. Jack lifted his eyes to Libby's again to find them veiled by half-lowered lashes and staring at some point near the center of his chest.

"Well, are they?" Libby breathed.

Jack had no idea what she was referring to.

"Are they what?" he asked as he backed away from Libby's flushed face, trying to make his suddenly clouded mind pick up the threads of their conversation.

When Libby raised her eyes to gaze into his, he remembered. "Oh, your pupils," he said. Lifting his shoulders in what he hoped looked like a casual shrug, Jack went on, "Damned if I can tell. I guess I'll have to leave that for Shawn to determine."

"Shawn?"

"My brother. One of them, anyway. Shawn's a doctor. I called him about you earlier, and—"

Jack broke off at the sound of a knock at the door, then finished speaking as he got to his feet, "And if I'm not mistaken, that's him now."

As Libby watched Jack move toward the door, she drew in a deep breath and prayed for her cheeks to cool. It was too much to hope that Jack had missed seeing her face redden. However, she consoled herself, there was no way for him to guess at the reason behind her sudden blush. Most likely he would simply assume it was some odd reaction to her injuries.

And, in a way, it was.

If she hadn't just gone through the most terrifying experience of her life, if her head hadn't continued to throb to the beat of a dozen drummers, she was sure she would have recognized his features earlier. It was just her dumb luck that he had been so very close to her when she finally remembered the face in the oval frame that hung on her bedroom wall, the photograph of the man who bore an uncanny resemblance to Jack McDermott.

Libby had never expected to meet this person in the flesh. As far as she knew, the man in the picture was solely the product of her imagination, a result of her early experiments in combining several negatives to produce a composite image.

Using photos of several men, some famous and some not, she'd blended a hard-edged facial structure that defined strength of will with eyes that held the ability to dream, to care. To the lean, sculptured cheeks she'd added deep dimples that hinted at a sense of humor, and she'd carefully chosen a wide, full mouth that promised both tenderness and passion. Only Jack's mustache and the deep cleft in his blunt chin was missing from her photograph.

"So, this is the patient."

A strange male voice interrupted Libby's thoughts. No doubt it belonged to the doctor Jack had mentioned. With a shiver, Libby drew the afghan closer, reluctant to have another stranger examine her. She wanted to forget the horrors of the night, as well as the dream image she'd childishly called upon to ease her fears. She wanted to tell these men that she didn't need a doctor, just a short nap before she'd be up and on her way, but suddenly it seemed beyond her power to speak, difficult even to form coherent thoughts.

"Libby. I need you to look at me."

The quiet voice startled Libby into opening eyes that had somehow fallen shut without her notice. The man standing next to the couch had red-blond hair, and a matching mustache like Jack's, but was half a head shorter.

"I'm Dr. Shawn McDermott," the man said as he took a seat on the edge of one of the cushions.

Libby found that an annoying ring in her ears garbled his words. It took several seconds for her to interpret them and a few more to form the simple reply, "Hello."

"I'm here to take care of your bumps and bruises, and make sure there isn't anything seriously wrong with you."

The only words Libby heard clearly were, "Take care." They made her body go rigid. *You're a big girl,* a voice rasped in her mind. *If you're going to live under this roof, you'll have to learn to take care of yourself.*

Libby managed to push herself higher on the pillows as she shook her head. "I don't need anyone to take care of me. I'm just fine."

The strength of her voice pleased Libby, made her almost believe the words she'd uttered. The man in front of her shook his head, obviously not buying her protest.

"Well, you don't *look* fine." Shawn smiled. "I promise this won't take long, and I'll do my best not to hurt you."

The note of concern in his words and the worry shadowing his light blue eyes made Libby wonder just how badly injured she appeared to be. She soon had a pretty good idea. As Shawn's examination proceeded, she found that hardly a square inch of her body didn't hurt to some degree. The doctor's touch, gentle though it was, made each sore spot seem momentarily more noticeable than the piercing throb in her head. And that pain soared to torturous proportions when he softly probed the back of her skull.

"Nasty bump," Shawn said a moment later as he eased Libby back to the pillows. "The cut's still oozing, but it's not deep enough to need stitches. You did a pretty good job of cleaning it up."

Libby stared blankly at the man. By the time she realized that his last words had been directed at Jack, Shawn was shining a bright light in her eyes.

"Head hurts, does it?"

Libby managed to nod as she blinked away from the narrow beam that flashed first into one eye, then the other.

"How about nausea?"

Libby hadn't given any thought to her stomach one way or the other. "No," she replied.

"Good. I'm going to give you something for your headache, then I'll leave you alone so you can get some rest."

After swallowing the pills, along with another glass of water, Libby collapsed against the pillows, closed her eyes and listened while the two men discussed her welfare.

"I'd say she probably has a concussion," Shawn said. "A slight one, most likely, but you can never tell. It might be a good idea to have her spend twenty-four hours at the hospital, where the nurses can watch over her."

Libby shook her head at this. She tried to open her eyes, but her recent battle with the bright light made her eyelids feel too heavy to lift. She parted her lips to tell these men that she *was* a big girl, to repeat her earlier claim that she didn't need *anyone* to watch over her, but before she could utter one syllable, Jack asked, "Are you really worried that this might develop into something serious, or are you just being cautious?"

"Just cautious."

"Then she stays here. I'm stuck with her until I get further orders."

A long pause followed these words, a pause in which Libby's heart took a painful twist. *Stuck with her.* Just like her aunt and uncle had been after her granddad had died and her mother had abandoned her.

The pain in Libby's chest hardened into anger as she opened her mouth to inform these men in no uncertain terms that she had no intention of burdening Jack with her presence. Her efforts to speak produced only a pitiful moan, and this was lost in Shawn's reply.

"All right, but I want you to wake her at least once an hour. If she doesn't respond, you get her to a hospital. Now then, how are *you* doing? Is that leg coming along?"

Shawn's voice seemed to fade on each word as the irresistible urge to sleep pulled at Libby's mind. Jack's answer sounded far away and even dimmer, but there was no missing the anger that sharpened his voice as he replied, "*I* am just fine. Libby's the one I brought you out here to see. So, tell me if there's anything I should . . ."

Light. A blazing shaft of brightness beat upon Libby's eyelids and made her frown. She rolled her head from one side to the other, then winced at the dull throb produced by the motion. Lord, she was stiff. And still so tired. She didn't want to get up, but she had to. Nature was calling, summoning her with an urgency that could not be denied.

Libby opened her eyes and blinked against a harsh glow. Her frown tightened as she squinted at the wide window in the wall beyond the end of the couch, trying to figure out just where she was. Then memory came flooding back. She was at Jack McDermott's place, and it was Jack's window that framed the wide stretch of blue ocean.

The brilliance of the yellow-pink sunset striking her eyes made them close. Sunset. Libby vaguely recalled waking several times, remembered being urged into semiconsciousness by a deep voice and gentle hands, then lulled back to sleep by a low whisper that could have been Jack's voice or the muted rush of waves onto the shore.

Forcing her eyes open, Libby glanced around the room. No sign of Jack. She thought of calling to him, then remembered those words, *I'm stuck with her until I get further orders.*

Defiance tightened her jaw. This man was *not* stuck with her. *No one* had to take care of her, not now that her head felt better. A dull ache still pulsed behind her eyes, but the wild, piercing pain was gone.

Which only made Libby all the more aware of another source of discomfort.

The water she'd consumed the night before was pressuring her to search for relief. Looking around again, Libby noted that Jack's place seemed to be just one large room beneath a high, sharply pitched ceiling. The living area and the small kitchen were divided only by the line where the orange shag carpet gave way to faded mustard-colored linoleum.

The rough-hewn table in the kitchen and the rustic look of the room's wood paneling made her fear that the facility she was searching for might turn out to be a shack outside with a half-moon cut into the door. Shifting to look around the corner of the couch, the sight of a ladder lead-

ing up to a large platform and the wood stove sitting in the
opposite corner next to a sliding glass door, reinforced her
concern.

Things were getting desperate. Scooting herself up, Libby
gazed over the back of the couch. An open door revealed a
room floored in more yellow linoleum, a floor that supported an old, clawfoot bathtub. At last. Just the room she
needed. Now.

Or as soon as possible, anyway.

Libby's muscles protested the moment she tried to lift the
afghan from her body. Her legs cramped in protest at being forced to bear her weight, and as she rose, her head began to spin slightly. She ignored the sensations. None of
this could be allowed to interfere with her very pressing
mission.

The bathroom floor chilled Libby's bare feet as she entered the small room. Without thinking about it, she shut
the door behind her and just as automatically performed as
nature was so persistently requesting. It wasn't until she
stood before the sink, washing her hands, that she happened to look into the mirror and saw the visible evidence
of her night of horror.

The face staring back at her was nearly as white as the T-
shirt she wore. Her pale flesh was marked by an angry
scratch over her left eyebrow and several small bruises on
her right cheek. Studying the faint ovals, Libby could almost feel the hand that had smothered her screams before
the gag was tied in place.

She squeezed her eyes shut tightly in an attempt to block
out the memory of fighting for her breath behind unyielding fingers, trying to banish those moments of terror to the
back of her mind, reluctant to let them darken this room
where fading daylight flowed through the small window to
her left.

After a moment, Libby opened her eyes. This time her
attention was drawn to the oversize T-shirt that hung so
loosely from her shoulders. She frowned. Not only did she

not own a white T-shirt, she certainly didn't possess a garment as large as this.

Glancing down, Libby could see that it hit her mid-thigh. As she stared beyond the hem at the bruises marking her legs, her stomach tightened. Quick heat flooded her face, not at the sight of the ugly purple welts, but at the knowledge that Jack McDermott had seen them, too, and so much more.

The T-shirt was obviously his. Logic told Libby that removing her fog-dampened clothing and getting her into something dry had been the correct thing for him to do. She should be grateful for his actions, relieved that she at least still wore her bra and bikini panties. But the embarrassing fact remained that Jack McDermott had seen more of her body than any man had in over five years.

Even as a blush scalded her cheeks, Libby chided herself for being so silly. Jack was a policeman. He'd only been doing his job. And besides, the bruises blooming on her legs, arms and who-knew-where-else would hardly be likely to arouse any kind of lustful attraction.

Libby lifted her gaze to the mirror again, and almost laughed out loud. Not exactly a fetching sight. Dust robbed her black hair of all shine and the tangled knots made it look as if a pair of birds had tried nesting atop her head. Smudges of dirt marked the tip of her nose and grazed the side of her jaw.

No wonder the man feels he's "stuck" with you.

The echo of Jack's words put an abrupt end to Libby's moment of amusement. The man's tone had made it clear that he had no interest in her beyond carrying out his responsibilities as a cop.

Chagrin twisted through Libby as she recalled how her bruised mind had placed him in the role of savior, of hero. Of course, this did have a logical explanation of sorts, Libby reminded herself. Just before she'd blacked out, she had conjured up the photo of her "dream man." When she'd opened her eyes to find Jack holding her, in the dim light of morning her semiconscious mind must have recognized Jack's resemblance to that made-up face.

Not that this was any excuse for the mortifying things she had said and done next, of course. She didn't want to believe it, but her memory was painfully clear on this point. She had actually called the man "her hero" before she kissed him, then fainted.

Fainted! Libby shut her eyes tightly and gritted her teeth. In a life full of foolish mistakes, she had never managed to do anything so pitifully idiotic before. And it only got worse. At least when she'd done that she'd had the excuse of being only half-conscious to explain her irrational behavior. This had not been the case when she'd awakened on Jack's couch, then continued to respond to his ministrations like some feeble damsel in distress.

Libby opened her eyes and again focused on the image in the mirror. As she tried to untangle a particularly large knot of black curls, she consoled herself with the knowledge that Jack McDermott could not possibly be aware of the ridiculous thoughts and feelings that had run rampant through her mind and body these last few hours. However much he'd seen of her bruised flesh was far less embarrassing than the idea that he might have a hint about the fantasy behind her whispered words about heroes. Libby knew better. The *last* thing she needed in her life right now was a hero.

What she *did* need was a bath.

Libby released the twisted strand of hair and turned to the oversize tub. With thoughts of warm water soothing her aching muscles, of soap and shampoo washing away the dirt, along with some of the terror that made her insides shiver each time she thought of how close death had come, she turned on the faucets.

The moment Jack stepped in the door, he noticed that no slender form huddled beneath the faded afghan on the couch. With a muttered oath he turned toward the kitchen, kicking the front door shut behind him as he moved, calling her name as he placed the bags of food on the table.

"Libby!"

No response. A quick search of the floor behind the orange sofa revealed no sign of a collapsed body. Jack didn't bother to glance up at the sleeping loft, for he knew that Libby was far too weak to climb the rough-hewn ladder. That left only one other area to check. Turning, his long legs took him to the bathroom door where he raised his hand to knock. The sound of splashing water made him call out, instead.

"Libby?"

The splashing stopped. He heard the soft hum of liquid whirling down the drain before a small voice replied.

"Jack?"

"Of course, it's Jack. What the hell are you doing?"

"Taking a bath."

Her tone of voice seemed to ask, "What do you think I'm doing?" as if having a woman take over his bathroom was an everyday occurrence for him.

It wasn't—hadn't been for far too long. Despite this fact, or perhaps because of it, Jack found himself picturing Libby Stratton stretched out in that old tub, her pale pink flesh softly shimmering in the surrounding liquid.

The image made Jack's blood run hot. He'd undressed the woman and draped her in one of his shirts with quick efficiency. Now he clenched his jaw as he found himself recalling far more about Libby's slender form than he remembered consciously noting.

The fact that he was reacting to this woman as a male animal, rather than as a cop, made Jack's jaw tighten further. Libby Stratton was not in his house to ease his needs in any way, he reminded himself, but as a refugee from danger. The fact that her sapphire eyes were easy to get lost in, that her long legs seemed expressly made to wrap around a man and that her gentle curves invited close exploration, could not be allowed to make him forget that she was in his bathroom, in his life, as a result of mistakes he had made.

And if not for the slow recovery of his injuries, he would be back at work right now, fixing this mess himself.

Anger and frustration curled Jack's left hand into a hard fist and sharpened his voice as he raised his voice to be heard through the door.

"You shouldn't be in there."

A longer silence followed these words. Jack opened his mouth to say more, but the door gave a loud snap then jerked inward so quickly that he could only straighten away and stare at the woman in the doorway.

Libby's damp hair fell in rich ebony waves to her shoulders. The oversize T-shirt clung to her slight body, making Jack instantly aware that she was no longer wearing the bra he'd left on her the night before. She stood straight, one slim hand gripping the doorframe. Anger flashed in the dark eyes narrowing up at Jack.

"I apologize for taking over your bathroom," she said angrily.

Jack stared at Libby, fighting the impulse to grab her shoulders and shake her for those heart-stopping moments when he'd entered and found her missing. For that would hardly be fair. She could have no idea how important it was to him that he oversee this little part of the case to the best of his abilities. Slowly he shook his head.

"Look, you can use the damn thing anytime you want. But you have a concussion. You shouldn't be up on your own, taking the risk of becoming dizzy and perhaps falling. The last thing you need is to crack your head again."

"No," she said tightly, "that probably wouldn't be a good idea."

"Then why did you come in here on your own?"

Libby lifted her eyebrows. Some of the anger in her eyes faded as she replied. "I *had* to."

Her expression made it clear that she expected those three words to explain everything. They only made Jack shake his head in confusion.

"I *had* to," she repeated pointedly. "Given the urgency of that need, it didn't occur to me to wait for someone to provide an escort." She paused to shrug. "And once I got in here, I decided I might as well take advantage of the tub."

Jack got the picture at last. Heat rose to his cheeks as he took two steps back.

"Oh. I see. Well. I guess there was no harm done. I'm . . . sorry I wasn't here to help."

To help *what?* a mocking voice in his head asked. Help her undress for her bath? Help yourself to another peek at that tempting body? The warmth in Jack's cheeks became a deep burn. He gestured toward the kitchen table as he spoke quickly.

"I went out to get some dinner. I thought it was about time you woke up and tried to eat something. Are you hungry?"

For the first time since Libby had opened the bathroom door, she appeared to relax. Her eyes widened as she breathed, "Oh, God, yes. I'm famished."

She released the doorframe as she spoke, took one step toward him, then one more before she stopped. A look of dismay crossed her features and the expression in her eyes softened into an unfocused gaze.

Jack reached for Libby as she began to sway, grabbed her, then swung her up into his arms. She was very light, yet his left leg protested slightly at the added pressure, a dull ache which was rendered almost unnoticeable when he became aware of the soft breast that brushed his chest as he crossed the room.

When he reached the couch and bent forward, Libby's free hand came up to grasp his neck as he lowered her to the pillows. Now both breasts teased him with their cushioning warmth. Clenching his jaw against the sudden tightening of his loins, Jack released Libby, then sat down next to her on the edge of the couch. He shifted uncomfortably as he watched her eyelids flutter open.

"Well," she said. "Do I have great timing, or what?"

Jack stared into the innocence in her dark blue eyes. Realizing she was unaware of the effect she had on him, and wanting to keep it that way, he shrugged. "Well, now you know why I was so upset to find that you'd gotten up by yourself."

He hadn't meant his words to sound like a reprimand, but apparently that was how Libby took them. Her eyebrows moved together and her eyes narrowed to a mutinous glare as she said, "I did *not* faint this time, you know. I just got a little dizzy."

Her words reminded Jack of the way she'd roused herself from a near stupor the night before to insist, "I don't need anyone to take care of me." He found himself wondering what would cause a lovely young woman to be so defensive. The next second, he told himself it was none of his business. It was enough that he recognized a case of wounded pride when he saw it.

After all, he had a nearly terminal case of it himself.

Libby Stratton was a sharp reminder that he had no official place in the case that had brought her into his house. And the stiffness resulting from his early-morning exertions was making it clear that he wouldn't recover full use of his leg or hand as soon as he wanted. Not that any of this was an excuse to take his frustrations out on her.

"Hey." Jack placed one finger on Libby's cheek. "I'm not angry, just concerned. I'm responsible for your welfare, you know."

She stared at him darkly. For a moment, Jack thought she might try to stand again, might attempt to stomp off in a huff. Then slowly her frown faded. She sighed as she lifted her eyebrows.

"Are you going to send me to bed without dinner?"

Libby's attempt at easing the tension between them brought a smile to Jack's lips. "No," he replied. She smiled back, then started to get up. He placed a gentle palm on her shoulder. "I think it would be safer if I brought the food to you."

"Oh? Dinner in bed?"

"More like dinner in couch," he said as he stood.

Libby felt her bright smile fade the moment Jack turned and started toward the kitchen. The fact that her head was still spinning, even though she was half reclining, bothered her deeply. She could only hope that the food would ease the last of the "giddies," for as soon as she was finished filling her empty stomach, she planned on insisting that he take her home.

It would be lovely to stay here one more night, she admitted, to bask in the sense of security she found in just being near this man. But danger resided in this cozy cabin, too, and not only because of the searing gaze Jack had leveled at her as they'd faced each other at the bathroom door, a look that had made her cling to the doorframe in order to keep her knees from buckling.

The threat came from herself, from the way she grew warm and weak each time this man's dark green eyes looked into hers, the way her pulse raced at his touch and the persistent manner in which her poor bruised mind tried to fool her into believing that beneath Jack's angry outbursts lay the strong but sensitive man she thought she'd given up looking for.

Hero worship.

Libby recognized the malady with ease. Her psychologist believed that Libby would always suffer from it to some degree, given the unresolved issues with the father she'd grown up imagining, longing for. Libby had no reason to doubt this prognosis. After all, the woman's counsel had led Libby out of the darkness following Dan's self-destruction and her former husband's attempts to pull her down with him, a painful process that had taught Libby that hero worship was most definitely a lousy basis on which to form a relationship.

The rattle of paper made Libby blink away these musings and see that Jack had set several fragrant white bags on the coffee table. She took the wrapped burger he handed her, and they sat across from each other as they ate, Libby propped up on the wide couch with the afghan over her bare legs, Jack sitting in the worn leather armchair facing her.

The hamburgers were juicy, the fries deliciously greasy and the chocolate shake thick and frothy. Libby refused to allow herself to compute the meal's fat count as she ingested the food, just as she tried to ignore the fact that dinner conversation was noticeably absent. By the time she'd eaten half of her burger, the silence had become so uncomfortable that she began to look for any excuse to break it.

"You know," she said at last, "it just occurred to me that I have no idea where I am."

Jack looked up. "My place," he said with a shrug. "Or to be more accurate, my older brother's 'hippie hideout'."

This reply raised more questions than it answered. "Okay," Libby said as she lifted her shake. "I don't suppose you'd mind telling me just where 'your place' is located, and what you mean by 'hippie hideout'?"

Jack gave her one of his rare smiles, brilliant white teeth beneath a lifted mustache, bracketed by those deep creases. "You're just across the highway from Muir Beach," he said. "In a small place that Mike bought back in the sixties, right out of law school. After his practice grew and he moved into more palatial digs in Sausilito, Mike kept this as a place to get back to his 'roots.' He likes to think he hasn't lost any of those sixties' ideals, so as you might have noticed, he refuses to redecorate."

Libby glanced around the earth-toned room, noting the area beneath the loft where two sets of shelves crammed with books, albums and framed photographs formed an L-shaped nook around an orange beanbag chair. The sliding glass door next to this area was curtained in strands of yellow and orange beads, and beyond that, a cast-iron stove sat atop a raised stone hearth.

Truly a blast from the past.

Returning Jack's smile, she popped her last french fry into her mouth and relaxed against the pillows. A moment later, she frowned as she realized she was already battling the desire to drift off to sleep.

With a tightening of protesting muscles, Libby fought the weariness stealing over her limbs. Now that she was clean and warm and at least half-alert, she was aware of how odd her situation was. She felt self-conscious each time she thought about having been cared for so intimately by a complete stranger, and was disturbed by the heat that twisted in her belly each time Jack touched her, clinical and professional as these encounters had been.

More than anything else, she wanted to go home, where she could moan or cry out in pain as she felt the need, where she didn't have to play the part of the "big girl," where she could curl up and recover alone.

"Well, dinner was delicious," she began. When Jack nodded his reply in deference to the fact that his mouth was full, she went on, "I really appreciate all you've done for me. Now, if you'd just tell me where my clothes are, I'll get dressed. Then you can take me home and have your couch, and your bathroom, all to yourself."

Jack stared at her, then shook his head as he swallowed. He put the remaining half of his second burger on the table alongside him, placed his elbows on his knees and leaned toward Libby. His green eyes held hers as he spoke.

"I can't do that, Libby. To all intents and purposes, you were killed last night. And for the time being, you're going to have to stay dead."

Chapter 3

"*S*tay dead?"

Libby stared at Jack as her heart raced. Slowly she shook her head as she went on in a strangled voice, "No. I have to get home."

"Libby, you can't do that." Jack spoke as if he were reasoning with a small child. "While you slept, I talked to my chief. Tomorrow morning, a cop pretending to be a hiker will "find" your body. By noon, the coroner's van will arrive to remove an apparently full body bag. By five-thirty, your death will be on the evening news."

Each sentence was a blow to Libby's chest. With this last bit of information, she felt as if her heart had been forcibly stopped.

"Why?"

Jack's frown formed a deep furrow between his eyebrows as he sent her an assessing gaze. "To protect Matt," he said at last.

"Matt?"

"Yes." Jack nodded. "I told you about him. The undercover cop who pretended to shoot you."

Libby could only blink uncomprehendingly. Jack stared at her another long moment then sighed and reached for his shake.

"Look," he said at last, "it's a long and complicated story you've fallen into, but I suppose you deserve to know all of it. Are you familiar with Foresters Restaurants?"

Libby shrugged. "I've heard of them. They're a bit too pricey for me to be *familiar* with."

Her reply seemed to ease some of Jack's tension. The corners of his mouth sketched a smile, but the expression didn't reach his eyes as he said, "One of the owners, Frank Forester, recently stood trial for murdering his wife, Marie."

When he paused, Libby nodded. "I remember. He was found guilty, but on the way to the courthouse for sentencing, Forester was killed by a police officer. If I remember correctly, Forester had somehow gotten possession of a gun, and before he could be stopped, he had shot the two cops who—" Libby halted, then took a deep breath before going on. "You were one of those cops."

"Right. I was wounded. My partner, Gary Halston, was killed."

Jack took a long pull on his straw. He held the cup in his hands, elbows resting on his knees again and stared at the container as he went on.

"Gary handed the D.A. what we felt was an open-and-shut case of a man who covered the fact that he'd killed his wife by staging a robbery. It turned out not to be so simple."

Jack paused as he lifted his eyes to Libby's. "Forester's twenty-year-old daughter, Louisa, came to us and insisted that her father had been framed."

The words hung in the air for several seconds. Libby gazed at him, then lifted one eyebrow. "I would imagine that's a pretty common claim."

The corners of Jack's eyes crinkled slightly. "And sometimes a legitimate one, if you believe detective novels and TV cop shows, that is." All hint of a smile faded as he shook his head. "In most cases, I would have shrugged the claim off, but the girl was pretty convincing. Her father's lawyer, Adam Monroe, backed her up. That was pretty hard to ignore." His lips twisted wryly. "For three years, Adam Monroe was my father-in-law. Despite the problems I had with his daughter, Adam treated me with complete fairness. He's also one hell of a lawyer, with a reputation for strict ethics."

Libby brushed away the inappropriate questions flitting through her mind about the woman who had been Jack's wife, and concentrated on the matter at hand.

"Did the lawyer say *why* Forester was being framed?"

"I went directly to Frank for that information," Jack replied. "When I visited him in jail, I was served a long involved tale about an agreement to run dirty money through the two Foresters restaurants. Frank claimed that his brother, Robert, had been approached a year earlier to set up the system in the branch managed in Los Angeles. Six months later, Frank was convinced to do the same in the San Rafael store. Things apparently went smoothly until the third brother, Nick, let the cat out of the bag in front of Frank's wife. Marie demanded that the criminal activities stop. Shortly after, she was killed. Frank insisted that the man who'd set up the money laundering plan was the person responsible for her death."

A frown creased Jack's forehead and his eyes narrowed as he stared at the waxed paper cup in his hands. After a few seconds of silence, Libby asked, "And what did this person have to say about Frank's accusation?"

"He wasn't exactly available for comment." Jack's lips curved in a wry smile. "This silent partner of theirs is also something of an invisible man. According to Frank, the Forester brothers only met with this character in dark rooms or alleys, under circumstances that would conceal the man's identity." Jack glanced sideways at Libby. "Not your normal way of doing business, of course, but clandestine deals are often handled in a rather, well, clandestine manner."

Jack took another sip of chocolate shake. While he swallowed, Libby connected this information to the details she remembered reading so many months ago and began to see where the story was going.

"So this 'mystery man' supposedly set up Marie's murder in such a way that Frank would be accused?" Libby asked.

"That's what he claimed. And I must admit, on first hearing, the story sounded pretty farfetched. But the pain in Frank Forester's eyes when he spoke of his wife made me agree to look into his claims."

"What did you find?"

"Very little. The accounting records at the local Foresters came up clean, but that didn't surprise me. This sort of thing is normally handled with two sets of books, the bogus, totally innocent ones being the only ones available for public consumption. My questions to brothers Robert and Nick on the subject of dirty money brought quick denial. Again, no big surprise. But it was a different situation when I double-checked everything we had on Marie's murder. Under further scrutiny, some of the evidence looked less conclusive than it had the first time out. Evidence *I'd* helped provide."

Jack's words slowed. He stopped speaking after the last one and gazed past Libby. When the silence had stretched on for several moments she asked, "And you couldn't convince anyone else that Frank might be innocent?"

His eyes narrowed as they shifted back to hers. One side of Jack's mouth quirked up bitterly. "That's right. Gary disagreed with me vehemently. He stood by his original assessment of the evidence, as did my commanding officer and the D.A. During the trial, I was hardly surprised when the prosecutor avoided asking me any questions that might let me indicate my doubts about certain items. The defense team tried to introduce reasonable doubt on cross examination, but each time Adam's associate tried to bring up the contradictions I'd uncovered, the D.A. managed to get the line of questioning overruled. It must have appeared to Frank that I'd gone back on my word to help him."

Libby watched Jack's eyes narrow again as he stared straight ahead. "So he blamed you for his conviction," she said softly.

"Frank and a lot of other people."

The self-condemnation in Jack's voice rang loud and clear. Libby opened her mouth to assure him that he'd done all that he legally could, but before she could utter a word, he straightened his shoulders and spoke quickly, as if he'd read her thoughts and wanted her words of support to be left unsaid.

"Ironically, it's due to the fact that some unknown party managed to get a gun to Frank that my superiors decided his claims of a mystery man running a money-laundering scheme might warrant another look. So, that's how Matt came to be called from his division and placed undercover, and why he was on that dock last night."

Libby nodded slowly, her thoughts on something Jack said earlier, something that had triggered a memory buried within the morass of terror from the night before. She frowned, growing more frustrated by the moment as she tried to make the connection, until a name echoed in her mind.

"You said that Forester had a brother named Nick," she said suddenly. "The third man on the dock—*his* name was Nick."

She looked up, expecting Jack to be excited by this revelation. Instead, he smiled blandly. "We know all about Nick Forester. Matt approached the man over a month ago, posing as the former owner of a New Jersey restaurant that had been closed down by the vice squad. When Matt inquired about employment, Nick seemed thrilled to find someone to fill the flunky gofer job that had been his prior to Frank's arrest and death, when Nick was promoted into the position of manager of the Foresters in San Rafael.''

Jack's lips twitched into a wry smile as he shook his head. ''Believe me, Nick is *not* the brains behind any of this. After rather clumsily feeling Matt out on his willingness to slip onto the wrong side of the law, Nick hinted that Matt might soon be meeting someone who would ask him to do just that, and pay him well for doing so. No, whoever set all this up is very clever. Clever enough to use the confusing blend of media, cops and lawyers as cover to slip a gun into Frank's pocket as the man made his way up the courthouse steps.''

''Hold on a moment.'' Libby held up her hand in a gesture that matched her command. ''I thought you said Frank had never met the man in charge of the money laundering. Why would Frank take a gun from a stranger? If he had any idea that this was the man who had killed his wife and framed him for the crime, I would think Frank would have turned the gun on *him*. Why shoot you and Gary?''

Jack lifted his shoulders in a weary shrug. ''Captain Lowry feels I give this mystery guy too much credit, but I think the fellow planned everything down to the last detail. My theory is that Mr. Moneylaundering was in contact with Frank in some other guise, where he could convince Forester that both Gary and I had been bought, that I wasn't serious about getting the truth about Marie's murder out at all.''

A lopsided smile twisted Jack's lips as he glanced at Libby, then went on, ''Crazy as it may sound, I not only think our mystery man poisoned Frank's mind, I believe that he set it up so that Frank would try to off two cops with half the force looking on, knowing that Forester would be shot and killed himself, thus eliminating the last of Mr. Mastermind's problems.''

''Could he...'' Libby hesitated. ''Could the man you're after be a cop?''

"Absolutely. Or he could be someone who has a cop or two in his pocket. Like he had Gary."

Libby took in a quick breath. "Your partner?"

"Yes." Jack spoke softly, his tone as hard as steel. "An investigation of Gary's effects revealed that he'd paid off several large delinquent bills and a huge gambling debt right after he and I concluded the original investigation into Marie Forester's murder. This, along with evidence that Gary had arranged for certain items at the crime scene to point to Frank's guilt, made it pretty clear that my former partner was on the take."

Libby watched Jack frown, saw his face tighten in an expression that could be remembered pain or anger, before he turned to her and went on, "Anyway, it is precisely because the man we're looking for might be a cop, someone with easy access to an untraceable weapon, that the captain and lieutenant have limited the number of people who know that the investigation has been reopened. Matt was to meet our mystery guest last night. We've eliminated Nick for that role, so that leaves man-in-the-hat, which he no doubt wore to obscure his features. You're sure he was the one who furnished the tie used to secure your hands?"

Libby nodded.

"Well then, our mystery man may have unwittingly left us with a calling card of sorts." Jack stood, crossed the room to the shelves in the corner beneath the platform, then returned with a crumpled strip of silk.

"Normally matching such a mundane item to its owner would be impossible," he said as he placed the necktie on the trunk. Libby stared at it, fighting the absurd desire to shrink from the tangle of blue, purple and pale pink silk as she would a snake while Jack said, "But as you can see, this tie is quite unusual. It looks like it's been hand-painted. There's no designer label, which leads me to believe it may have been produced by a local artist. There's a remote possibility that we can find out who sells such items and trace our fellow that way. *Very* remote, of course. Our best chance is still to make sure the guy comes to trust Matt and pulls him into the moneylaundering part of the business.''

When Jack paused, Libby looked up. He gave her a slow smile that deepened the creases bracketing his mouth, revealing the dimples that time had elongated.

"You've already helped in that area," he said. "Matt was expecting to face some form of test before he would be trusted. Your presence on the dock, and Matt's apparent willingness to kill you, provided the perfect opportunity for my cousin to prove himself. However, just in case someone decides to verify your death, we have to have the media report it.''

Jack's smile faded and his last words held a note of don't-argue-with-me finality to them. Libby understood his concerns regarding his fellow officer's well-being, she even shared them. But she had worries of her own, responsibilities that had been forgotten in the world of pain and fear in which she'd dwelt for the past day. These demands now clamored for attention, robbing her surroundings of all sense of security.

As Libby visualized her life outside this place crumbling in her absence, the cabin's rustically paneled walls seemed to shrink inward, making her feel hopelessly trapped. Her heart began to race again as problems multiplied in her mind. To control her rising panic, Libby took a deep breath.

"How long?" she managed to ask.

"How long will you have to play dead?" Jack shrugged. "Matt should be pretty close to the man we're after. I'd say a couple of days. A week or two at the longest. But don't worry, you won't have to stay *here* all that time. The department will find you a safehouse, somewhere more comfortable.''

Libby was only half listening to Jack's reply. Above the sound of these words, she heard his deep voice repeat his earlier pronouncement: *You're dead, and you're going to have to stay dead.*

The wild pounding of her heart became painful. Two weeks was an eternity. Even though her work was beginning to sell well, she was still living the hand-to-mouth existence of most artists. In the following several days alone, she had five different sittings scheduled. Two weeks away loomed the deadline for the calendar proposal she'd been working on when she fell into this mad rabbit hole. If she missed those appointments and lost out on the fat fee she'd been hoping to receive from the calendar deal, it was very possible that the life she'd spent years piecing together in the wake of Danny's death would collapse under the weight of her financial obligations.

"No," she said. Libby shook her head as visions of the abyss she had barely escaped five years earlier blocked out all of Jack's careful explanation. "You can't keep me here. I'm a professional photographer. I have pictures to take, bills to pay. I have pets to feed. I have a *life*."

Jack frowned as Libby finished on an anguished note. He saw fear darken her eyes, knew he should sympathize with her plight, but he couldn't feel past the cold knot forming in his chest. Libby Stratton had taken him in completely, with her wide-eyed vulnerability and undemanding disposition. So unlike his ex-wife, Sheila, he'd imagined, whose needs and desires had come before anyone else's.

Now he knew better. "*You* have a life?" he started softly. "What about Matt? Did I mention that he is my cousin, my best friend? He has a life, too. A life that will be placed in deadly peril if you're spotted alive *anywhere*. Are you going to measure missed *photo opportunities* against the life of the man who saved yours?"

By the time Jack finished, he was shouting and Libby had retreated against the pillows. Moisture welled up in her eyes as she shook her head.

"No," she said. "Of course not. I'm sorry. I guess I'm not thinking too clearly."

These words, and the slight quaver in Libby's voice, softened the shell around his heart. That organ gave a quick twist as he ground his teeth and cursed himself. Libby didn't deserve this. She hadn't set these events in motion, wasn't responsible for placing Matt's life in jeopardy.

"No, I'm the one who's sorry," he said. "This isn't your fault."

Libby shrugged. "True. But you're right about Matt, about keeping him safe. My work will...just have to wait."

She glanced away. Jack watched her blink as she stared out the dark window. When she looked back at him, the moisture was gone, but deep concern still shadowed her eyes. "My cats," she said softly. "I keep them indoors. They haven't been fed since yesterday morning."

"Surely you have friends who'll feed them."

A confused expression pleated her delicate features. "Well, yes. But my friends won't know..."

Her voice trailed off. Jack reached over and took her hand. "About your sudden demise? They will by 5:00 p.m. tomorrow."

Libby stared at him blankly, then shook her head. "How? Nick searched me that night, but I'd locked my driver's license and purse in my truck when I parked near the dock. So if this plan of yours is to go right, the body that's found tomorrow will have to be reported as unidentified."

Jack closed his eyes. Damn. She was right. He'd have to call Sergeant Semosa and make that clear. This could have been a major slipup. It seemed that more than just his leg and his gun hand had gotten rusty lately.

"You have a point," he said. He opened his eyes again to see Libby take a deep breath.

"Look," she said as she leaned forward, "take me home tonight, while it's dark. I can set out some dry food for the cats, enough to last them several days. It'll only take a few minutes. I could grab some clothes, too."

Her tone dropped on these last words and her cheeks flushed pink as she glanced down at the white T-shirt draping her form.

Jack felt a quick heat rush to his own face as he frowned and replied, "*You* won't do anything except give me your address and directions for locating the cat food and which clothes to get. You have a head injury, remember?"

Libby looked up. "But you can't go into my house alone," she said. "In the first place, the keys to my pickup and house are at the bottom of the bay where they were tossed last night, along with my camera equipment. Second, there's a special trick to breaking into my house. Even if I gave you directions, you'd never get it right. And third, my cats would tear you to shreds."

Jack felt a smile tug the corner of his lips. Attack cats. Sure. He shook his head.

"You're too weak. You almost collapsed less than a half hour ago."

"I got a little dizzy," she corrected. "And that was before I ate. I'm much better now."

Jack studied Libby closely. Her skin was still pale, almost translucent, like the finest white silk. But a wash of pink lit her high cheekbones and her eyes no longer had that unfocused look.

Other than the story about the danger her cats posed, she had a point. If he went in alone, he ran the risk of breaking something. Eventually, someone might recognize the picture that would be run of Libby as "Jane Doe." If that happened and officers were sent to search her house, he didn't want to be the cause of any awkward questions. Besides, with her along, the two of them could get in and out more quickly.

"All right," he said at last. "I washed the clothes you were wearing and hung them on the line. They should be dry by now. I'll bring them in, then you get dressed quick, before I change my mind."

* * *

"Are you all right?" Jack whispered to the slight form standing in his loose grasp.

Libby's white face, framed in a dark tangle of curls, lifted to his. The midnight blue eyes blinked twice before she nodded.

"Of course."

Jack knew her words were a lie. Her voice was weak. Wearing a black sweatshirt of his over the clothes he'd found her in, Libby swayed slightly within the circle of his arms. As he tightened them, drawing her close to his chest, he felt her tremble.

Getting into Libby's backyard unseen hadn't been as difficult as Jack had imagined. They'd parked the VW bus a block from her quiet street in San Rafael, where rows of Victorian houses presented still-respectable faces, despite their advanced age. Libby's two-story home sat on the corner. The front yard was bordered by a white picket fence. Tall and narrow, with a bank of bay windows on one side and a round tower on the other, the house rose like a white shadow in the night.

Its location had made it easy for them to slip behind the bushes along the side street and climb over the six-foot fence, but it was obvious to Jack that this physical activity had taken its toll on the young woman. Fearing she might faint again, Jack bent his head to tell her that the expedition was off. Before he even managed to open his mouth, Libby leaned away from him and whispered, "Let's get this over with."

The strength in her voice surprised Jack into loosening his grasp. Libby slipped away from him, grabbing his hand as she turned toward the house, then led him to a small window set at flower-bed level. After she released his hand and knelt, Jack heard a snapping sound, followed by a low groan as the window opened inward.

When Libby turned and placed her feet in the dark rectangle, Jack grabbed her arm. He had no idea how long her strength would hold out, and he'd be damned if he'd let her down into the dark without being there to catch her if she got dizzy again.

"I'm going in first," he said.

It was a tight squeeze, but Jack managed to slip through the narrow opening. Following Libby's whispered instructions, he let himself slide down slowly until his feet touched the concrete floor of the basement. He had just stepped back to make room for Libby's dangling legs, when he felt a slight, almost gentle touch on his ankle, a touch that instantly became a searing pain, as if a thousand needles were digging into his flesh. His leg jerked, and the needles sunk deeper.

"Damn."

Jack gritted the word through clenched teeth, then forced himself to stand perfectly still, enduring the torture as he listened to Libby finish her downward slide.

"What's wrong?"

Her voice was very near. Jack said tightly, "I think I've met up with one of your watch cats."

"Oh, darn."

A tiny beam shot through the darkness. Jack glanced down as Libby used the flashlight he'd given her, the light revealing a large black cat crouched at his feet. Its paws bracketed his lower leg between the tops of his running shoes and the hem of his jeans as the animal blinked amber eyes into the light.

"Ripley, honey," Libby crooned as she crouched. "It's okay. This is a friend."

She looked up at Jack. "Bend forward and let him smell the back of your hand."

Jack followed directions, trying to ignore his discomfort as the cat's tiny nose made darting motions toward his knuckles. Slowly, he felt the needles withdraw. Ripley then neatly removed his paws from Jack's sock and placed them both on the floor, before lifting one to be licked by a dainty pink tongue.

"You've passed muster," Libby said, smiling as she stood.

In the dim glow of the flashlight beam, Jack saw her smile waver. His arm shot out to wrap around her as she began to sway.

"Oh, my," she said at last. "I guess I should move a little slower for a while."

Her body was soft, pliant in Jack's arms. In the ambient glow of the flashlight, her dark eyes shone up at him, her full lips parted, a temptation that pulled at Jack's career-long resolve to keep personal relations separated from the line of duty.

"What you're going to have to do," Jack growled, "is make yourself stay down here, while I go upstairs and feed the cats, then collect your clothes."

Libby's body stiffened. "Don't be ridiculous. Even with my taking it slowly so that I don't get dizzy again, we'll get out of here more quickly with me leading than if you try to work your way through my house alone. Look."

With that word, she lifted the flashlight and slowly moved the beam around the room. It lingered first on a collection of wigs, hats and feather boas draped on a nearby coatrack, then shimmered on a shield and sword hanging on the wall above a full suit of armor. The light danced on, glinting over a carousel horse, then illuminating an eight-foot gorilla and three naked mannequins, before coming to rest on a large table in front of them.

"The upstairs isn't quite as cluttered," Libby said as she stepped toward the table, which was littered with camera equipment. "But it's still something of an obstacle course. Believe me, you'll be better off with a guide."

She grabbed a backpack from the center of the table as Jack stood behind her, trying to make sense of what he'd seen.

"What *are* all these things?" he asked at last.

Libby looked up as she finished loading cameras and lenses into the nylon pack. "Props," she said simply, then zipped the pack shut and slung it over her shoulder. "Come on now. I think Ripley has had enough time to get used to you."

Jack followed Libby up a narrow stairway, wondering as he watched the black cat lead the way in the flashlight's slender beam, what kind of photographs this woman took.

"Wait a minute."

Libby's whisper floated back to him as they reached the top of the stairs. Jack stopped just behind her to see another cat waiting for them in the circle of light, this one pure white with the palest blue eyes Jack had ever seen. They gazed up at him, round and unblinking.

"Is this one going to attack my other ankle?" he asked.

"No." A combination of amusement and affection warmed her voice. "Barnum is the proverbial scaredy-cat, and I don't want you to spook him. He'll run away, hide and won't eat for days if I'm not here to coax him out."

"I see," he said. "So what do I do?"

"Nothing." The word held a note of concern. "Just stand there for a moment. Let him lead the way."

Jack watched the cat. It didn't move, just fixed him with those almost-colorless eyes and stared, while Jack tried not to think of the dull ache that had awakened in his knee, the warning that always preceded debilitating pain.

This mission of mercy was beginning to seem even more foolish than it had in his living room. They needed to get in and out quickly, not stand around and wait for his old injuries or for Libby's new ones to incapacitate one, or both, of them.

Just as Jack was about to say something to this effect, Barnum stood up, then padded forward until he was right in front of Jack. After the briefest hesitation, the cat began to slide along the ankle that Ripley had attacked, as if trying to make up for his cohort's inhospitable greeting. Barnum's satisfied purr was clearly audible, as was Libby's sigh as she said, "Okay. He's accepted you."

Jack felt the illogical desire to smile. Instead, he frowned. "Good. Any more dragons to face?"

"You mean you didn't see the one hanging from the basement ceiling?" Libby gave him a wicked smile, then nodded toward the room in front of them. "Have a seat in one of the dining-room chairs, while I set things up for the cats in the kitchen."

As Libby disappeared through a door to his left, Jack flicked on his own small flashlight, then made his way over to the oak table. He sat down in one of the spindle-backed chairs before casting the narrow beam past the arched opening to the living room.

It didn't look so much like an obstacle course as an antique store. An overstuffed couch straight out of the forties was situated across from a Queen Anne love seat. A lamp with beaded fringe peaked over the shoulder of a wing-back chair and a maple table with an attached lamp crowded the arms of a bentwood rocker. The walls were crammed with picture frames of all sizes and shapes.

Jack wondered if these held examples of Libby's work, but he didn't want to risk knocking something over just to get a closer look, so he turned his attention to his immediate surroundings. The table before him was a jumble of envelopes and stacks of bills, but in the center, he saw a matted eight-by-ten-inch picture done in black and white.

The print focused on a dappled horse running beneath a crescent moon. Something odd about the shot caught Jack's eye, and when he leaned forward to look closer, he saw that what he had taken to be ground beneath the horse's prancing feet was actually the upper surface of a cloud bank. Silver printing on the lower left-hand corner of the dark blue matting formed the words: DREAMSCAPES by Libby Stratton.

"The cats are all set."

Libby's whisper startled Jack. When he looked up he lifted the flashlight, nailing her with the narrow beam. The

sight of her blinking and weaving brought him to his feet
and to her side just as she steadied herself.

"My bedroom is upstairs," she said as she stepped away
from his hand. "I can quickly pack and get us out of here
with no one the wiser."

Jack wanted to tell Libby that she looked far too pale to
do anything more than let him carry her back to the VW,
but there was a challenge in her dark eyes and a stubborn
tilt to her chin that told him she knew just how shaky she
appeared, and was determined to go through with her plan,
anyway. Arguing would only create a delay.

"All right," he said. "You're in charge of this expedition. Lead on."

They skirted the knot of furniture in the living room then
mounted the stairs. When they reached the top, Jack stood
directly behind Libby, feeling her body shift from side to
side as she drew in several deep breaths before preceding
him down a short hall to a dimly lit room. The curve of the
far wall told Jack they were inside the round tower portion
he'd noticed from the outside. Moonlight seeped in through
the lace curtains, giving the room the gray cast of dusk.

"I won't get much," Libby said. "Just some T-shirts and
jeans."

"Don't forget to pack something heavy," Jack said. He
turned as she opened a narrow door on their right. "It can
get pretty cold on the coast. And turn off that damn light."

He said this last as a bright glow spilled out of a doorway, revealing a neat but crowded closet that was lit by a
naked bulb hanging in the center. Libby reached up to pull
the chain, and darkness returned with a soft click.

"I'm sorry," she said. "Force of habit."

Jack frowned at the closet, now a black rectangle next to
the large wrought-iron bed. As the metallic whisper of
hangers sliding along a rod filtered into the room, he leaned
against the wall, hands in his pockets, and glanced around.

Through the gloom, he noticed that several rectangular
and oval frames dotted the wall between the spot he occu-

pied and the tall dresser near the windows. Curious, Jack levered away from the wall as he turned to examine the closest picture. A slit of moonlight illuminated a photo of a dark-haired child wearing a cowboy hat, toy gun and holster set, sitting astride a spotted pony. Noticing the uneven surface of the picture, Jack looked more closely and was surprised to see that the little girl had been cut out of another photograph and glued on to the pony's back.

A puzzled glance in Libby's direction revealed that she was standing beside the bed, quickly stuffing clothes into a large duffel. Not wanting to interrupt, Jack filed away the questions raised by this picture and moved on to the next.

At first glance, this appeared to be a straightforward family portrait, featuring an old house much like Libby's. A wide stairway led to a porch, where an elderly man sat in a rocking chair. Behind him stood a thin woman with long hair, parted in the middle, wearing an apron over a T-shirt and jeans. Both of these figures were sharply defined, unlike the shadowy form that seemed to fade into the corner behind the woman.

Jack switched on his flashlight and cupped his hand over the beam. By directing the muted glow onto the photo, Jack could see that the nearly transparent figure belonged to a man. Two of the three children sitting on the steps were similarly pale and out of focus, and yet the delicate features of the dark-haired girl seated in the middle were perfectly distinct, down to her wide midnight blue eyes and the shimmer of her long dark braids.

Jack heard drawers opening and closing to his right, followed by the ruffling sounds of clothes being stuffed into the duffel. He didn't move. The eyes belonging to the dark-haired girl seemed to hold him, haunting him with their expression of utter abandonment, as if the child was completely oblivious to the people surrounding her or to the two cats, one black and one white, that crouched at her feet.

These were hardly your average photographs, he thought as he shifted to his right once more, preparing to study the next photo. A single face seemed to be the subject of the oval frame hanging closest to the dresser, but before he could do more than catch a glimpse of masculine features, he felt long fingers tighten around his arm. Turning, Jack found dark eyes, exactly the shape of the girl's in the last picture, gazing up at him in the moonlight.

"I'm ready," Libby said.

Jack nodded, then tipped his head toward the photo of the house. "That your family?"

Libby glanced at the people on the porch. She knew this portrait well, had spent painstaking hours at the enlarger, getting the collection of negatives just the right size in order to produce a photo of a home and a family that she could call her own.

"Well, yes and no," she answered.

Conscious of the telltale catch in her voice, Libby shifted her gaze to Jack and gave him a smile. His frown told her that he was going to ask her just what she'd meant by that reply. Although she preferred to keep the reasons behind the creation of her "family portrait" to herself, she would definitely rather explain this particular picture than the one he'd been moving toward—the composite image that bore such a startling resemblance to Jack himself.

Libby wasn't able to explain this phenomenon to *herself*, let alone anyone else. Too many things had happened in too short a time for her to consider this amazing fluke. Her friend Grace would no doubt quote Shirley MacLaine and insist there were no such things as accidents. Grace believed wholly in clairvoyance and ESP. Libby had enough to do dealing with things as they came up in her day-to-day existence; she had no time to worry about what the future might bring.

She didn't in any way, shape or form think she had "seen" Jack's entrance into her life. He just happened to be a man who possessed the type of rugged, been-around-the-block-more-than-once good looks she found attractive. That didn't mean, however, that she wanted him to know that. So, she opened her mouth to reveal the pain that had urged her to create a "family" grouping that included people who existed only in her mind.

But she was spared this embarrassment. In the moment of silence before she spoke, a loud clicking sound echoed somewhere in the house, then a voice, high and uncertain called out, "Libby? Libby, are you home?"

Libby drew in a soft gasp, then held her breath and listened to the silence until a deep male voice floated up the stairwell, "I *told* you, she's not here, Grace. Her little pickup isn't out front."

The disdain in her friend Barry's voice made Libby close her eyes and pray that Grace would listen to her husband.

"And I told you that *someone* is here," Grace replied. "I saw a light in Libby's room as we drove by. Besides, something is wrong. I feel it."

Libby choked back a groan. She was highly aware of the man next to her, standing tall and stiff, his very posture seeming to condemn her for that moment when, forgetting that they were supposed to be invisible, she'd turned on the closet light. She felt him bend toward her, expected him to berate her for her foolishness. Instead, his whisper was soft, without a note of criticism.

"We need to hide. They might come up to investigate."

Libby nodded. She tiptoed across the room, stopping to retrieve the backpack and duffel from the bed, then drew Jack into the closet just as she heard Grace say, "I saw it clear as day as we drove by."

Libby heard a creak from the stairway, then Barry's reply, "You see light everywhere. White light, golden glows, auras, halos. What you saw tonight was probably only the reflection of your headlights on the window. Come on. We shouldn't be here when Libby isn't home."

The brass knob was slick in Libby's hand as she held the closet door a narrow slit away from closing, conscious that the man standing inches away from her was as tense as she was.

"Libby said I could borrow that blue shawl of hers," the female voice said. "So, now that I'm here, I might as well get it. And while I'm at it, we can make sure there isn't anything funny going on."

Another creak warned Libby that her friends were nearing the top of the stairs. She drew the door silently closed.

"We're trapped, aren't we?"

Jack's deep voice was the merest of whispers in her ear, spoken on a soft breath that sent a quiver spiraling down the center of Libby's insides, a quiver that built as she shook her head, and her cheek brushed against Jack's.

"The shawl is hanging on the wall with my scarves and belts," she managed to whisper back. "But just to be safe, come with me."

The tiny enclosure was pitch-black. She couldn't see Jack's outline, but she was vitally aware of the powerful form brushing against hers as she guided him toward the back of the closet. Behind the clothes hanging on the rack and the shoes lined up on the floor, there was just enough space for the two of them to stand toe-to-toe, chest-to-chest, breath to shallow breath.

And as the voices grew closer, Libby found herself fighting the insane desire to laugh, battling the irrational response that often took over whenever she was upset or afraid. Not that she was scared of being found. These were her friends, for God's sake. The only danger in her discovery might be to them, for it would be far safer if they were truly ignorant of her whereabouts once the police began to investigate her "death."

No, she had the wild urge to laugh because in the middle of all the trouble she was in, the only thing she could think of was Jack McDermott and the way his mildest touch sent her blood singing, how his husky whisper made her knees buckle and his musky scent filled her senses. Of how much she wanted to draw his head down to hers, to touch her lips to his warm mouth and make him want her as much as she wanted him.

Chapter 4

Jack drew a slow, torturous breath, inhaling the essence of the woman he held. He couldn't remember the moment he had placed his arms around her, nor the thought that had urged him to do so. He figured it must have been some instinctual, protective reaction to being shut in a closet, hiding from possible discovery.

He told himself, as he felt the rise and fall of her soft chest against his, that in Libby's weakened state, the support of his arms around her slim body was necessary to keep her from tumbling to the floor of the closet. She'd fainted once before, after all, and had experienced several episodes of dizziness.

He assured himself that the fact that his blood was racing through his veins and his heart was pounding rapidly beneath the slight pressure of Libby's cheek had nothing to do with the tempting body pressed against his. Fear was a well-known aphrodisiac. It was quite normal that he should find that his jeans were suddenly painfully tight in one particular area.

"Look, Gracie. Not a soul up here."

The deep-voiced words pulled Jack's thoughts away from his body's undisciplined reaction to the woman in his arms. Staring through the row of hangers on the rod, he saw a sliver of light seep through the space at the bottom of the closet door as the woman's voice responded.

"Okay, so you were right. But something *is* wrong. I feel it. It isn't like Libby not to be home at this time of night."

"Did it ever occur to you she might have a date?"

"It often occurs to me that she *should* have a date, but I would know if she'd met anyone. Now, I wonder where…"

The sound of a drawer opening and closing covered the next few words, then the male voice echoed through the door.

"Wonder later. I'm not comfortable being here when Libby isn't. There's a blue something hanging on that rack by the closet. Is that what you're looking for?"

"Yes."

"Well, grab it and let's go."

The sliver of light vanished. Footsteps echoed down the hall, then on the stairway. When the front door slammed shut and Libby jumped slightly, Jack realized just how tightly his arms circled her slender form. He heard as well as felt her take a deep breath as he slowly released the pent-up air in his own lungs. His lips twitched as a loose curl feathered across them, then firmed as he realized that this brief touch had made him once more excruciatingly aware of the body pressed to his, of the lips mere inches away.

"Do you think we can leave now?"

The muffled words drifted upward. Jack nodded and released Libby, then stood back while she stepped through the hanging clothes. She opened the closet door as he ducked between the folds of fabric that held her slight, elusive scent, then joined her in the relative lightness of the moon-drenched room.

Libby's eyes gazed up at him, dark in her pale face. Her hair was a tousled, dark nimbus that made her look as if she'd just risen from the bed she stood next to. An image of her doing just that teased Jack's mind, making him frown as he asked, "Are you all right?"

Jack heard his whisper echo harshly in the silent room again, heard Libby take a quick breath, before she answered firmly, "I'm just fine. I think we should go now."

We shouldn't have been here in the first place, Jack wanted to say. He kept the words to himself, knowing they would come out as gruff-sounding as his earlier inquiry. He frowned as Libby returned to the closet, then took one of the two nylon bags she withdrew from the small enclosure. When his hand brushed hers, he felt her fingers tremble and knew she must be tiring again, but refrained from commenting on it as he led the way out the room, only whispering to her to hold on to the banister as they started down the stairs.

"Are you all right?"

When Libby gave Jack a brief nod and a tight, "Yes," he returned his attention to the road.

The moment his eyes left her, Libby took a deep breath. It was the third time he'd asked the question since their escape from the closet. Each time, she had given the same answer. Each time, it had been a lie.

That moment in her room had been the most difficult. How could the man think she was fine when he'd just released her from his arms? Of course, she could hardly fault him for not sensing her reaction to being held so securely, to the gentle strength in that embrace, to the allure of his closeness. Not only did she not blame him for his ignorance, she was darned grateful. It was bad enough that *she* knew what a fool she was to react so strongly to a man who was a virtual stranger.

He had again inquired about her well-being after they left the house and made it over the fence. It had taken all Libby's strength of will to reply at all as she clung to the boards and fought waves of dizziness. But the brief delay had helped steady her, made it possible to get to the VW, climb into the passenger seat and collapse, as much as an upright position would allow.

Now, again, he wanted to know if she was all right. Sure, she was fine. It was perfectly okay that she was leaving most of her life behind, that she could only hope that this nightmare would end before her cats starved or her abandoned house was burglarized or burned down or subjected to any of the images of catastrophe that were flitting through her exhausted brain.

Libby closed her eyes and took a deep breath. She was tired and scared and not a little angry at the unfairness of all of this. But when had she begun to expect life to be fair? She knew better. She prided herself on having learned to deal with the rough spots and move on.

So what if she was sore and getting stiffer by the moment? True, she was so tired, she could fall asleep sitting straight up, but she had a place to stay, and someone who would watch over her. And despite all the romantic fantasies that had insisted on weaving themselves into her mind while his body pulsed warmly next to hers in the closet, she was damned lucky that Jack McDermott was unaware of them.

As much as it grated on her to be viewed as a victim, the situation had obviously raised Jack's cop instincts, making him see her as someone who needed protection rather than as a woman who might be attracted to him. Considering that they would be sharing his very small house until the other arrangements he had mentioned could be made, this was for the best.

She knew very little about the man, she warned herself. Her feelings for him could only be based on physical attraction, even if she factored in his similarity to that picture she had made years ago. After all, "dream men" were just that, fantasies that responded at will to their creator's slightest whim. Jack didn't strike her as the kind of man that would respond to anyone's whims, not even his own.

"What would you say to a moonlight dip?"

Jack's question seemed to counter Libby's last thought. She turned to him in surprise. "A dip? As in the ocean?"

"No. As in my hot tub." Jack gave her a quick sideways glance. As he returned his attention to the road, his mustache lifted in a smile. "No Marin County place built in the late sixties or seventies is complete without one, you know."

Libby stared at the small house that loomed in front of them as Jack turned in to the gravel driveway. Marin was known for stately, expensive places that dotted the hillsides. This little A-frame cabin, sitting across from the beach and backed up against the cliff beneath the picturesque Coast Highway seemed to belong to another world all together.

"I forgot to tell you to bring a swimsuit," Jack said, "but there are several in the closet next to the wood stove. My sisters have been known to converge on the place for weekend getaways and gabfests."

"Sisters?" Libby turned her head toward him in a quick jerk.

"Yes. I have four of them."

Four sisters, and at least two brothers. Libby sighed as she thought about the picture hanging on her bedroom wall, the one Jack had been so curious about. Even with the addition of the two girls that flanked the likeness of her younger self, the photo seemed empty when she contrasted it with the mental image of a family filled with seven rambunctious children.

"How nice," she whispered as the car rolled to a stop.

"Well, if you think it was life on Walton's Mountain, think again."

The slight edge to Jack's voice, combined with what sounded like a suppressed chuckle, drew a quick glance from Libby. The hand brake creaked as Jack pulled on it, then turned to her. "For one thing, it was damned crowded at times, in spite of the house my father built after Kate was born. I didn't have a place all to myself until I was twenty-three, out of college and the academy. For someone who is known in the family as "The Loner," the lack of privacy I endured was something like slow torture."

Libby stared into his shadowed face. Wonderful. And here she was, interrupting the peace of the hideaway he had retreated to after being wounded. Shrugging off the image of the hot tub that had so tempted her, she pressed on the door latch and glanced at him.

"Well, I did stuff a swimsuit in my bag, but I don't think I want to get into it tonight. I'm very tired, and just want to sleep."

Without waiting for a return comment from Jack, Libby opened the van door and exited, pausing to take her duffel and backpack from the floor. As she came around the front of the vehicle, heading for the cabin steps, she became aware that Jack was walking next to her. His left hand closed around her left arm as he reached down and took the handle of the larger bag.

She should protest this move, she told herself, should tell him that she was not in need of such gallant acts. But it was taking all her concentration not to groan as she exerted muscles that had tightened all out of proportion to the short time she'd sat in the van. The stairs were slow torture. She moved up them so stiffly that she wasn't surprised, once they were inside and Jack had flicked on the light, that he turned to her and said, "I think you should reconsider my offer. If I can admit that my knee is very sore and in need of a soak, despite the macho posturing I tend to indulge in, then you should be able to admit to a similar need."

Looking into his green eyes, Libby saw a glint of self-effacing humor. Some of the tension in her shoulders dissolved and her lips softened slightly.

"Where can I change?"

"The bathroom. I can use the loft. When you're ready, come out the back door. And bring a couple of towels with you."

It took Libby longer to change than she had expected. Her aching muscles fought her as she dug through her duffel bag for her swimsuit, making each movement a battle as she slipped out of her clothes and into the stretchy fabric. A glance into the full-length mirror attached to the door made her frown and reconsider the offer of warm water that her muscles now cried out for.

Though she owned skimpier suits, this one-piece bit of shiny midnight blue fabric fit her tight enough to be a second skin. The straight neckline that ran from shoulder to shoulder was modest enough, but the low back and high-cut leg openings revealed a lot of skin. Much more flesh than she would normally expose to someone she knew as little as she knew Jack McDermott.

And much less than he had already seen.

She had almost forgotten that Jack had undressed her the night before. Staring at the black-and-blue marks on her legs, bruises that would hardly be considered sexy, she watched her skin turn pink, and felt the rush of heat spread up her body.

Libby pivoted from the mirror. What an idiot she was being. First, she imagined the man as some knight in shining armor, and now she was worrying he might be some lecherous fiend, planning on seducing her. She had to get herself in hand. She was not on a date. She was going to sit in a tub of warm water and soak away her aches in the company of a man who suffered similarly.

With flustered speed that made her clumsy, Libby turned to the shelf behind the door and pulled down a large white towel. Her fingers fumbled as she wrapped it around her, sarong-style, tucking the end to secure it around her waist, then grabbed another towel before leaving the small room.

The curtain of beads whispered softly as she closed the sliding glass door leading onto a redwood deck. The air was cool, salt-scented. The moon revealed a small yard enclosed by a six-foot fence separating Jack's property from the yards on either side and the hill that rose behind it.

Framed by a smaller fence of lattice panels, the deck she stood on was just large enough to hold a picnic table and gas barbecue on her right. The left-hand corner was filled with a redwood tub, measuring about two-and-a-half feet high and six feet in diameter.

Jack's head and broad shoulders rose above the mist floating atop the water as Libby approached the tub. Moonlight glinted off his muscles. His chest was dark with hair, except for one coin-size circle that glittered in the center of his left pectoral with the shine of newly healed skin.

When Libby realized that she was blatantly staring at the man's sculpted upper torso, she averted her eyes quickly. He was not looking at her, thank God. He hadn't seen the concern for his wound nor the admiration for his physical shape that she was sure must have been obvious in her gaze. His attention, she realized as she grew closer, was on his left knee.

Beneath the water, Libby could see that Jack was slowly flexing the joint up and down, pausing occasionally to massage it with his hands. Libby watched him as she removed the towel from her waist and deposited it, along with the folded one, on a bench attached to the deck railing. It wasn't until she placed one foot slowly into the water that Jack looked up.

He seemed startled. A frown dropped over his eyes for several seconds. Then the muscles in his shoulders bunched as he lifted his arms to rest his elbows on the edge of the tub, not once taking his eyes off her.

"I hope the water's not too warm for you," he said at last. "It feels pretty hot at first, but you'll get used to it in no time."

She might get used to the water, but Libby didn't think she'd so easily become accustomed to the glint in Jack's eyes as he continued to look at her. So, although the water did feel hot, she sank into that heat, drawing in a quick breath as the shimmering surface rose to provide some cover from Jack's gaze.

Jack had stared at her that way once before, when she'd come out of his bathroom earlier that day. Lord, she could hardly believe that had only been hours ago, and that this time the previous night she had been packing her camera gear, setting out to capture a shot of the late-August moon.

"Are you all right?"

The soft words made Libby blink, then look across the two feet of water that separated her from Jack. She smiled and asked, "Do you realize how many times you've asked me that question?"

Jack shook his head. "No. How many?"

"I'm not sure of the exact total since you first found me, but I count four times this evening alone. Just where in the birth order of that large family do you fall, anyway?"

"I was number four." Jack eyes narrowed. "What makes you ask that?"

"Oh, I thought maybe you were one of the oldest. I read a lot about birth orders when—" Libby shut her mouth over her words and backed away from memories of the child-rearing books stuffed onto the bottom shelf in her bedroom. "I've read about these theories in magazines," she managed to say. "In doctors' offices and stuff. Anyway, they say that oldest kids tend to be care-takers."

A deep chuckle echoed over the water. "Well, I wouldn't know about that. I was the middle one. Middle boy, middle kid. You know, the one most likely to be rather shiftless."

"Lacking direction? You? Mr. I-must-see-to-it-that-you-are-well-and-my-partner-is-out-of-danger? You hardly seem to be suffering from middle-child-itis."

"No, not these days." Jack's voice was suddenly soft. "I guess I'm making up for what my father calls my wasted youth. Not that *he* thinks I've made proper restitution. Playing cops and robbers is not his idea of a proper adult livelihood."

Libby glanced down at her legs as they floated in the now comfortably warm water, uncertain how to respond. Jack's words were straightforward enough. It was the tired, sad note underscoring them that kept her silent.

"I told you, remember, that it wasn't always life on Walton's Mountain."

The note of humor in Jack's voice brought Libby's head up. Her eyes met his across the water, eyes that crinkled slightly in the corners as he went on.

"Of course," he said, "that has its upside, too. I don't ever remember wearing overalls or having to say good-night to every member of the family. And we were certainly far from poor, so we had plenty of creature comforts."

"Along with plenty of kids to play with."

Libby's words hung in the air, so full of pain and longing, she almost imagined she could reach out and pull them back as she badly wanted to.

"Yes, we had that." Jack spoke slowly. "As well as plenty of people to pick fights with, and lots of competition for our parents' attention. But I'm sure you found that, too, even with only two sisters."

"What sis—" Libby stopped midword. She didn't have to finish the question. She knew Jack was referring to the figures he'd seen in that family portrait she'd patched together. If there had been anything good about Grace and Barry nearly discovering them in her room, it was that she'd been spared the necessity of explaining that particular photo. Obviously, she was not going to get off so easily now.

"I don't have any sisters," she said slowly.

"But in the photograph..." Jack's voice trailed off as Libby shook her head.

"I made that picture up."

"Made it up?" Jack gave her a quick frown. "What do you mean?"

Libby shrugged. "It's a composite. The base of the picture is an old photo of my grandfather's house, with my granddad sitting in the rocking chair, my mother standing behind him and me sitting on the steps. The girls on either side of me, as well as the man in the corner, and even the cats on the sidewalk, are figures pulled from other negatives and superimposed on the original.''

"Your attempt to produce the perfect family?"

Jack's question made Libby study his face, looking for signs of amusement, or pity. She saw only an intense interest.

"Very good, Sherlock," she said quietly. "Are you always so quick with your deductions?"

Jack's smile was slow and uneven, with one side rising farther than the other as he lifted his right hand from the water and slowly began flexing his fingers. Libby caught a glimpse of a jagged scar marking his right elbow, before he covered it with his good hand to massage the joint.

"No. Sometimes I seem to miss them altogether."

Libby stared at the lean fingers that promised such strength, recalled them soothing around her arm, remembered the moment of clumsiness with the glass and his resulting anger.

"What do the doctors say?" she asked softly.

"About my hand? That I've made a lot of progress. More than they'd hoped for, they tell me. It's what they don't say that bothers me."

"And what *don't* they say?"

Libby held her breath after asking the question, not sure if she was getting into an area that might be too personal on such short acquaintance. Jack continued to stare at his flexing fingers for several seconds before he shrugged and glanced over at her.

"That this is it. That the bullet that slashed my elbow did irreparable damage to the nerves affecting my hand, and that I won't recover any further than I have. That I should forget my plans of returning to my old job, should just become a desk jockey and be damn glad I'm alive to do that.''

The bitter sarcasm underscoring Jack's words made Libby's shoulders tense, but didn't prevent her from responding.

"And taking a desk job. That would be bad?"

Jack lowered his hand and stared at the water in front of him. "My father and I don't agree on much, but he's right about one thing. I've never outgrown the cops-and-robbers games that Matt and I played as kids."

He paused, then lifted his gaze to meet Libby's. "You hit the nail on the head when you called me Sherlock a few moments ago. That's what they call me at work. Or did before I screwed up." Once again his lips quirked into a half smile. "I love everything about being a detective. Searching for clues at the crime scene, interviewing and psyching out the suspects, following a trail to its proper conclusion. You don't get that sitting behind a desk. What you get there are mounds of meaningless paper to file, computer leads that someone else gets to follow and an ugly roll of flab around your waist."

By the time Jack finished speaking, his lips had firmed to a tight, straight line. Libby watched him flex his fingers repeatedly in the water for several moments as the anger and suppressed fear beneath his words echoed in her mind.

"So when will they decide your fate?"

Jack shook his head. "*They* won't. Give me a few more weeks and I'll be able to muscle through any test the department puts me through. My leg will throb for a week afterward, but my superiors won't know that. As for my shooting ability, I look damn good on the firing range. There I can take my time, wait for my trigger finger to respond to directions from my brain. But it's a different story when I try to shoot in a hurry. The way my hand is now, I'd be damned unreliable as anyone's backup. I won't put myself back on the street unless I know I can do the job right."

The hard edge to Jack's words completely failed to hide his pain from Libby. A sharp ache seared her heart as she stared into the dark eyes frowning at her, eyes narrowed as

if defying her to offer him comfort. She knew better than
to try that. Never again would she attempt to take someone's pain from them, never again would she rob another
person of the chance to find their own inner resources. She
would not be responsible for creating another Dan.

"It seems you've thought this through pretty thoroughly," she said.

Jack shrugged. "I've had a lot of time for thinking."

"So, if it comes down to it, and you have to take yourself off the street, what will you do?"

Her question brought Jack's head up sharply. His eyes
narrowed again. "I haven't the faintest idea. Perhaps you
can advise me. You might as well join the club. Plenty of
others have come up with a suggestion or two. In fact, everyone I know seems to have an opinion on how to fix my
life. Why not a perfect stranger?"

Libby's heart began to pound as he leaned forward to
stare more directly into her eyes.

"What do you say?" he asked roughly. "Want to try to
fix my life for me? It'll give you something to do until my
captain arranges a safehouse for you."

Libby felt suddenly cold. The skin on her arms puckered into goose bumps despite the warm water surrounding her. Fix his life? Like she had tried to fix her husband's?
No way. Nothing in the world could induce her to take on
such pain, to face such failure, ever again.

"No."

Libby choked the word out as she rose to her feet. She
turned to get out of the tub, but before she could move Jack
was standing next to her, his hands on her shoulders,
twisting her around to face him.

"I'm sorry."

The genuine regret in Jack's words brought Libby's eyes
up to his. "No. *I'm* sorry," she replied. "I asked about
things that are none of my business."

Jack gave her a slow smile and lifted one eyebrow.
"That's true. But I suspect you were just making polite

conversation. I shouldn't have taken my anger out on you. None of this is your fault.''

"I'm here," she said with a shrug. "You came to the beach to be alone, to heal in private, didn't you? And here I am, a total stranger, asking questions that are far too personal and generally making a nuisance of myself.''

The smile widened, gleaming white in the night. "True again. But that beats the alternative.''

"Which is?''

"Me, alone, staring at the law books on the shelves and trying to convince myself that I want to go back to school and become the lawyer everyone thinks I should be. If you hadn't come along, needing to be rescued, I might not have remembered how good it felt to do my job.''

The fingers gripping Libby's shoulders gentled as Jack spoke again. "Now that I think about it, I haven't had much time for feeling sorry for myself since your arrival. For that alone, I should be thanking you, instead of growling at you.''

The now-raspy timbre in Jack's voice banished the night chill from Libby's arms. His eyes were no longer narrowed in anger, but open and gazing down at her, studying her. She found it difficult to breathe, found that the cool night air had become as thick and charged as the atmosphere between them in her bedroom closet.

Her skin, too, seemed to recall those moments in the dark, crowded enclosure, growing suddenly hot as her heart raced and her body swayed toward the strength she'd found more than once in this man's arms. It wasn't rescuing she wanted now, or comfort. It was simply his touch, the feel of his body against hers, the caress of his lips on her mouth. She wanted to take all the romantic dreams she had infused into the composite image of the man that looked so much like Jack and make them come true.

And it seemed as if she was going to get her wish. Jack's hands had slid down her arms, his fingers had firmed around her flesh to draw her nearer to him. The tips of her breasts were barely touching his chest, but they blazed with heat. His head was lowering, his lips moving closer by the second, hers were parting softly to receive his kiss . . .

"Jack, where the hell are you?"

The loud voice echoing from behind her made Libby jump back, as a gate slammed shut and the voice went on, "Are you lolling about in that damned hot tub thing again? You know, if you don't watch it, you're likely to prune up perm . . . an . . . ently."

This last word came out slowly. Libby turned to stare at the dark-haired man who had stepped around the corner of the house to stand beside the deck. Her heart raced. She knew that voice, her ears echoed with the memory of it whispering for her to "play dead." Though Jack was still holding her arms, his touch was gentle, too light to keep a sudden chill from sweeping her body.

"Libby Stratton, I presume," the man said. At Libby's jerky nod, he smiled widely. "Allow me to introduce myself, since Jack has apparently been struck dumb. I'm Matt Sullivan, your assailant from last night, and I want to say I'm sorry for all the trouble I've caused you."

"No trouble," Libby breathed, then shook her head at her idiotic words. "Well, yes, I guess I *am* in trouble. But I have a feeling things would have been worse for both of us if you hadn't been able to convince those other men that you'd killed me."

"Well, you were the one who did that." Matt mounted the wooden steps as he spoke. "Such a good job, I decided to see for myself that you're really all right. And it does seem that you are indeed in good hands."

Jack's touch fell from Libby's arms as he moved toward the edge of the tub. "We were just finishing our soak, Matt. Libby was beginning to stiffen up from that little tumble she took last night."

"I see. And you got in with her to make sure she didn't lose consciousness and drown, I suppose."

Jack had stepped onto the deck. He snapped the folded towel out and began drying himself off as he replied, "Not at all. I have those pesky exercises to do for my arm and leg, remember?"

Libby shivered as she looked from one man to the other, noting Matt's widening grin and Jack's lowering scowl. Another shiver raced through her and she forgot about their somewhat confusing emotional battle. Stepping out of the tub, she reached for her towel, wrapped it around her like a shawl and announced, "I'm freezing."

When Jack turned to her, she asked, "Do you mind if I take a quick shower before I get into dry clothes?"

Jack shook his head, then watched as Libby turned and headed for the glass door, his eyes drawn to her long, slender legs as she disappeared into the house.

Good God, he had been about to kiss her. What had he been thinking? She was a victim of a crime, a victim that had been placed in his care, and he had been about to forget all that and pull her into his arms, kiss her lips and any other part of her body his mouth could reach.

"She really *is* all right?"

Matt's question pulled Jack's attention to the man next to him. "She says she is. What about you? Is it safe for you to be here?"

Matt grinned. "Yes, Jack. I made sure no one followed me. Your little cousin *can* take care of himself."

The sarcasm in Matt's voice brought a reluctant smile to Jack's lips. "Says you. Well, then, come on in and tell me what's happened since last night."

Chapter 5

"What do you mean they won't put her in a safe-house?"

Jack frowned as his head popped through the neckline of his gray sweatshirt, then glared at Matt as he closed the glass door on the front of the wood stove he'd just fired up.

"The captain feels that it would mean at least three more people would have to be let in on our operation." Matt shrugged out of his dark blue pin-striped jacket and adjusted the burgundy suspenders that matched the tie knotted in the center of his mauve shirt. "It's a case of who're ya gonna trust? We have no idea who the inside connection might be."

"So that means I'll have to stay *here*?" Libby said.

Jack glanced up as she emerged from the bathroom dressed in an oversize pink sweatshirt over matching leggings, her hair a tangle of curls pulled atop her head. Before Jack could respond, Matt stepped forward, ran a hand through his slicked-back dark hair and answered quietly.

"That's right. I know it's adding insult to injury, insisting that you stay with my cousin and continue to put up with his nasty temper and his ugly face, but with any luck, it won't be for long."

Libby gave Matt a long, somber stare before her lips curved into a slow smile. "Well, considering that the house comes complete with such amenities as a hot tub and a wood stove to keep me warm, I guess it won't be *too* awful."

Matt's answering smile was dazzling, displaying the dimple in his right cheek that women seemed to find so irritatingly irresistible. No less irritating to Jack was the glint of interest he saw sparkling in his cousin's eye as Libby crossed to the black stove and turned her tiny backside toward it.

"It'll warm up in here in a couple of moments," Matt said. "In fact, the place is so small, it will get quite toasty very quickly. If I were you, I'd insist that Jack keep it that way all the time."

"Oh, and is the force going to supply me with wood for all this?" Jack asked.

Matt turned his smile to his cousin. "Of course not. It's hardly in the budget. But hey, you're on the payroll, collecting money for doing nothing more than sitting out here on the beach. This is the least you can do in the way of earning your keep."

"Oh, like nearly losing my life four months ago isn't enough?"

Matt's smile faded and a frown dropped over the green eyes that were the exact color of Jack's. Realizing that a matching scowl creased his own forehead, and embarrassed by the bitter, humorless words that still echoed in the room, Jack turned and walked toward the kitchen.

"I'm going to make some coffee," he said over his shoulder. "You two want some?"

The two subdued replies in the affirmative increased Jack's anger at himself. He was acting like an idiot. Matt had been teasing him about being lazy since the moment Jack had woken from surgery following the shooting. Jack had been grateful for the lack of sympathetic words, happy that his cousin respected him enough to continue their life-long verbal sparring act. Tonight, however, Jack had gone over the line, reacting with unwarranted sharpness.

And there was only one reason for his behavior. Libby Stratton, with those just-out-of-bed tendrils framing features that still flushed pink from her shower. She had smiled at Matt in spite of the heavily oiled hair that made the guy look dark and dangerous, had fallen right in with his cousin's teasing as if she'd completely forgotten that Matt had been the one to get her into this mess in the first place.

And Jack was jealous.

His hand shook as he measured the grounds into the filter. Jealous. The cop who prided himself on his ability to stay detached under any circumstance had almost chewed his best friend's head off over a woman he hardly knew.

No, that wasn't true, he thought as he poured water into the coffeemaker and readied the pot to receive the hot liquid. He'd been with Libby less than twenty-four hours, but already he knew more about her than he'd known about the woman he'd been married to for three years.

Libby was strong-willed, for one thing. He knew several men who wouldn't have fought back from their injuries the way this slender young woman had. That she had a kind heart was easy to figure. How else could one describe a woman who would ignore her own weakened physical state in order to see to the welfare of a couple of crazy cats, or who would agree to turn her life upside down to safeguard the life of a man she didn't know? And she was quite stubborn. That had been easy to spot, for Libby reacted the same way he did to any offer of sympathy.

Jack's lips twisted into a half smile. She was also very attractive, with her half-gypsy, half-lost-waif looks. He liked her eyes, large and dark and oh so solemn, until something he said made them crinkle with laughter, flash with anger, or soften with pity.

No, not pity. Jack measured the brown brew into three mugs. Understanding maybe, sympathy perhaps, but nothing as demeaning as pity. Libby Stratton was a woman who insisted on standing on her own two feet even when her legs were almost too weak to hold her up. She would understand that need in others, and respect it.

"I have cream and sugar for whoever wants it."

Jack returned to the living area, balancing a tray in his left hand. Matt moved from the stone hearth where he had been conversing with Libby. His green eyes met Jack's from beneath raised eyebrows.

"What service! Look, a tray and everything. Just when did you become so very domestic?"

"This is not domestic. It's practical. It saves me a trip, not to mention that it keeps me from dropping things." Jack placed the tray on the trunk in front of the couch, then lowered himself onto the worn leather chair. "Come and get it. I made the stuff, but I'm not about to wait on you hand and foot."

"I don't know why not," Matt said as he came around the end of the couch and took a seat on the far end. "If you don't keep working on that hand and foot of yours, you're never going to get back to work. Or is that the idea?"

Jack squinted at Matt as he took a sip of coffee. "That's it. You've got me pegged, cuz. I'm just going to sit here and stare at the green sea and the blue sky, and spend the rest of my life contemplating past glories."

"Oh? Well, that should take all of five minutes. Then what? Write that mystery novel you're always talking about? Or have you finally decided to become a lawyer so you can get paid big bucks for your lies?"

"Not on your life." Jack chuckled.

"Well, then. How about doing something more than baby-sitting Miss Stratton here? Like some detective work."

Jack paused in the process of lifting his mug to his mouth, every muscle in his body instantly tense. "What kind of detective work?"

"Well, while you were playing Sally Homemaker in the kitchen, Libby told me about the necktie that our Mr. Mysterious so graciously wrapped around her wrists last night. She said the tie appears to be handcrafted and that you felt it might provide a lead."

"It might. I planned on getting it into the station tomorrow with just that in mind. I think the possibility of learning anything from it is pretty much a long shot, though, wouldn't you say?"

"Yeah, I would. But the way things are going, it could be months before this guy decides to use me in my guise as Tony Minetti. And no one else is available to check this thing out. Sue Greene and Larry Stenzel from L.A.P.D. are busy working undercover as servers at Foresters." He ticked the names off on his fingers. "Under Sergeant Pete Semosa's supervision, Jamal Williams, Terri Hague and Robert Ames are taking turns on that special phone line. That's it, except for Lieutenant Cooke and Captain Lowry, and they have to act as if everything is business as usual. Any backup you can give us just might break this thing earlier. Besides, I figure giving you something to do will keep you from driving Libby crazy with your annoying personal habits."

Jack grinned and glanced at Libby to check her reaction to this banter. Her face was completely expressionless. In fact, her eyes were closed, and the rise and fall of her chest told Jack that she'd fallen asleep sitting straight up in the corner of the couch. Shooting a warning frown at Matt, he reached across to remove the cup of coffee resting in her lap, loosely bracketed by her hands.

"I think it's time I left."

Matt spoke softly. Jack nodded as he placed both his cup and Libby's on the tray, then rose to follow Matt to the glass door at the back of the house. Jack held the bead curtain back as Matt turned, his hand on the aluminum frame.

"She's quite a sport." A slight frown rode over Matt's eyes. "When she wakes up, thank her again for helping me out of a tight spot."

"Sure. But she'll only say something to the effect that you were the one who helped her."

"Oh, really? Into mind reading these days, are you?"

"No. She's just like that. You know the type."

"What? The anxious-to-please, doesn't-want-to-hurt-anyone's-feelings type?"

Jack shook his head. "No. She's too honest for that. Honest and decent."

Matt's frown deepened as he appeared to consider Jack's words. Slowly, he shook his head. "No, can't say that I'm familiar with that sort of woman. Kinda makes me wish I were the one stuck out here with her."

Matt's slow smile and the wicked glint in his eyes sparked sudden anger in Jack, an irrational possessive response that he tried to hide behind a quick grin and a shrug.

"Well, what can I say? Some of us get all the breaks." He paused, brushing his moment of anger away, then stared evenly at his cousin.

"You watch your back out there, all alone."

"Ah, hell. I'm not alone. Like I said, I have Semosa, Williams, Hague or Ames just a phone call away." Matt's smile widened as he pushed open the door and stepped onto the deck. "You're the one in trouble."

Jack raised his eyebrows. "How's that?"

"Her." Matt lifted his chin in the direction of the couch. "Just don't forget what your mother always told you about those strays you used to take in. She can only stay until her real home is found. She isn't yours to keep."

Before Jack could reply, the glass door slid shut and Matt's grinning face disappeared. With a sweep of his hand, Jack let the beads click in place and turned to gaze at the back of the couch. The curls dancing above the top edge told him that Libby hadn't moved. But was she still asleep, or had she woken and heard any of Matt's idiotic words?

Jack smiled as he came around the end of the couch. Sleeping like a baby. As well she should be. It had been a very long day, even for someone who hadn't rolled down a hill and suffered a slight concussion.

He didn't want to wake her, but he had to. For one thing, she really should be lying down and for another, he needed to check her eyes as Shawn had instructed. Reluctantly, he took a seat next to her on the edge of the couch, put one hand on her shoulder and softly called her name.

Libby heard Jack's voice. It seemed to come from quite a distance, but she recognized it immediately. Her eyes opened to find his face very near hers, so near that his breath made the tendrils at her cheek flutter slightly, a fluttering in her stomach echoing it.

"What?" she asked as she stared deep into his eyes.

"It's time for bed."

Bed? Libby glanced around. The end of the couch, where Matt Sullivan had just been sitting, drinking his coffee and teasing Jack, was empty.

"Matt's gone," Jack said. "He told me to tell you thanks again."

Libby shook her head as she shifted her eyes back to Jack's. "He saved my life. I owe him."

"I told him you'd say that."

The quick smile beneath Jack's mustache and the warmth in his green eyes brought a sudden and rapid increase to Libby's heartbeat. "Oh, you did, did you?"

"Yep. And now I'm going to tell you that it's time you got some decent sleep."

"And where am I going to do that?"

Jack lifted his shoulders in a quick shrug. "Here, on the couch, I guess. I'd gladly give you my bed, but I think we want to make sure all danger of dizzy spells has passed before you try climbing up to the loft."

"Here will be fine. It's a comfortable couch."

"I think you might want to wait to pass judgment until you've spent some time on it when you aren't near exhaustion. Now, don't argue with me. It's obvious you're beat. I'm going to get you some sheets and a blanket, and you are going to lie down and go to sleep like a good girl."

Jack was looking deeply into Libby's eyes as he spoke. She wanted to smile at his words, but her mouth had other ideas. As Jack's face moved closer to hers, she felt her lips soften and part, just as they had during those moments she stood in the hot tub, waiting for him to kiss her.

"Your pupils seem to be the same size," he said slowly. "I guess it's safe to let you sleep through the night without waking you to check them again."

Jack's words hit Libby like a slap. Shutting her eyes, she bit the inside of her cheek until the pain drove the tingling and the longing from her lips. Oh, God, what was wrong with her? What had made her think he was going to kiss her? Why in heaven's name did she continue to react like an idiot around this man?

"I'm sure you're right," Libby forced out as she opened her eyes again. "And don't worry about making up the couch for me. Just tell me where the sheets and such are, and I'll do it myself."

Jack refused to go along with this, and rather than face a protracted argument, Libby escaped into the bathroom to brush her teeth and scold her reflection for fantasizing about a man who very clearly, very properly, viewed her only as a part of the job he'd been given.

Once she was settled on the couch, burrowed beneath a blanket and the crocheted afghan, Libby listened to the sounds of Jack preparing for bed. As her eyes drooped shut, she found herself thinking back to the days when the sounds of a man in her room and her life were as familiar as her own breathing.

Familiar and increasingly sinister.

The sound of running water followed Libby into sleep. Instead of fading out, it grew louder and louder, filling her ears, drawing her back into a terrifyingly familiar scene.

A whimper escaped Libby's throat as she found herself standing in the living room of the house she'd shared with her husband, surrounded by the furniture that Dan had so proudly surprised her with after their whirlwind romance had led to marriage.

The room was a painful reminder of the happy days, back when his photos were selling, when showings of his work had promised him such a bright future. The green leather couch and the white lacquered end tables seemed to rebuke Libby as her fingers tightened around the folded sheaf of papers she carried.

And the water continued to run, accusing her in a sibilant whisper, as it had so very many times before.

The sound echoed softly from the basement, from Dan's darkroom. Libby didn't want to go down there, but she couldn't seem to prevent her body from turning and moving down the narrow stairs, into the blackness that grew deeper with each step.

It was a little lighter at the bottom. A red bulb glowed above the door at the far end of the narrow brick room. Libby stared at the scarlet light, listened to the water hiss sibilantly. Behind the door, a sound demanded she walk forward even as she fought to stay where she was.

When she came to stop beneath the light, she told herself to obey the warning not to open the door. This time she would stand outside and wait for Dan to turn the knob and walk out to her. This time would be different.

No, it wouldn't.

Without her touching it, the door swung inward slowly. The crimson beam from the overhead bulb flowed into the room beyond, staining the table that held developing trays, bleeding into the water that gurgled from the faucet into the already full sink, then gushing onto the floor where it pooled darker at the edges, drawing color from the thicker liquid that trickled from a source somewhere beyond the doorframe. Libby tried to turn, but like countless times before, she found herself drawn forward instead, forced to stare at the deep slash in the wrist floating in the water, to look into the wide, sightless eyes of Dan Stratton.

And again, for what had to be the thousandth time, her mouth gaped and released an anguished, "Noooo!"

The sound of her own voice woke Libby instantly. Her eyes opened to a dimly lit room, a room that seemed totally unfamiliar to her. She started to sit up, but a firm hand pressed on her shoulder, and held her against the pillow.

"Take it easy, there," a deep voice soothed.

Jack. It was Jack's voice, Libby realized. It was his weight on the edge of the couch next to her, his gentle hand warm against her shoulder. With that thought, her constricted chest relaxed a little, enough for her to take a deep, steadying breath.

"That's good. Are you okay now?"

Libby nodded.

"Liar."

She turned toward the sound of his voice and was surprised to find that she could see his features quite clearly. A faint golden glow filled the room, filtering down from somewhere behind and above her. His sleeping loft, no doubt.

Libby didn't need to ask Jack why he was there, sitting next to her, taking her hand into his as she stared into his dark green eyes. She had heard her own scream, and could only assume that her earlier whimper upon finding herself once again reliving that five-year-old nightmare had echoed into the darkness, as well, bringing him down to investigate.

"No, really," she said. "I *am* all right."

She tried to sit up again, and this time his hand gave her no resistance. It didn't move from her shoulder, though, just rested there, offering strength and comfort as she pulled herself up and thought back to her grisly dream.

"Want to tell me about it?"

Libby's first reflex was to shake her head. She'd shared the horror of her past with very few people, despite her therapist's warning that Libby's reluctance to discuss the subject might be prolonging her sense of guilt. Slowly, she changed her original gesture to a nod.

"If you don't mind. Some people find other people's dreams rather boring."

One corner of Jack's wide mouth lifted. "It depends on the dream. Go ahead and try me."

His deep voice, so gentle and soothing, urged Libby on. "It was about my husband," she started.

"I didn't know you were married."

Libby met Jack's frown. "For three years. Dan died. I was the one who found his body."

The sightless eyes she'd just looked into rebuked Libby again. She swallowed and blinked away the vision, then stared at the cleft in Jack's blunt chin.

"Is that what you were dreaming about?"

Libby lifted her gaze to his and nodded. Jack regarded her through narrowed eyes. "And you expect me to believe that this hasn't affected you?"

"I didn't say it hadn't affected me. I said I'm all right with it." Libby took another deep breath as she turned to stare out his front window at the moon hanging low over the sea. "I'm used to it. It's one of those recurring dreams you hear about. My therapist says I'll keep having it until I forgive myself."

"Forgive yourself?"

"Yes. I've never been able to stop thinking that I was somehow to blame, that if I had only tried a little harder, I might have been able to prevent Dan's death."

"Libby, accidents happen."

Turning to Jack, Libby replied softly, "This wasn't an accident."

"What do you mean?"

"Dan killed himself."

Again Jack frowned. "How could you blame yourself for that?"

"Oh." Libby laughed softly. "You would be amazed at what I could blame myself for. Where would you like me to start? The failure of my marriage? My grandfather's death? Why don't I go right back to the beginning, with the fact that my birth ruined my mother's life?"

"What do—"

Libby stopped Jack's words with fingers pressed lightly to his mouth. As she shyly drew her hand away, she said, "I know. That's ridiculous. I've worked all that out in therapy." She took a deep breath. "Or most of it, anyway. And none of that really pertains to Dan's suicide."

The last word came out very softly. Libby saw the questioning look in Jack's eyes, mixed with a quiet expression that said it was up to her to go on or to stop.

"I met Dan when I was eighteen and he was twenty-six." Libby let the words flow out of her, into the night. "I went to work in his father's photography studio the day after I graduated high school. Dan came in from time to time, to use the darkroom and other equipment. Tall, boyishly handsome and a talented photographer, he was very easy to fall in love with."

Libby took a deep breath, then shook her head slightly as she went on. "I suppose it isn't surprising that someone who'd had as little experience with men as I'd had would fail to see that Dan had never outgrown his need to compete with his very demanding father. I didn't realize that he was challenged by the fact that his father had taken me under his wing. I only saw the romance, the excitement of having a man fall in love with me, of being swept off my feet. Our courtship had lasted all of two weeks before Dan suggested we drive to Lake Tahoe and get married. How could I refuse? He was exactly what I'd dreamed of, a hero come to whisk me off my feet and save me from my wicked stepmother."

An apologetic smile lifted the corners of Libby's lips. She glanced at Jack with a shrug. "Okay, my wicked aunt. Anyway, I thought I'd found the happy ending I'd prayed for. I was wrong."

Libby felt the smile fade from her lips as she dropped her gaze to stare at the tightly entwined fingers in her lap.

"Oh? What happened? Did your knight run out of dragons to slay? Or did his armor simply tarnish?"

The harsh, sarcastic edge to Jack's words brought Libby's head up. The frown above his eyes made her own forehead tighten. "That's not how it happened at all," she said. "I was happy working as Dan's assistant, thrilled to be learning so much from the man I had married. I desperately wanted both our marriage and artistic partnership to be successful. But it takes the efforts of two people to pull that off, a fact that completely escaped Dan's awareness."

Libby paused. Old wounds deepened her frown as she continued, "When his work stopped selling, I wrangled a couple of photo assignments from an ad agency so we could pay the bills. Instead of being pleased, my husband told me I should be above such "hack" assignments. When the critics attacked his newest style, I told him what insensitive idiots they were. But *my* opinion wasn't enough for Dan. His life wasn't going as planned, and rather than try to fix it, he turned on me."

Libby stared into Jack's eyes, saw him shake his head as he spoke softly. "I'm sorry. I've been on the receiving end of a wife's disappointment, you see. Not that this excuses me for projecting my life onto yours, but it's the only one I have. Please, go on."

The defensive anger that had fueled Libby's tirade collapsed like a leaky balloon, leaving her with little energy. "I'll spare you the gory details," she said. "Things went from bad to worse, but I hung in there, clinging to my dream of a happy family life, telling myself that we had just reached a bad spot in the road."

A shiver trembled through Libby's body as she recalled cowering in body and spirit as Dan railed at her. She felt herself begin to shrivel inside, just remembering. With a shake of her head she lifted her chin to look again into Jack's quiet eyes and continued her story in a near monotone.

"When we learned I was pregnant, I was thrilled. Dan was furious. He said he wasn't ready for the responsibilities of fatherhood. Then I had a miscarriage. Dan's callous reaction to the grief I felt over this loss opened my eyes. I started seeing a therapist. Dan hated the changes in me, the growth that came with learning to be strong, to be my own person. We separated. When Dan continued to refuse my pleas to attend therapy with me, I asked for a divorce. I was bringing the papers to him the night I found his body."

A long moment of silence followed these words. Then Jack's voice, deep with reassurance, echoed in the dimly lit room. "Libby, lots of men are faced with divorce. Very few kill themselves over it. In fact, for some of us, it's even a relief."

Libby let her lips sketch a weak copy of Jack's smile as she shook her head. "I *know* I'm not responsible for Dan's actions. But I sometimes wonder if I was so busy trying to build myself up after all the verbal abuse I'd suffered both before and during my marriage, that I ignored the pain Dan was enduring. For someone who was having trouble dealing with failure, anyway, confronting the end of our relationship must have been the last straw."

Libby dropped her gaze, stared at the holes in the crocheted material covering her knees for several seconds, then sighed one last time and looked back up at Jack.

"There's no answer to that," she said. "I wasn't expecting one. But thanks for listening."

The tiny half smile that Libby was coming to count on curved Jack's lips, lifting one side of his mustache and dimpling the crease in his cheek. He tightened his hand over her shoulder. "No problem. Thank you for trusting me with it."

Libby nodded as she gazed into his eyes. She did trust this man. Not just because her grandfather had taught her to respect police officers, or because Jack had come to rescue her like the knight in shining armor she'd once dreamed of. At one point, she'd thought of Dan as a savior, as well, and look at what a mistake that had been. No, she trusted Jack because something in his eyes told her that he'd heard beneath her story to the other deeper pain that still festered, and had respected her enough to leave it alone.

Unless, of course, he just didn't care.

Suddenly, the room felt like ice. As a chill ripped through Libby, she caught the edge of the blanket and pulled it up to her chin.

"Cold?" Jack asked. At her nod, he reached down and tugged the afghan up to be even with the blanket. As he did so, Libby noticed for the first time that he was not wearing a shirt, was dressed only in a pair of rather tight-fitting boxer shorts.

"Are you going to be okay?"

Libby took a deep breath. "Sure. I'm warmer already."

This was no lie. The sight of Jack's bare chest, the well-formed muscles beneath the curly red-brown hair, bathed her entire body in a quick flush. As he asked the question, Jack's hand had cupped her cheek and the skin beneath his touch blazed with sudden heat.

"You are one brave lady, do you know that, Libby Stratton?"

Jack's words sent a giddy sensation squirming down to the pit of Libby's stomach. She shook her head slightly.

"No, not really," she whispered.

"Yes."

Jack smiled as he leaned forward. His chest radiated a heat that grew even hotter as he came nearer. Libby's lips parted, half in surprise, half in invitation as his mouth hovered over hers.

The kiss started with a mere brush of flesh over flesh. Libby held her breath, hoping that he would repeat the action. In an instant, her wish was granted with another kiss, this one almost as tentative, but with a little more pressure. As his lips lifted from hers this time, a small cry caught in her throat, a sound that brought Jack's mouth down on hers with a passion and strength that caught her completely by surprise.

And with much the same surprise, she found herself returning his kiss with matching heat, drawing her hands from beneath her covers to wrap them around his broad back. Jack's skin was warm and firm beneath her fingers, his chest hard against her breasts. She arched up, pressing against him to answer the throbbing need his kisses were awakening, allowing his arms to slip around her.

Jack's kisses and the slow caress of his hand down her backside, held all the tenderness and passion that Libby had ever dreamed of, filled every corner of her swelling heart, touched every inch of her body with growing desire. No, it was *better* than she'd imagined, better than she'd ever hoped love could be.

Except this wasn't love.

A sudden shiver swept Libby's form. This was nothing more than pure lust, and her feelings for this man were nothing more than infatuation. How could it be otherwise? This time last night she had been lying on a mountainside, dreaming of a hero. Now, a mere twenty-four hours later, she was ready to believe she'd found him.

She knew better than this. If five long years of working through her past had taught her one thing, it was that her instincts about men were not to be trusted. It didn't matter how much she loved the way this particular man mixed gentleness with need. She might be able to trust this man with her body, with her passion, but she didn't know him well enough to trust him with her heart, with her love.

Chapter 6

It was only supposed to be a good-night kiss.

Jack had planned on simply brushing his lips over Libby's, much the way he might with his nieces as he tucked them into bed. He should have known better, should have realized that once he kissed Libby, he wouldn't want to stop. Considering how his body had reacted to more impersonal brushes with hers earlier on, he should have expected the fierce, hard desire that made him want to pull her even closer to him.

Unfortunately, it was painfully obvious that Libby wasn't as eager for him. The body that had been soft and pliant in his arms moments before had become suddenly rigid. The lips that had welcomed his kisses, that had returned them with fervor, had suddenly slipped from his as Libby tucked her head beneath his chin and shivered within his grasp.

Drawing on more self-control than he thought he had, Jack stilled the motion of his right hand, holding it above the curve of her buttocks that had tempted him so many times in the past day. He held her to him for another second, reluctant to break the contact that seared him to the very core of his being. Then slowly, using the cushion beneath Libby as leverage, he pushed himself back to gaze at her as she reclined wide-eyed against the pillows.

"Go back to sleep," he said. "I'll see you in the morning."

He couldn't say any more. He refused to apologize for his actions, would not lie and say he was sorry for those few moments of passion, even though he knew he should not have allowed them to happen. So, he stood, and turned from the dark eyes staring out of Libby's pale face, and crossed the room to climb into his loft.

"I've written down lettuce, tomatoes, cucumbers—the normal salad fare, along with steaks and chicken breasts and milk. Is there anything else you think I should pick up?"

Jack glanced from his position at the kitchen counter to where Libby sat in the leather chair. She looked up from the mystery novel she'd pulled from the dozens that filled his shelves. Her dark blue eyes gazed into his for several seconds, then she began to shake her head. Breaking off in midshake, she said, "Yes. Ice cream and film."

"What kind?"

Libby shrugged. "Any flavor. As long as it's chocolate," she said wryly.

"No, what kind of film."

"Oh." Libby gave him a wide grin. "Whatever brand they have. Thirty-five millimeter. Three rolls of color with a two hundred speed and two of black-and-white four hundred. Thirty-six exposures, if they have it. I grabbed some film from home last night, but I tend to go through it very quickly."

"And just where and when do you plan on using this film?"

Libby shrugged. "Around here. I never get tired of shooting the beach, there are a million ways to—" She brought her words to an abrupt stop, then stared long and hard at Jack before she went on. "I *am* going to be allowed out of the house, aren't I?" she said tightly.

Jack studied her for a moment. She looked a little better this morning. The shadows beneath her eyes were lighter and the bruises on her cheek, faint to begin with, were now barely discernible. And she seemed full of energy. She had already showered and had dressed in a denim work shirt tucked into jeans by the time he'd finally climbed down from his sleeping perch.

Not that the loft had seen much sleeping after he'd left Libby's side. He'd tossed and turned until dawn, trying to forget the feel of her in his arms, trying to tell himself that what had happened was never going to happen again.

In the clear light of day, he could almost convince himself that those moments on the couch had been some part of a romantic, erotic dream, especially since Libby had apparently decided to act as if nothing had happened between them.

The glint in her eyes as she glared at him right now told him she was no more likely to accept unnecessary restrictions today as she had been the day before.

"Can you leave the house? Well, I don't know about that." Jack paused, fighting a grin at the way her eyebrows lowered in mutiny. "The way I see it, you're under protective custody."

"Which means?"

"Which means, you stay indoors until I say it's safe to go out. And *that,* my dear Miss Stratton, won't be until I can escort you."

Libby stood as Jack crossed to the front door. "Why?"

She wasn't aware just how sharp and demanding her question had sounded until Jack turned, his eyes narrowed. Libby stood her ground, met his frown with one of her own as he replied.

"Because, in case you have forgotten, you're recovering from a blow to the head. You were ordered to rest, and you

have done very little of that. Until you do so, and I'm
thoroughly convinced that you're not likely to fall down
and do yourself more injury, you are to stay put unless I'm
with you. There is also the matter of making sure that no
one catches sight of you and starts asking awkward questions. The neighbors on either side only use their places on
weekends, but several others live here full-time and com-
mute to their jobs in the city.''

Libby hated this. She knew he was right, for even though
she felt stronger than she had the day before, her head did
tend to spin ever so slightly when she moved too fast. It was
doing its little dervish dance even now. She wasn't close
enough to Jack to blame this sensation on his presence, so
she figured it must be due to the speed with which she'd
gotten to her feet.

Which was just as well. She could deal far better with a
little physical weakness than the thought that her silly heart
was causing this particular giddy spell, making her feel as
weak-kneed as a love-struck schoolgirl.

"That sounds like I might not be able to go out at all."

Her words echoed with stubborn challenge. A smile
creased Jack's face as he replied, "Don't fret, Princess. I
promise I won't lock you in the tower forever. As soon as I
devise a cover for you, I'll see to it you get out of here often enough to keep you from going completely stir-crazy.''

"And what am I supposed to do in the meantime?"

Jack's smile faded and the frown returned in one quick
moment. "In the meantime, you can make some room in
the closet over there for your clothes. Then try to get some
rest, you hear?''

"I hear."

After a long, searching look into her eyes, which made
Libby grow tingly all over, Jack gave her a brief nod,
opened the door, stepped out and pulled it shut behind him.

Libby stared at the door for three beats of her heart, then
lowered herself to the comfort of the worn leather armchair. Resting her head against the overstuffed chair back,

she released a slow breath filled with frustration, anger and fear. Frustration at the situation she'd fallen into, anger at herself for the way she'd so eagerly responded to Jack in the middle of the night and fear that she would give in to temptation and repeat that same mistake at the slightest indication that Jack McDermott was interested in another encounter of the romantic kind.

Libby's breath caught in her throat as she thought of those moments she'd spent in his arms. Never in her wildest fantasies had she imagined that a few kisses and caresses could so quickly elicit such a strong response from her. She had been married, for goodness' sake, had assumed that she was familiar with her own sexuality. But intimate relations with Dan had never heated her up like those few moments on the couch.

She should have expected this, of course. Her therapist had warned her not to judge all men by the perfectionism of Daniel Stratton, had promised that there were men who were as interested in giving pleasure as they were in getting it. But the woman had never warned Libby that she might run up against anything as potent as Jack McDermott.

Or as dangerous.

The man was wounded, both in body and soul, and Libby knew herself well enough to recognize that she longed to be the one to ease his hurts. She had spent years analyzing her marriage, examining her need to help Dan recover from the injuries inflicted by his controlling parents. She had fallen into the trap of so many before her, slipping into the role of rescuing angel, believing that if she was the one to ease his pain, Dan would love her and care for her forever.

Even when he turned on her repeatedly, she couldn't see how his kind of need fed on itself. She knew now that men like Dan never healed, because even though they refused to acknowledge that they were in pain, they never stopped needing. She'd seen similar warning signs in Jack, the reluctance to rest when his leg was hurting him, his insistence on pushing himself past the point of pain, his frustration when his body refused to cooperate.

Libby got to her feet. The last thing she wanted was to become enmeshed in another hopeless cycle of pain that was beyond her ability to help heal. She had grown past that, had learned she had to see to her own needs first. At this particular moment, she had a job to do, the daunting task of making room for her things in Jack's crowded, minuscule closet. That would keep her busy, keep her mind from dangerous dreams of a relationship that could never be.

Moments later, having emptied her duffel onto the floor beside her, Libby stood next to the wood stove and stared at the open closet. Impossible. There was absolutely no way she was going to fit one more thing into the tightly packed tangle of clothes and sporting equipment. She was going to have to take everything out, then try to—

The sound of a door slamming made Libby turn from the closet and gaze out the large front window. A rusted yellow truck had pulled in to Jack's driveway and was now parked diagonally to the cabin. A man stood by the passenger door, a dark-haired, wiry fellow with a thin face and small eyes that shifted back and forth behind the black frames of his glasses as he glanced around, then turned to the man that had just emerged from the driver's seat.

This one was taller, with longish, sandy hair that danced in the wind as he glanced at the house, then back toward the road before starting around the front of the truck to join his friend.

Libby didn't like the looks of either man, didn't trust the spotless khaki coveralls they both wore, the spatters of mud that nearly obliterated the logo on the truck's door or the way they stared at the cabin. She particularly did not like it when they each started to pull on thin latex gloves.

She didn't think they'd seen her yet, though they had both stared at the front porch. Most likely the sunlight on the window created too much glare for them to see inside until they got closer. And it was entirely possible that they had a legitimate reason to be here. Possible, but highly improbable. At any rate, Libby wasn't going to be stupid enough to answer the door when they knocked on it and find out. Nor was she going to let them know she was in the house. She would hide behind the couch, and wait for them to leave.

Libby grabbed the backpack holding her cameras and crawled over to her hiding place, preparing to settle in. As she did so, a beam of light fell onto the nylon case. She glanced behind her, then groaned at the sight of the sliding glass door, covered in nothing more substantial than a curtain of orange and yellow beads. They'd be able to see her through the door.

She was being paranoid, she knew, to imagine that these men might check the back door if they got no response from the front. But considering the events of the last couple of days of her life, paranoia seemed to come with the territory at the moment. And it was better to be safe than sorry.

Better to find a better hiding place now, while she still had the chance, than to sit here and be found by these men if they decided to fulfill the worst of her fears and come into the house.

The closet was out. She doubted she could wedge her big toe in there. All the cupboards in the kitchen were too tiny, and the bathroom held no safe nooks, either. That left the sleeping loft. With the strap to her camera bag clutched in her hand, Libby lifted her head slowly to peek over the back of the couch. The truck was still there, but the men were gone. For some reason, that fact only increased her fear, made her turn and crouch low as she made her way to the ladder three feet behind her.

She had managed to climb halfway up, when the knob on the front door squeaked. The sound sent her scrambling upward. She made it over the top ledge and plunged onto the bed in the corner of the platform just as the door clicked and a voice floated into the room.

"What did I tell you? Cops are the worst about getting good locks. Think they're invulnerable, or something. I suppose it has to do with those guns of theirs. It was the same with that other cop we did last year, remember? I wonder what makes these guys feel so sure that no one would have the guts to—"

"Save the analysis, Metzker," a second, gravelly voice interrupted. "We've got to get this done and get it done quick."

"Piece of cake, Joe, you know that. Two bugs will take me all of ten minutes."

"Yeah. Well, our instructions are to do the phone first. You see to that and I'll search out a likely spot for the one in the room."

Not up here. Please not here. Libby's heart was racing as fast as if she'd just run two miles, her respiration was labored. She tried to control it, to quiet the rush of air past her lips, but her heart only pounded more rapidly and her breathing grew more ragged.

Enough. Quit panicking, or you'll give yourself away.

Libby took a deep breath, held it for several seconds, then forced herself to release it slowly, softly. Closing her eyes, she drew on the relaxation technique her therapist had taught her, ordering her tight muscles to soften one by one. With her ears attuned to scuffling and scraping sounds below, she repeated the procedure a second time as a voice floated up.

"Jeez, look at this place, will ya? Reminds me of a pad I had back in seventy-one. Bead curtains. Candles. A beanbag chair. God, even a lava lamp. This other furniture is vintage, too. I wonder where—uh-oh."

The raspy voice identified the speaker as the one named Joe. Something about the way he said those last two syllables made the tension creep back into Libby's shoulders.

"What's up?"

"Well, Metzker, we might have a little problem here. Come look."

The sound of footsteps rose to Libby's ears, followed by an annoying male whine. "Okay. A pile of clothes. So the guy doesn't pick up after himself like his mama taught him. You interrupted my delicate work for this?"

"You can do that *delicate work* with your eyes shut. And these are not guy's clothes. They belong to a woman."

"Oh, yeah. Nice stuff. I like those little lacy things. But so? The guy has a guest. Big deal."

"So? He was alone in the van when he drove by."

"Oh. I get your drift."

Libby didn't move. She couldn't. She didn't even think she was breathing as she pressed herself into the mattress, certain she could feel two pairs of eyes staring up at the loft.

Move, a voice whispered in her mind. *Hide.*

But where? Libby raised her head mere inches from the mattress. To her right, the bedclothes formed a long jumbled pile next to the wall. It wasn't much, but since the bed was the only thing up there, her only hope was to bury herself beneath the pillows and the thick quilt and hope that whoever came up to investigate would take a quick glance and leave.

"You check in here, Metz. I'll have a look outside."

"Outside?"

"Yeah. She could be sunbathing, or something."

"Oh, that's right, Joe. Take all the good jobs for yourself."

Libby took advantage of their bantering to scoot toward the wall, dragging her backpack with her, then burrowed beneath the bedclothes, trying to make sure that every bit of her was covered by as many layers of blankets and pillows as possible.

Sounds were muffled beneath the layers of fabric, but she was sure she heard a couple of doors open and close, then Joe's voice.

"No one on the deck."

"Bathroom's clear."

"Well, I guess that leaves the platform thing. Be my guest, Metz."

"Not me. You know about me and heights. You check it out. I'll get the phone back together."

Libby heard the scape of a leather sole on the bottom rung of the ladder. The grating sound repeated itself five more times, then silence. She knew the man was staring at the bed, could almost feel his eyes boring through the tumble of cotton and batting that covered her, that threatened to suffocate her.

She waited, certain any moment he would step onto the platform, would spot the toe of her shoe, which she was not certain was completely covered up, or notice that the blankets moved each time she drew the slightest breath. It was only a matter of time, she feared, before he would lean forward, yank back the covers and discover her cowering there.

Chapter 7

Jack parked the van in front of his cabin, then shook his right hand rapidly, trying to rid it of the annoying tingle that had spread through his fingers as he drove home.

Great. Something new for the doctors to wag their heads over and mumble about next time he went in. Maybe he'd blow it all off, he thought as he slid the van's side door open. Maybe he'd forget all about the doctors, about getting back into shape and just give up on his career.

Yeah. Like someday the pope would take a wife.

Jack started to lift the plastic shopping bag that contained Libby's film, then stopped and reached in to pull out a small, flat package. Frowning at the sudden heat that flared on his cheeks, he stuffed the object in his back pocket before slipping his right hand through the bag's plastic loops and gathering the necks of the other three bags into his left fist.

Thirty-three years old, and embarrassed about buying condoms, he chided himself as he balanced on one foot and slid the van door shut with the other. He felt like a damn teenager, thinking with his hormones. The worst part was, he had no idea if he'd have the occasion to use the damn things. There had been no question in his mind that Libby had wanted him to stop kissing her the night before. But, he'd told himself, that could have been a reaction to the awkwardness of her situation, being a virtual prisoner in the house of a man she'd known for little over twenty-four hours.

He was probably being a fool, he thought as he started up the porch steps. He wanted to believe that she was as attracted to him as he was to her, so he was using any evidence at all, no matter how flimsy, to convince himself of this. Most likely, the condoms would end up rotting in the bathroom medicine cabinet. As they should. He had no business even considering an involvement with someone as mixed up in one of his cases as Libby was.

Except it was really no longer *his* case. He wasn't fooled by Matt's suggestion that they needed him to check out this tie thing. And, damn, if last night was any indication of his lack of willpower, the least he could do was be responsible enough to see that he was prepared, should the temptation arise again.

Tightening numb fingers around his house key, Jack approached the front door. He was barely inside before Libby was at his side, holding a pad of lined paper at chest level and speaking in a rapid, breathy fashion that was nothing like her normal voice.

"Oh, Jack. I can't tell you how glad I am that you came back. I went out right after you left, and walked all the way to that gas station. You won't *believe* this. They said they have no idea *at all* what caused my Harley to break down like that, and it could be another *week* before they figure it out and fix it. It's such a bummer."

Harley? Gas station? Jack stared at Libby's wide dark eyes and shook his head. The pupils *seemed* to be the same size. But how was he to tell when she kept jerking her head down, then staring at him with a frantic, expectant expression? Maybe this was some delayed reaction to the bump on her head, making Libby suddenly talk like an airhead on speed, or maybe it was the stress of—

"I really don't know what to do." Libby's voice, strained and urgent, broke into his thoughts. "I know I should probably get out of your way, you know, get a motel room, or something, but then I won't have any money to pay for those repairs."

As Libby finished speaking, she lifted the pad of paper and held it directly in front of Jack's face, forcing him to read the words: THE ROOM IS BUGGED.

Oh, God. It was worse than he'd thought. The girl had become delusional. With a kick of his foot, Jack shut the door, then moved toward the kitchen. Once he had his hands free, he could attempt to calm her down, try to make some sense out of—

"Jack!"

The note of desperation in Libby's voice made him drop the groceries on the counter. Attempting to free his right hand from the plastic loops, he turned to her to see that she held up a fresh note.

There were more words on the new sheet, written in a quick hand, smaller and harder to make out. As Libby began to babble on about her fictional Harley-Davidson and someplace she had to be in three days, Jack read the message: Two men came. I hid. They placed a listening device in the lava lamp.

The *lava lamp?* It sounded highly improbable. So improbable that he knew he had to check it out before he made another move. Freeing his hand from the plastic trap at last, he turned to Libby and mouthed, "Show me," before speaking out loud.

"All right..." He hesitated over her name. Most likely an unnecessary precaution, since there was probably no listening device to be found. But just in case. "Jill," he said in response to her quick scribble. "Calm down, Jill. We'll figure something out."

As he spoke, Jack moved over to the shelves lining the area beneath the loft, where his brother's prized sixties trophy sat on a shelf with Mike's law books. Slow examination of the tapering cylinder, from the clear liquid on top to the blue ooze on the bottom, revealed nothing. He began to move back from his close inspection, when a slender, feminine finger pointed at the black base.

There it was, tiny, almost invisible, sharing the circular opening that housed the electrical cord.

Jack grabbed Libby's arm and towed her back toward the kitchen before speaking again. "I'll tell you what. As soon as I get the groceries unpacked," *and figure out how to handle this,* "I'll give the garage a call. Maybe they can tell me something more about your chopper. You know how it is, sometimes they just won't talk to women about engines and things."

Libby replied, "Don't I just," as she held up a note that said, *the phone is bugged, too.*

Jack nodded as he began loading the groceries into the refrigerator. "On the other hand, maybe we should take a drive down there, and talk to the guys in person."

After placing the meat, milk and vegetables into the tiny refrigerator, he turned to Libby. She had moved back to the couch and sat staring out the window, no doubt suddenly exhausted now that she'd gotten her message across.

Getting her away from the house for a few moments might not be such a bad idea, Jack thought. It would help to know the whole story before he decided on his next move. But taking her out could be disastrous, as well. If he *was* being listened to, someone might be watching him, too. He doubted that whoever had hurt Libby two nights earlier would recognize her, but there was no way to know this for sure.

"Jack," Libby said suddenly, "I think you have company."

Jack turned to the front door, hand immediately swinging around toward the gun he'd wedged into the waistband at the back of his jeans before he'd left the house earlier. Just as his fingers touched the cold metal, he caught sight of a man with light brown hair getting out of a white Volvo. As he watched the tall, slender form make its way toward the steps, the muscles in Jack's shoulders relaxed slightly. He dropped his hands to his side, then lifted one to rake his fingers through his hair.

"It's my brother, Mike."

Jack had the door open before the man could knock. Mike's eyes, large and dark brown in his thin face, crinkled at the corners as he stepped in.

"Hi there, Jack. Just thought I'd stop by and see how you were doing. Shawn told me about your excitement the other night." Mike brushed back a lock of sandy hair that the wind had blown onto his forehead. He turned his smile to Libby and went on. "When I told Shawn I was stopping by, he asked me to see how—"

"*Jill* was doing?" Jack broke in. "Well, you can see that she's doing fine. She's recovered from that little fall of hers, but we can't say the same thing for the Harley."

"Harley? I thought—"

Mike stopped speaking as Jack put a warning finger to his own lips. Before Mike could even close his mouth, Libby spoke up.

"You thought it was a Honda, right? Well, that's typical. It's like no one thinks a little thing like me could handle that big bike. I really get tired of listening to that stuff, ya know. It ticks me off royally."

"Uh, I'm sorry. I didn't mean to offend you, or anything."

Jack watched Mike's eyes dart to Jack then back to Libby. A smile quivered at the corner of her mouth. As Jack bent to retrieve the first note Libby had held up for him, he heard her respond in a breezy tone. "Oh, that's okay. I shouldn't have jumped on you like that, ya know. It's just been something of a rather..." Libby paused, then finished in a voice that trembled slightly, "bad day."

Jack grabbed the note then straightened, afraid that all of this had been too much for Libby, had brought her close to tears. His eyes met her dark blue ones. Narrowed, crinkling at the corners, they weren't welling up with moisture as he'd feared, but brimming with laughter.

It was obvious from the way she trapped her lower lip between her teeth to restrain her smile that Libby was very close to an outburst of nervous, hysterical giggles. Jack crossed to her immediately, then with one sweep of his arm, he pulled her to him and held her face to his chest. As he handed the note warning that the room was bugged to his brother, he felt her shake with silent mirth.

"I suppose you also came to see if I've been reading those damn law books you foisted on me," Jack said.

When Mike raised questioning eyes from the note, Jack nodded and went on, "Well, you can save your breath. If I've told you once, I've told you a thousand times, I refuse to consider becoming a lawyer."

"I . . . see."

Mike stopped, as if unsure how to go on. Jack gave him a wide grin and forced anger into his next words.

"You know, I'm sick of you and Dad and everyone else telling me what I should be doing. I'm here to relax and heal, not to stare at reminders of what a failure you all think I am. So why don't just run along and take these damn things with you?"

As he spoke, Libby pulled away from him. She now stared at him with an expression every bit as stunned as Mike's. Jack glanced from one to the other as he moved toward the shelves in the corner. Pointing to the lava lamp, he mouthed, *help me*.

Libby nodded, but it was Mike who stepped forward and spoke. "Hey, settle down. Sure, I'll take them. If you help me put them in my trunk, I'll get out of your hair. Hey, watch it!"

The sudden order made Jack pause as he slid one book from the shelf. Mike crossed the room to grab the lamp and cried, "God, you almost knocked this off!"

Jack gave his brother a quick grin in recognition of Mike's inspired ad-lib, then came back with, "So what? Big loss. That's the most hideous thing I ever saw in my life."

"Hideous? It's a collector's item. Worth quite a bit at the right places. Do you have any idea how few mint-condition lava lamps are left?"

"Too many, as far as I'm concerned. If you like it so much, why don't you just take it with you?"

"I will. I should have put it somewhere safe long ago. Come on, let's get these out to my car, and I'll leave you to deal with your motorcycle mama, here."

Libby grinned at Mike as she reached for a couple of books, but Jack shook his head and indicated she should stay in the room. As she watched them slip out the door, their banter floated back, making her smile soften.

It might not have been life on Walton's Mountain, but to Libby it looked as if there had been a lot of love circulating in the McDermott house. At least enough to allow for the kind of quick, unspoken communication she had just seen between these two brothers.

A shaky sigh passed her lips. She blinked back tears of longing as she turned from the sight of the two men walking toward Mike's Volvo. The couch beckoned her and she moved to it. She wasn't sure why Jack had refused to allow her to help them with the books, but it was just as well, she thought as she collapsed onto the cushions. Suddenly, she felt as if every ounce of energy had drained from her body, leaving her barely able to sit up straight, when the two men came back in. When Jack gave her an inquiring glance, she managed a weak smile.

"That was the only bug," she said to his silent question. "That and the one in the phone."

Mike spoke first. "Well, I would love to stay around and hear the story behind all this, but I think it's best to move on. How about I put the lamp in my living room and treat our unseen listeners to a night or two of teen angst and parental frustration?''

Jack nodded. ''Perfect. We don't want to arouse any suspicions. It's going to look pretty coincidental to our buggers, as it is, that I somehow managed to get that device out of the house so soon.''

''Oh, I don't know,'' Mike said as he cradled the last of the books in both arms. ''I think we all did a pretty creditable job with our little radio drama.''

He paused in the doorway, speaking softly. ''And just for the record, Jack. You can do anydamnthing you want with your life. I wasn't trying to interfere, just help.''

The left side of Jack's mouth crept slowly up as he shook his head at his brother. ''Yeah, well, I guess that's what big brothers are for. You made up for your *helping* today. See ya.''

''Take care. You too, Jill.''

''Libby,'' she corrected. Mike nodded, grinned then turned and started down the front steps.

''All right.'' Jack turned to Libby as he closed the door. ''Tell me the story. What happened after I left?''

Libby sighed. She was exhausted, and her head hurt. All she wanted to do was curl up on the couch and sleep, but she knew this information was important. Trying to keep her voice from shaking as she reexperienced the fear of seeing those men get out of their truck, she described them, then recounted everything she had seen and heard.

''You actually came out from under the covers to watch them?'' Jack asked.

Libby thought back to the moments she had listened to her heart beat hard and loud while the one called Joe had stood at the top of the ladder. Slowly she nodded.

''I thought I heard him go back down, but I was too afraid to move. Then I heard them speaking again. Their voices were muffled, so I lifted the covers a little. Metzker was bragging about how quickly he'd set his bug in the phone. Joe said there was no artistry to that, then challenged the Metzker guy to step into the bathroom while he set his bug in the main room, then try to find it.''

"So you decided to watch?"

"Yes. Was I wrong?"

Jack sat on the couch next to Libby. He placed his hand on her cheek. "You were very brave. Not to mention foolish. I don't like to think about what might have happened if one of them had looked up and seen you."

A shiver ran through Libby's body as she replied. "Well, as it turned out, Joe was beneath the platform. Since I couldn't see him, I knew he couldn't see me. The only bad moment was when I noticed that Metzker had quietly opened the bathroom door and was watching his friend. I retreated to the bed then, certain I'd never learn where the bug was hidden. If they hadn't played a quick game of I Spy and actually mentioned the lava lamp, we'd probably still be looking for the bug."

"And then you concocted that ridiculous story about the Harley-Davidson."

Libby shook her head. "No. I didn't have time. I was afraid the bug would pick up any noise I made, so I had to literally creep down the ladder and tiptoe to the kitchen to scribble those first two notes on the pad you'd been using for the grocery list. I'd barely finished that, when you walked in the door."

"Then that Harley business was pure improvisation? Very good."

The warmth in Jack's voice, the glint in his eyes, made Libby flush. The cheek covered by Jack's hand began to burn. As the other cheek ignited and the heat began to spread down her neck, Libby glanced away.

"Well, you did pretty good yourself, once you realized I hadn't gone batty on you," she said softly.

"Yeah, and Mike did a great job, too." Jack's chuckle drew Libby's eyes back to his. "He's got to be going crazy, wondering what this is all about, you know."

"Can you tell him?"

The amusement faded from Jack's features. "I can hardly explain what I don't know. I have to assume that someone has somehow learned where I'm staying, but since I'm on medical leave, I can't help wondering why whoever it is would be interested in my comings and goings. You're sure that neither one of these men mentioned why they were here?"

Libby sighed. She'd been interrogated on this point already. "No. As they left, they were arguing about the unusual payment arrangements, but I could hardly follow them and listen for more details."

"And you're sure that they said they'd bugged another cop last year?"

"Well, that's how it sounded."

Jack nodded slowly. "It could have been Gary. When we checked his place out, we found a listening device in his phone and one in his living room. I think I'll have one of our guys visit Mike and see if they can compare the equipment used. It probably won't give us anything conclusive, but at this point, even the tiniest lead might help. So—" Jack gave Libby's cheek a brotherly pat as his lips sketched a smile "—I'm going to need to make some calls."

"But the phone—"

"I know," he said as he stood, then crossed the room to pick up the mustard yellow receiver. "I want whoever is listening to hear this first one. I don't want them to think we've shut them out entirely."

The call to the gas station went quickly. Jack issued a series of threats about fixing "Jill's" fictional Harley-Davidson, not giving the person on the other end any chance to reply and tip off any listeners. Jack hung up and grinned at Libby.

"Poor Fred. I'll have to stop by the shop and fill him in, as much as I can, but in the meantime, that should back up our little one-act play. Now, I have to make some real calls, which will require a trip to a pay phone. I have a cellular in the van, but I think it's a good bet that whoever arranged to bug my phone has probably tapped into the frequency on that line, too.''

Libby got to her feet. "You aren't going to leave me here, are you?''

Jack frowned, then stepped forward to place his hand on her shoulder. "I have to, Libby. I have no idea if this place is being watched or not. I won't be gone long, though, and I don't think our friends could get back this quickly to re-place the listening device. In fact, they wouldn't, since they must have heard us talking and know that someone is here. Why don't you climb back into my loft and rest while I'm gone. You look as if you could use it.''

She probably looked like death warmed over. That was certainly how she felt, all still and shriveled inside. Except for the very core of her stomach, which curled and twisted with a slow heat in response to the feel of Jack's gentle touch and the look of concern in his green eyes.

That heat spread throughout her body as Libby curled up in Jack's big bed, beneath the covers that held his musky smell, surrounding her with the warmth and security she had found in his embrace. It wasn't as good as being in his arms, she supposed, but it was probably safer. This way the warmth did not flare into an uncontrollable heat, it just lulled her into the sleep she needed so badly.

A loud knock brought Libby out of her deep slumber. She sat up, feeling drugged, her mind fuzzy as she caught the murmur of male voices. Immediately, her muscles tensed, her heart stopped beating. Not again.

"Perfect. Yeah, keep the change. It's a long drive out here.''

The sound of Jack's voice released Libby's fears. After a long stretch and a deep breath that did wonders to clear her fogged brain, she slipped from beneath the covers and started for the ladder. When she glanced over the edge of the platform, she found Jack at its base, one foot resting on the lowest rung.

"Well, hello," he said. "I was just coming to wake you. Dinner is served."

Libby turned to start down the ladder. "Dinner?" she said over her shoulder.

"Well, pizza, anyway. I hope that's okay."

Libby pivoted as she reached the floor, then shook her head. "No, that is not okay." She paused a moment to watch a worried look crease his forehead, then grinned. "It's *perfect*. I hope you got a large."

"Extra large." Jack returned her grin. "I like it cold for breakfast."

"You're kidding! So do I."

"Well, I think this one's big enough for tonight and to-morrow morning for *both* of us. At least. I ordered a salad and bread sticks, too. You go wash up, and I'll get the table set."

The "table" again consisted of the trunk sitting in front of the couch. As Libby took her seat on the couch, she noticed that the television wedged onto one of the shelves beneath the sleeping loft had been turned on. The local newscast theme was just playing as Libby lifted the first wedge of pizza to her mouth. The delicious blend of dough, tomato sauce, chopped veggies and cheese disappeared in moments, and as she separated a second slice, she glanced at Jack.

"Did you make your calls?"

"Yes." Jack paused as he balanced pizza in one hand, then went on, "Sergeant Semosa agrees with my theory that the only person who might be interested enough in my... 'welfare' to bug this place is the guy behind the Forester murder and money laundering. We think it might mean that the fellow wants to be sure of my whereabouts before he makes any move. Hopefully, this means he's planning something soon, so the team is getting word to Matt so he'll be ready, just in case."

"How will they contact him? Don't you worry that Matt's phone might be tapped, too?"

Jack shot her a grin. "Hell, we count on it. The guys call 'Tony Minetti' all the time, orchestrating the messages meant to add to his cover. We also have several code words that tell Matt to call one of the three officers who man a message phone set up exclusively for this case."

"What about you, are you going to have to use the pay phone all the time now?"

Jack took a quick bite, then shook his head as he swallowed. "I can still use the cellular under certain conditions. As with my phone here, we don't want to stop using it altogether and let our buggers know we're on to them. I have to run into the station tomorrow to pick up a pager and a bug sniffer."

"A what?"

"That's my name for a sweep—an electronic device that reveals the presence of listening devices. The pager will be the kind that prints out the telephone number of the person calling. The caller can include a prearranged set of digits to let me know if I should use my phone, the cellular, or if I'll have to find a pay phone to return the call. When I use the cellular, I'll have to talk in code, just in case anyone is listening in. A little precaution we've learned from those embarrassing conversations intercepted between certain members of the British royal family."

Libby gave him a weak smile. She chewed her pizza slowly as Jack took a swig of soda, then turned to her again. "And having Metzker's name might be our first real break. The guys are going to ask around for someone fitting your description of him. If we find the fellow, we can look into his calls and see if we can find out who hired him."

"You wouldn't just ask him?"

Jack shook his head as he swallowed a bite of pizza. "Too tricky. Metzker could tip off whoever hired him, let the guy know that I'm onto their surveillance."

The grin creasing Jack's face brought a smile to Libby's lips.

"What?" he asked.

"You're loving this, aren't you?"

Jack took a sip of soda, stared at the can as he placed it before him, then nodded.

"It feels good," he said as he lifted his eyes to Libby's. "I'm moving forward, no longer sitting around feeling sorry for myself. My hand even feels better. You're good therapy, Libby Stratton. The best I've had."

Libby was blushing again. She could feel the heat seep from her cheeks up to her forehead and down her neck, but she couldn't pull her eyes from the intense gaze of the man next to her. An announcer's voice droned from the television as the pizza sent up a tempting scent, but she felt as if all of that belonged to another solar system. It was all separate, outside the place where Jack McDermott looked at her as though she had given his world back to him, where his eyes told her he loved her for it.

"The body of an unidentified young woman was found today in the Marin headlands."

The words sounded as if they'd been shouted in Libby's ear. She jumped and turned to stare at the television as the voice went on, explaining that so far the coroner had only been able to determine that the victim had died of a bullet wound. On the screen, Libby watched two men drag a green zippered bag down the hill to a waiting coroner's van as the anchor sadly informed his audience that no identification had been found anywhere near the body.

Jack watched Libby stare at the television. Even after the story involving the discovery of the "body" that Sergeant Semosa had arranged ended, and the weatherman came on and started talking about upper-level lows, her eyes remained fixed on the little screen.

"Libby," he said softly. "What are you thinking?"

Her face turned to him slowly. Her eyes met his, but there was no spark there, no hint of any emotion at all.

"I'm thinking how odd it feels to be declared dead," she replied. "To realize that, if it weren't for Matt's quick thinking, I would actually be in that body bag, that my life would amount to nothing. My house, my cats, my work would be left, but all that would be meaningless, like an elaborate picture frame surrounding a blank canvas."

Jack reached across to take her hand. "You're not nothing, Libby. You're a wonderful, loving person. And you *are* alive."

"Am I?"

Her eyes widened, revealing a small flash of anger. Or was it fear he saw there?

"You don't know me very well, Jack," she said. "In some odd sort of way, you've seen me at both my best and my worst. I've vacillated from damsel in distress to valiant heroine. Normally, I'm neither of these. I do my best to play that first role as little as possible, and the second role is one that I've never had a chance to explore before. The plain fact of my life is that I have lived it far too carefully, always fearing that I might say or do the wrong thing and make all the people in my life disappear."

Libby stood and walked over to the window. Jack watched her gaze into the night, then stood and crossed the room to join her. When he reached her side, Libby turned to him, eyes shimmering like the moonbeams that danced atop the waves on the other side of the beach.

"You know," she said, her voice shaking, "for all that care I took, for all that tiptoeing around, trying not to offend anyone, attempting to please, I'm still alone. I have nothing to leave of any value."

Jack watched as her eyes filled with tears. He gazed into those dark, brimming eyes, his chest tight with emotions that struggled to surface, that nearly caught in his throat as he asked, "Just what is it you think you should have? What do you want?"

As if you could give it to her, he thought as he watched her blink. She drew a deep breath, then released a sigh as she lifted her shoulders in a shrug.

"A husband. Children," she said with a catch in her voice that was a half laugh, half sob. "You know, all the things that my liberated self, the one who works so hard at her craft and is so proud of supporting herself, likes to pretend she doesn't need. I want . . . I have always wanted to matter deeply to someone."

"You do," Jack said. "You matter very much to *me*."

These words hovered in the air between them. Jack didn't remember them crossing his mind before he spoke. It was as if they'd come from somewhere else. If he didn't know better, he would have thought they'd come from his heart.

But that organ had been permanently damaged long ago. His ex-wife had inflicted a deep wound that had left it able to pump blood, but completely incapable of any true emotion, except perhaps anger.

Or so he'd thought. There was no doubt that he cared for the young woman standing before him. The tears she was blinking back so valiantly moved him deeply. The hope glittering in the eyes gazing into his made Jack long to fulfill her every wish. His hands moved up, one to slide around her waist, the other to cup the back of her head and tilt her face up to his as he lowered his lips.

The moment his mouth touched hers, Jack's blood began to race, pulsing with instant, insistent desire. When her lips parted beneath his, he took it as an invitation to taste her more deeply, to test the velvet of her mouth with his tongue. At her moan of pleasure, his left hand tightened around her waist, drawing her body to his, easing his need to feel her against him, to show her how strongly she affected him.

When Jack slid his lips from hers, to trail down the softness of her neck, another soft sound escaped her. He smiled as he used his tongue to make love to her ear until her breath came sharp and ragged and her arms tightened around him.

Chapter 8

Jack continued to draw Libby to him, wrapping his arms around her slender body and tightening them so that he could feel as much of her softness against him as possible. Moving his lips back to Libby's, he kissed her long and deep. Her lips tasted of salt. No more tears, he told her in his mind. I have you. Everything is all right now.

Just who is saving who here? a voice asked. You, the broken-down hero? Hell, she's stronger than you are. When was the last time you had the courage to face failure, to really deal with life?

Jack frowned as he lifted his lips from Libby's once more. Tunneling his fingers into the hair at her nape, he eased her head onto his shoulder. With his fingers twined within her silken curls, he stared out the window into the night. Good God, what was he doing? Comforting Libby, or building himself up? Using her need to make him feel better about the next-to-useless man he feared becoming?

She was a virtual prisoner in his house. Women had been known to fall in love with jailers' far harsher treatment. Not only was this unfair to her, it was dangerous. This sort of thing interfered with clear thinking, blurred a man's perception, slowed a fellow's reflexes. And his could hardly afford such interference. This had to stop. Now. Maybe later, after all this was over, once he'd proved to himself that he had something to offer he could...

Jack felt Libby shift in his arms. Her lips touched his neck, her hands caressed his back, making his body react with a flare of heat that brought a stern frown to his forehead. And just *what* would he have to offer her? If things went the way he wanted, he'd soon be back on the street. He'd be a cop. Libby would return to creating her photographs, mixing with gallery folk and intellectuals, the kind of people that Sheila had courted so intently.

Had he forgotten how Sheila had thrived on the stimulation she claimed those people offered, how she had found his stories of perps and clue trails boring, tasteless? Libby's career demanded she associate with these intellectuals, and after several months of comparing their struggles with line and imagery to his sordid tales of murder and larceny, Libby would long to be free of him, just as Sheila had.

The alternative was worse. If his hand never healed, if he had to place himself in a desk job, he'd be less than the half man he was now. His soul would shrivel, his bitterness would block out all the warmth he felt for this soft, vulnerable woman. Better to stop now, hard as it was to deny himself the pleasure, better to forgo the healing that Libby offered, before someone got hurt.

"Libby."

Jack angled his head back to look down at her face. Her deep blue eyes opened, shimmered into his, tempting him with the glitter of desire that matched his, testing his resolve. A quick cough deep in his throat cleared the longing that had lodged there and Jack spoke again.

"We can't do this."

He watched Libby's eyes darken as a frown slowly formed over them. She blinked twice, then nodded as she slowly loosened the arms clasped around his waist and stepped away from his loose grasp to stare up at him. He knew he could say more, could at least apologize for his actions, but he was not truly sorry, and to say any more would only embarrass them both.

"I have to go out," he said at last. "I haven't jogged for several days. I need to keep working on my knee."

Libby simply nodded again, then turned from him and began to clear the trunk of the remains of the pizza they'd shared. Jack gave her one last glance, then stepped out into the night.

When he got home, the only light was a small one over the kitchen sink. Libby was already asleep on the couch, curled up beneath the blanket and afghan, with her back toward him. He climbed to his loft and lowered the body that ached with exhaustion from the grueling workout he'd just put it through, but he didn't sleep any better this night than he had the one before.

He kept telling himself that he had done the right thing by ending that embrace before he drew Libby into a relationship with a man who was having as much difficulty facing life as the one in her recurring nightmare. He kept assuring himself that he had done the noble thing, then wondering why he felt as if he'd just performed the most cowardly act of his life.

"I can't believe you thought to grab a wig when we were at your house the other night."

Jack glanced at Libby as he pulled away from the San Rafael police department and headed the VW bus toward Highway 101 South. The platinum blonde sitting in the passenger seat turned to him with a shrug.

"It was a last-minute thing. I saw it as we stepped back into my basement the other night. I grabbed it off a hook on the wall while you were trying to prop open the window so we could climb out, and stuffed it in the backpack with my cameras. I didn't see it until I decided to take some shots this morning.''

Jack had finally fallen asleep shortly before dawn. He'd woken and climbed down the ladder to find Libby standing on his back deck, camera aimed at a hawk as it soared above the ridges of the hill behind his house. She'd shown him the wig then, a long, nearly white fall of Lady Godiva proportions, and they'd decided to cut the top and spike it with hair spray to fit the biker-mama image they'd created for their unknown listeners.

Not that Jack thought he was being watched. He knew how to spot a tail, and he'd seen nothing suspicious on the trip to the police station, where he'd picked up his beeper and the electrical sweep that would make sure his place stayed "bug free." No one had followed as they left the station, either.

"I'm glad I found the wig." Libby's words broke into his thoughts. "I think I would go really crazy if I had to stay in that place one more day, especially as nice as it is outside today."

The August sun had burned off the early-morning fog and now warmed the interior of the van as Jack sent her an apologetic smile.

"Well, I can't promise that today will be much of an outing for you, following me around, looking for a needle in a haystack."

"We're not looking for a needle," she said with a wide smile. "We are looking for a tie that resembles the one that was wrapped around my wrists. That means stores. I love to shop, though I rarely have time to do it. Maybe we can pick up some black boots to go with my new look. I always wanted a pair of those thigh-high jobbies, but I didn't figure I had anyplace to wear them."

Jack negotiated the freeway on-ramp, then let his glance sweep Libby's slender form. She wore a tight turtleneck, white and sleeveless, and even tighter jeans that empha-

sized her exquisite curves, reminding him how her lean
body had felt beneath his hands. One of his black leather
belts cinched her waist and the spiky blond wig framed a
face he barely recognized. Libby had applied what looked
like several layers of mascara to her eyes, along with black
liner that made them look twice as large and dark as usual.
The rest of her face she'd left pale, completely devoid of
any hint of blush on her cheeks or lips.

The only thing that didn't fit the role she was attempting
were the white high-top aerobics shoes on her feet. Other
than that, she looked like any of the biker girls he'd taken
in to the station, young things dressed defiantly in out-
landish clothes, their faces masked by layers of makeup
that did little to hide the fact that they'd found themselves
in a world that scared them half to death.

"How did you know to dress like that?" he asked.

"Oh, it's part of my job."

At Jack's quick glance, Libby went on, "Many of my
clients want to be photographed as something other than
their normal everyday selves. I've had to study all sorts of
people, so I can help my customers achieve just the right
look for the photograph they have in mind."

Jack lifted one eyebrow. "You have clients who want
pictures of themselves as Hell's Angels mamas?"

He shot a quick look her way, saw her shrug and give him
a small smile, before he shifted his eyes forward again.
"Well, not yet," she said. "But you never know. I've done
lots of clowns, a couple of ballerinas and an Indian maiden.
Most recently, I've gotten some requests to superimpose a
person's features over the face of an animal or a bird, like
a wolf or an eagle. Most of my work, however, is more reality-based."

Jack sent her a questioning glance. "Reality-based?
Since when is it rooted in reality to have a photo taken of
yourself in *any* kind of a costume?"

"I was speaking of *relative* reality."

Jack gave his eyebrows a skeptical lift, then turned his attention to the road again, noting the sign for the off-ramp to Sausilito, where he knew of a store that carried unusual items of masculine attire. It had been Sheila's favorite shop, and she'd hated it that Jack wouldn't be caught dead wearing any of the "hot" things she insisted on buying for him there.

This was just another example of what a disaster their marriage had been, based on unsubstantiated assumptions about each other. That was one mistake he never wanted to make again. When he gave his heart the next time, if there *was* a next time, he wanted to know that other person as well as possible before committing his bruised soul.

As the van eased into the deep curve that led from the freeway and onto the surface street, Jack glanced at Libby. Already, this young woman was coming close to holding his heartstrings in her hands, and he knew next to nothing about her. What in God's name was "relative reality," for example? He thought back to the things he'd seen in Libby's basement, the gorilla, the shields and swords, the feather boas, and wondered as he had that night, just what kind of photographs this woman took.

"I don't do any kind of kinky shots, if that's what you're thinking."

Jack turned to her as he pulled up to a stop at the red light. "Reading my mind, are you? If so, you must know that I am wondering just what a dreamscape is? I saw the photo of the horse in your dining room and you explained about the composite of your family. Do you—"

A loud, high-pitched beeping broke into his words. Jack pulled the small black square off the waistband of his jeans and stared at the number on the narrow display screen.

"I have to find a pay phone."

Libby noted the instant change that had come over Jack. Gone was the relaxed, teasing air, replaced by a quiet, frowning intensity as he made a right turn and began shifting his attention from the road to the buildings that lined the sidewalk as they moved along with traffic.

She was impressed, and not a little relieved. She didn't want to talk about her work just now, didn't feel like revealing so much about herself, not after her foolish display of vulnerability the night before.

Drawing a deep, shuddering breath, Libby glanced to the right as Jack turned in to a small gas station, parked in front of the pay phone and got out of the van. What an idiot she'd been, she told herself as she watched him approach the telephone booth. What had she been thinking of, opening herself to him so completely, revealing things about herself she had only shared in the privacy of her therapist's office? And how could she have been so unfair to him, asking him to care, coercing him into filling the emptiness inside her?

And fill her he had, Libby thought with a shaky sigh. Every inch of her had glowed as he kissed her. Each caress had promised the answer to all her prayers, prayers that someone somewhere might find her worth loving, that she might meet some kindred soul who would want what she wanted, to be together, to make a home to replace the long-ago one she'd known so very briefly.

Libby shook off the sudden warmth seeping into her muscles. Jack's home couldn't be hers. It was enough that he was giving her somewhere to stay while she and Matt were in danger. He was right to have pulled away from her, to have given her a look that said more plainly than words—*I can hide you, but I can't save you.*

Only she could do that. And she'd never manage it if she continued to act like a victim, letting tears fill her eyes in a way that begged for attention, as she had the night before.

"Change of plans."

Libby blinked away her thoughts and glanced at Jack as he slid into his seat. "Oh?"

"Matt left a message for me. He needs to talk. We have to meet him."

Libby glanced at the beeper on his hip as the engine coughed to life. "Well, it must be important. Good thing we picked that thing up."

"Yeah. I've worn them before, of course. Makes me feel like a doctor. Would almost make my father proud."

"I thought he wanted you to be a lawyer."

"Doctor, lawyer." Jack shrugged. "It didn't matter. Anything but a cop."

It was on the tip of Libby's tongue to ask Jack just what his father's objection had been to that particular profession, but he turned to her first, his features hard and unreadable as he asked, "What about your dad? What did he want you to be?"

Libby stared at him a moment before breathing her reply. "Nothing. As far as I know, my father doesn't even know I exist."

Jack's expression sharpened. A puzzled frown highlighted the sympathy in his eyes. "What do you mean? What about the man in that picture on your—" He stopped, the creases disappeared from between his eyebrows, and he went on, "Oh. You made up that guy on the porch, right?"

Libby nodded. Her throat closed over any words she might have thought to say. She had no desire to reveal any more of her sad and woeful life than she already had. She stared at the road in front of them as they moved back onto Highway 101, going north now, but out of the corner of her eye, she saw Jack glance at her one more time. She tensed, preparing herself for his curiosity.

He didn't ask her a thing, though. After several moments, she relaxed, watching the roadside shops of Strawberry Mall slip by on her right and gazing at the wheat-colored hills as the van continued past San Rafael. A couple of exits later, Jack turned off the freeway to follow a narrow road that wound past some large houses and into an area that was fenced off with posts and barbed wire. A small herd of cows grazed in the distance as they approached a large stand of oak trees.

Jack pulled beneath their branches, parking the van deep inside the grove, beyond sight of the road behind. He switched off the engine, then turned to look at Libby for several minutes. Noting the indecision in his eyes, she watched him frown as he said, "I think you should come with me. Matt might have some questions for you."

Jack continued to frown as he led Libby through the shade beneath the trees, following a path he and Matt had blazed in long-ago, simpler days. Days when the crooks they followed were imaginary, and no more dangerous than a shadow behind one of the trees that they darted between as they pretended to stalk and corner their prey.

Things were so much easier then. There were no thieves they couldn't trap, no murders they couldn't solve, no wide-eyed young women plagued with mysterious, tragic pasts to pull at their heartstrings.

It was no use denying his feelings. He may have thought he'd buried his ability to care beneath the bitterness over his failed marriage and despair over his physical wounds, but Jack wasn't so stubborn that he would refuse to admit the obvious. He was not only intrigued by Libby Stratton, he was strongly attracted to her. He also cared enough about her to respect her obvious reluctance to reveal her past, no matter how curious he might be.

"Hey, cousin. You made good time."

Jack glanced up to find Matt standing between two tree trunks, dressed in tan pants and an ivory shirt, sporting a brown tie and matching suspenders that made Jack feel grungy in his green T-shirt and jeans.

"Yeah, we did. What's up?"

The two fell into step as they continued up the hill. "Well, first off," Matt replied, "Semosa sent Jamal Williams to your brother's for a look at that bug on the lava lamp. Mike told Jamal all about Libby's biker imitation, by the way. Anyway, it appears that the bug this Metzker fellow placed in the lamp is identical to the ones we found at Gary's place."

Jack nodded slowly as his mind treated him to a unbidden vision of his former partner, lying on the ground next to him, the look of surprise fading from Gary's face as his life seeped onto the concrete sidewalk.

"I doubt we'll ever know exactly what part Gary played in all this," Jack said. "He messed with the crime scene at the Forester home at the very least, shifting the position of the shards of glass from the patio door to make it appear as if it had been broken from the inside, like a botched attempt to fake a robbery. He did a good job, too. If I hadn't gone back and had forensics check the angle of the pieces left in the door, proving it had been broken from the outside, and if Frank Forester hadn't come across as being too smart to hide his wife's jewelry in his own garbage can, the person who actually committed the murder would have pulled his cover-up plan off with no one the wiser. And unless we're very lucky, he might just get away with it, anyway."

"No. Not with the two of us on the job." Matt punched Jack's good arm and grinned at his cousin's quick glance. "You were the one who suggested we check out Gary's place after he died, remember?"

"Yeah, well it was just dumb luck that Semosa decided there might be more to my suggestion than the mutterings of a wounded and delirious man, then managed to convince Captain Lowry to reinstate the Forester investigation."

"Well, the luck still hasn't run out. The guys have located this Metzker character, and they're working on his past phone records as well as tracing his current calls. They can't do much else, otherwise someone might connect our sudden interest in him with that visit he paid to your house. And *that*, of course, might raise questions about the little lady who is staying at your house while she waits for her

Harley to be fixed. The last thing we want is for someone to make any connection between the two of you."

Jack heard Libby gasp. He turned to see her standing three feet behind them, staring at Matt with wide eyes and a half-open mouth.

"You don't think this person, the one who tried to kill me that night, would try to find out who I am, do you?" she asked.

Jack shrugged. "I don't know how he could. You said your ID was in your truck."

"Yes," she replied. "And the pickup is still at the dock. If this guy is as thorough as you say he is, he might have ordered someone to break in, look for my registration, then visit my house to make sure it's empty."

Jack sent a quick glance at Matt. The vehicle was a loose end he hadn't thought of. Someone was going to have to pull it into an impound lot before anything resembling the scenario Libby had just painted came to pass.

"It could happen," he said, half to himself, before giving Libby what he hoped was a reassuring grin. "But if it does, no harm would be done. We didn't leave any trace that we'd been to your house the other night."

The fear stayed in Libby's eyes as she shook her head. "You don't understand. We have to go back to my house. We have to get the picture."

"What picture?"

"The one of you." Libby paused to shake her head. "Well, it's not you, but it looks like you. The only details missing are your mustache and the cleft in your chin."

Jack frowned, both at the jumble of incomprehensible words and at the deep blush that turned Libby's pale face a bright pink. She took a deep breath, then went on, "You asked about my dreamscapes. Well, they're sort of collages, formed out of several negatives. Like the family portrait I explained about. Well, when I was learning the technique, I used photos of several men with features I admired to create a portrait of one man. The resulting composite looks a lot like you."

"How flattering." Matt's dry humor lent warmth to his words.

Jack was grateful that his cousin had spoken, for he was speechless at the moment. He could see that Libby was having difficulty, too, until she turned to Matt and spoke quickly.

"If someone sees that picture, some person connected to that trial where Jack was shot, they might assume that I'd known him previously. They might decide to do more than simply listen to his phone calls."

"Don't worry about it, Libby," Jack managed to say at last. "I'll see to it that someone from our team gets into your place and removes that picture. No, don't give me that cat argument again. I'll tell the captain that whoever he assigns should wear talon-proof knee-high socks and take goodies to keep your feline friends happy. They can put down more food while they're at it. And I promise to warn them not to spook Barnum."

Libby stared up at him for several moments, her eyes clouded with worry, her cheeks flushing. Finally, she gave him a resigned shrug.

"Got it all under control?" Matt asked.

Jack turned to him and nodded.

"Good. Now, I asked you to come up here so I could tell you what's happening. I leave today for L.A. I got a call this morning and recognized the voice as belonging to the guy who ordered me to shoot Libby. As usual, he's being very careful. His call was too short to trace. All he said was that I was to pick up a package at a warehouse in San Rafael at noon, then drive down the coast and check into a motel on Melrose, where I'm to sit and wait for the phone to ring. More instructions will, I assume, be forthcoming."

"The captain has arranged for backup?"

"A team is being put in place even as we speak. The San Francisco Police Department and the California Highway Patrol will be with me on the way down. L.A.P.D. will take over once I get to Malibu."

Jack nodded slowly as a knot formed in his stomach. He should be the one sticking his neck out, putting his life on the line, not Matt, not his laughing, happy-go-lucky best friend in all the world.

"You've packed, I assume," Jack chided. "And you remembered clean underwear."

"Yes, Mother." Matt grinned widely. "Hey. I need to kill some time before I head on down the Yellow Brick Road. My appointment in San Rafael is a couple of hours off. How about some target practice? Libby can judge our little contest."

Jack glanced over his shoulder. Libby's backpack hung open on one shoulder and she cradled a camera in one hand. The smile she gave Matt was a little lopsided.

"I've got a better idea," she said. "How about I shoot the two of you shooting?"

Jack followed his cousin up the hill to a wide clearing. Matt had already set up the first row of targets, several rusted cans, on an old stump. With Libby standing well to one side, Jack stood on his mark and in moments the sound of gunfire and the smell of powder blasted away thoughts of the danger that Matt faced, and took Jack back to those simpler days he'd been thinking about earlier.

His shooting pleased him, too. He didn't miss one can. Did better, in fact, than Matt. He had to fight a grin as his cousin frowned after missing two of his targets. But when Matt turned and prepared to toss a can into the air, every muscle in Jack's body grew suddenly tight.

"Ready?"

Jack wanted to shake his head, wanted to remind Matt that his hand still tingled sometimes, his fingers occasionally refused to respond on sudden demand. He nodded, instead, as he gripped the butt of his gun. The can flew into the air, he lifted his weapon, got the target in sight and pulled the trigger.

At least, that was what his brain told his finger to do. The message got short-circuited somewhere, freezing his index finger for a moment, just long enough for the can to begin to drop. Then the trigger came back, the hammer fell and the gun popped.

The cylinder of tin dropped to the ground, totally unmolested. Jack stared at it, his stomach twisting. That shot had once been his specialty. In the old days, he would have shot from the hip and hit the can four times out of five.

"Missed by a hair."

Jack looked into his cousin's face. Matt's smile was strained. His normally dancing green eyes didn't quite meet Jack's. He knew. Matt knew what Jack had been fearing for weeks, that his gun hand was never going to be what it had been, that Jack was going to have to let the game of cops and robbers go on without him.

"We'd try it again," Matt said, "but I think I'd better get going. Don't want to miss my appointment. And hey, who knows? Maybe we'll get lucky and our man of mystery will greet me in San Rafael in person, I can collar him and we can put an end to all of this today."

"Right." Jack forced a joviality to his voice that he was far from feeling. "And maybe all the hills of San Francisco will collapse in the space of one moment."

Matt lifted his hands. "Hey, watch what you say. *That* could happen."

Jack shook his head at the sick joke. His lips curved into a genuine smile as he punched Matt's shoulder lightly. "Watch your back and phone home often. You hear, sonny?"

"I hear, Mother. See you soon. Now, go get that poor girl out of the tree over there before she falls and hits that head of hers again."

Jack turned. Matt's receding footsteps echoed in his ears as he stared at Libby. Perched in the crook of a nearby tree, eight feet off the ground, she leaned over the limb, her camera held tight to her face.

"Libby!"

She jerked, then turned to him as he strode forward, her pale face questioning the anger that had echoed in his voice. Fear for her safety and frustration over his hand's momentary hesitation added fuel to that anger.

"Are you trying to get yourself killed?" He glared up at her from the base of the tree. "Get down here immediately."

Her lips twitched. "Yes, Mother," she said in a perfect imitation of Matt's sarcasm.

Under normal circumstances, Jack would have seen the humor, would have replied in kind. But nothing was normal anymore. He'd gone from being ecstatic over his marksmanship to abject misery over his failure to shoot under pressure. And the worst of it was, he couldn't let anyone know. It was bad enough that Matt suspected. But Matt was on *his* side. If anyone else found out, the bubble would burst at last, he would no longer even be able to pretend that he had a chance to keep his job.

"Knock it off, Libby. We have work to do. Get down so we can start looking for that tie. And be damned careful."

Libby found no joy in the rest of the day as she followed Jack in and out of a series of men's stores located in several shopping malls. His mood had been dark ever since they'd left the grove of trees, and it seemed to grow darker as the day went on. Not only didn't they find anything that resembled the tie that had bound her hands, but although several of the clerks admired the intricate batik style that formed the impressionistic faces decorating the silk, none of them had seen anything like it before.

"Maybe we should try some art stores," Libby suggested as they got back into the van. "Many of them carry one-of-a-kind items. Some of them have textile shows from time to time, too. They might know who does this kind of work."

"Could be." Jack's voice held absolutely no enthusiasm. He shrugged as he went on, "It's getting late. We'll work on that tomorrow."

These were the most civilized words he had uttered all afternoon. For two hours after they left the grove of trees, he had hardly glanced at Libby, hadn't said more than a word or two, and these had been a warning to let him do the questioning when they reached the stores.

As if she wanted to do his job for him, or something, Libby thought huffily as she frowned into the fading light of evening. How childish. And she hated this silent treatment of his. Dan had done this to her, too, whenever life had upset him and she had happened to do or say the wrong thing.

It might help if she knew exactly what Jack was so peeved at. She was aware that he hadn't been happy to find her in the tree, had refused to listen to her explanation about the squirrel she'd wanted to catch on film. He hadn't even relaxed when she demonstrated the relative safety of her perch by climbing down the close-set limbs that descended the trunk like a circular staircase.

Perhaps it was that business about the composite photo. She'd seen the stunned look on his face when she described how she'd put it together. She had to admit the explanation must have seemed absurd, must have made it sound as if she'd spent her life waiting for someone matching Jack McDermott's description to come into her life like some Prince Charming. Like she expected him to place a glass slipper on her foot and make her life perfect from that moment on.

Libby's jaw tightened. Well, he was wrong. She had *not* spent her life waiting for a conquering hero. Well, part of it, maybe. But ever since the day she realized that Dan only wanted her as long as she was willing to play the adoring bride, she had walked out that door and started to see to her own needs.

She did not *need* the man she'd created for that photo, *or* the one who sat next to her. As soon as she knew that Matt was out of danger, she would walk out of Jack's door and back to the life she'd created for herself.

Chapter 9

Libby was still fuming an hour later. Not that Jack had noticed. He had barely glanced at her when they got back to the cabin, other than to tell her to stay in the van until he could sweep the house electronically and make sure no more listening devices had been planted in their absence.

Once he gave her the all-clear sign and waved her in, he disappeared into the bathroom, then emerged in T-shirt, shorts and running shoes. Libby watched him cross the street then start down the beach for another jog. Well, here was one man who took running away from his problems literally, she thought as she turned to stare at the ever-narrowing walls and tried to figure out what to do.

What she was *not* going to do was waste any more time worrying about what Jack McDermott was so white-lipped upset about. She was not going to try to mollify him, as she had attempted to do with Dan whenever life frustrated him and he lost his temper.

Ten minutes later, she reassured herself that she was only in the kitchen, mixing a salad and peeling potatoes for mashing while two steaks marinated in the refrigerator, because it felt good to be doing something useful. Besides, she was in the mood for steak, for something cooked rare that she could sink her teeth into.

Libby had just heated up the gas barbecue on the deck behind the house when Jack came in. She glanced at the two steaks on the platter, then looked over at him as he started toward the shower. She *could* put her meat on to cook and let him worry about his own dinner when he thought about it. The way her temper was flaring, she was tempted to do just that, but her anger was hardly an excuse to waste all that fossil fuel.

"Jack?" she called through the open sliding door.

He stopped in the doorway to the bathroom and turned to her as she said, "I'm cooking dinner. How do you like your steak?"

He stared at her a moment with an expression that spoke of surprise, then gave her a small smile. "Well-done," he said, then shut the door.

The smile didn't ease Libby's ill humor at all. In fact, it only added to it. What a jerk. Not one word of thanks. She'd been in Jack McDermott's house for three days and now she was a fixture, someone whose proper place was to prepare his dinner, to see to his every need. Like *hell!* She should *burn* the damn steak for him.

Twenty minutes later, Libby placed a plate in front of Jack, who had showered and changed into jeans and the ivory fisherman sweater she remembered seeing the first time she'd woken on his couch. It looked every bit as good on his wide-shouldered body now as it had that morning. His hair was still a bit damp, falling in red-brown waves onto his forehead in a way that made him look young and vulnerable, that made it impossible for Libby to stay angry at him.

She'd gotten past that, anyway, she told herself as she took a seat on the bench at the kitchen table and began cutting the steak she'd cooked to pink-in-the-center perfection for herself. It *had* felt good, though, to react with anger to a situation that at one time would have reduced her to a cowering wimp. Now, she simply wanted to savor the food she had prepared, to enjoy it with no thought as to what effect the food might be having on the man sitting on the other side of the table.

Jack swallowed another piece of steak, followed by a glass of red wine. The run had done him a world of good, had put things back into perspective. The doctors had warned him that the nerves to his hand might be slow to heal. Forget that they'd added, *if ever*. It was clear that his injury had obviously affected his reaction time, but that only meant he would have to work harder, exercise his hand and fingers more, the way he'd done with his knee.

Three nights ago, he'd been about to give up hope on that, too, when it had threatened to give out on him as he carried Libby's limp form down the hill. Tonight, his leg had barely protested at all as he'd pounded down the beach, working up a healthy appetite.

An appetite that was being more than adequately satisfied by this meal.

"This is good." Jack looked at Libby as he indicated the steak with the tip of his knife. "What did you do to it?"

She barely lifted her eyes to his before glancing back down at the beef she was slicing. "Just marinated it for a while."

Something was wrong. Jack recognized the stiff reply, the refusal to look him in the eye. Sheila had treated him this way more times than he could remember, especially whenever he'd been late for dinner. Jack opened his mouth to apologize, but before he could say a word, his eyebrows dropped into a scowl. Why should he say he was sorry? He hadn't promised to be back at any special time.

"Look, Libby," he said, "I didn't ask you to play the 'little woman' and cook for me, you know."

These words made her dark eyes narrow slightly as she stared at him a moment. "I know that. I had time, so I put the steaks in a sauce while I made salad and potatoes. It's no more trouble to make two servings than it is to make one, you know. And as for the steak, I wasn't planning on waiting for you. I was getting ready to cook mine when you came in."

Libby held Jack's gaze one more moment, then returned her attention to her dinner. Jack finished his in silence, as well. She didn't seem angry, he told himself, just very distant. As if she'd pulled away from him and locked herself in a tower somewhere out of his reach.

Jack glanced at her again as he rose to take his plate to the sink. While she finished eating, he washed his dishes and utensils, as well as the bowl in which Libby tossed the salad and the pot in which she'd prepared the potatoes.

When he turned to ask if she was finished, Jack found that Libby had left the table and moved over to stand before the large front window. While she stared out into the night, from all indications completely unaware of his presence, he removed her dishes and washed them, too.

Her silence ate at Jack, worried him. Libby had been through a lot in the last few days, not the least of which was the ordeal of being shut up in a tiny cabin with a moody soul like himself. The outing she had looked forward to today must have turned into a nightmare for her, forced to follow him like a muzzled puppy as he ran in and out of stores.

"You need to get out," he said as he came to stand next to Libby. When she looked up, eyes widened into a question, he gave her a smile. "You've been cooped up too long. You need some exercise. Get something heavier on, and we'll go for a walk."

He didn't know what he'd expected from her. That she'd give him a hug, perhaps, and thank him for his graciousness. Smile, at least. He certainly hadn't figured she'd simply shrug, walk over to the duffel that still sat by his closet, pull out a thick hooded navy sweatshirt and slip into it as she wordlessly walked back to him.

Jack matched her silence as he led her out the front door and across the narrow street to the wide stretch of sand. He said nothing as they continued toward the whispering of the night waves, nothing until they stood staring at the moonlight shimmering on the wet sand at the ocean's very edge.

"So what's eating you?" he asked at last.

The sound of waves hissing as they slid down the sloping shore echoed in the silence following Jack's question. He stared at Libby until she turned her head toward him and replied.

"Nothing."

"Don't *nothing* me. I know when someone is ticked off and keeping it to themselves. I *should* know. I'm the king of the silent fumers."

He saw one side of her mouth lift slightly. "So you are. Well, I guess that makes me the queen. Or it would, if I were fuming. I'm not. I did that while you were gone."

"You were mad at me because I left the house?"

Her eyes flew open. "No. I was mad at you because you were mad at me and I found myself playing the same kind of wimpy, oh-what-have-I-done role I fell into every time Dan got angry."

Jack grabbed Libby's hand and pulled her around so that she was forced to look directly up into his eyes.

"Libby. Listen to me. I'm not Dan. I might get angry and yell. I might argue, or I might not, depending on my mood. But I've never been known to punish anyone, verbally or otherwise, no matter how ticked off I get. And just to set the record straight, I was *not* angry at you."

Libby lifted her chin ever so slightly. "You're lying. Look, I can take it. I know it was silly of me to climb that tree when I've been having dizzy spells, but I don't think of things like that when I see a shot I want to get."

Jack took a deep breath, then placed a hand on her shoulder. "Yes, it was silly of you, and it scared me when I saw you up there. But I overreacted to that because I was angry at something else."

Libby pulled her hand from his, crossed her arms over her chest and turned her head to stare at the rolling waves. "It was the picture, wasn't it?"

"The picture?"

When Libby looked back at him, her eyes glinted defiantly in the moonlight. "Yes, the one that needs to be removed from my bedroom. The picture of the man that looks so much like you."

"Libby, why would that make me *angry?*"

Her curls tossed around her face as she shook her head. "I don't know. I thought maybe the idea that I'd created the image of someone so like you might have embarrassed you. Dan used to get angry whenever I did anything that embarrassed him."

"I told you," Jack said, his voice lowering to a growl. "I'm *not* Dan. And besides, why would I be *embarrassed* by this composite photo? Intrigued, maybe, flattered, yeah, but not embarrassed."

His voice had deepened and softened as his mind played with this. He'd forgotten about the picture. He needed to call this little bit of info in, and now that he thought about it, he *was* going to feel a little foolish explaining it to the guys.

It was a little spooky to think of Libby creating a picture like that, especially considering the way she'd fallen into his life. It raised questions about fated meetings and predestined relationships that sent a tingle running up his spine and lit a strange glow in his chest.

"Okay then," Libby said. "Why *were* you angry?"

"What?" Jack pulled back from the fanciful road his mind had stepped onto and focused on reality, where he felt far more at home. "Oh—you mean those hours in which I acted like a wild animal looking for something to chew on? Simple. I missed a shot."

"A shot?" Libby stepped back from the light hold he had on her shoulder. "You mean you treated me like an unwanted piece of baggage because you failed to put a bullet in the middle of a tin can?"

Put that way, his behavior did sound ridiculous. Of course, Libby had no way of knowing the implications of the sudden glitch in his reaction time.

"Your trigger finger," she said suddenly, her voice much softer this time. "It froze up on you, didn't it?"

Libby reached out to curl her fingers around his, drawing his hand between both of hers as she gazed into his eyes. He was wrong about her, he thought. She *did* know. Her eyes were filled with sympathy, with understanding. But not with pity. And there was none in her words when she spoke again.

"You haven't been doing your exercises properly since I came into your life, have you? Matt's visit interrupted the ones you'd started the night before last." She paused, then went on, "I don't know much about this stuff, but it seems to me that it's far too soon to declare your career over on the basis of one can that escaped your marksmanship."

Jack felt his shoulders begin to tighten in response to her words, felt the old defenses come up, defenses that warned him to deny his weakness. Instead, he smiled at her. "You're right. Will you join me in the hot tub while I give the old digits a proper workout?"

Libby gazed up at the dusting of stars that marked the night sky as she rested her head against the edge of the hot tub. A breath of cool air brushed over her upturned face, leaving the scent of salt and chilling her cheeks. The rest of her body was warm, cradled as it was in heated liquid. A slight splash made her turn her head to watch Jack repeatedly open and close his fingers, then massage his right forearm and hand with his left.

"Can I help you with anything?" she asked.

Jack's head jerked toward her. The hooded look in his eyes, the tension in his mouth told her his guard was up again, that he was hurting and didn't want anyone to see. She said nothing, just continued to gaze into his eyes, waiting, as if her words were an offering of food tossed to a wild animal that needed taming.

"As a matter of fact, you can," Jack answered quietly. His gaze softened slightly as Libby sat up and moved closer to him.

"I need help stretching. Hold your left hand up, fingers splayed," he instructed. "Now, I'm going to fit each of my fingers to yours, then press forward. You resist, all right?"

Libby kept her hand steady while Jack pressed forward until his fingers were bent backward at almost right angles to the back of his hand. He held the position several moments, then relaxed, only to start the procedure again.

Watching his face, she saw his frown of concentration, imagined she could feel the desperation that fueled each motion.

When he stopped at last, his fingers curved around hers, as if drawing her into his battle. Libby squeezed back as her heart skipped a beat. She was only helping, she told herself. She was not trying to save anyone here. Those days were over.

"Thanks."

The simple word, so softly spoken, made Libby blink and look into Jack's eyes. He gave her a smile and said, "I'm done now. You can let go."

Libby uncurled her fingers. Her left hand slid back into the water, but her right hand remained clasped in Jack's. His smile widened. "You're stronger than you look."

"That's true," she said, and let her lips curve into a smile. I'm strong enough to be there for a man, she thought, to be there without losing myself. Try me, Jack. "I think maybe there's some sort of isometric value in holding a camera still for long periods of time."

"You don't use a tripod?"

"Oh, sure, but there are times it's just not practical to drag one of those along."

"Like when you're chasing squirrels up a tree?"

Libby slid her hand from Jack's loose grasp and glanced down at the water. "Yeah."

The pressure from Jack's wet finger beneath her chin brought Libby's gaze back up to his as he asked, "Tell me, do you always get so caught up in your work?"

"Yep. I'm a little dangerous when I have a camera in my hand. It's like I've stepped into another universe, where everything is defined by light and shadows and angles, and I'm invulnerable as long as I'm engaged in capturing that world on film. There's a certain magic involved in the process.''

Jack stared deeply into her eyes for several moments before asking, ''And the pictures you produce, are they magic, too?''

The way his eyes narrowed slightly puzzled Libby. Shaking her head slowly, she replied, ''No. The pictures I create are only reflections of reality.''

''Then why call them dreamscapes?'' A frown dropped over Jack's eyes as he went on, ''Why include people who never existed, or superimpose a human face over that of an animal?''

Libby turned from him to stare at the sky again. She had known this was coming. Her work was difficult to explain to people. So many of them misunderstood, wanted to label what she did as being ''spiritual'' or ''otherworldly'' or even just ''weird.'' Normally, she just let her photographs speak for themselves, but it was very important to her that *this* man understand.

''It began in therapy, after Dan died,'' she said. ''Although I had begun to work through years of verbal abuse and was starting to feel better about myself, I still had no sense of direction. In the past, I had always defined my life by the things that were lacking in it, a father, siblings, pets. Miriam White, my psychologist, encouraged me to try meditation, to create a vision in which all these elements were a part of my life. But every time I tried sitting around with my eyes closed to ''visualize,'' I fell asleep. So I started creating collages, first by taking photographs, cutting them up, then pasting them together to create a picture that depicted the life I wanted.''

Jack nodded as she paused. ''I think I saw one of those on the wall in your bedroom. A little girl on a horse.''

Libby's lips curved. "Yeah, that was one of my first attempts. The man who fathered me was an itinerant photographer, you see. He went around neighborhoods with a pony and a camera and took pictures of kids dressed as little cowboys and cowgirls."

Her smile faded. "My mother would never discuss my father, my granddad was the same way. I owe what little I know to my Aunt Susan, who told a sordid story about my mother ditching school toward the end of her junior year in high school, inviting the handsome 'devil,' as Susan called him, into the empty house and allowing herself to be seduced. Nine months later, I came into the world."

And ruined her mother's.

Libby shook away the intrusive thought, then hurried on, "Anyway, the picture of me riding a horse was my attempt to make some connection with this man, just as the photo of the people on the porch was an effort to heal what I perceived as the loss of a loving family."

She watched Jack's eyebrows pucker in a questioning frown. "And did it work?" he asked. "Were you *healed?*"

The slightly cynical note on Jack's last word made the skin on Libby's arms tighten. She gave him a quick shrug and replied, "The picture itself didn't make the wanting go away, if that's what you mean. But working with the *idea* behind the photo did help me see that those unfulfilled needs had been fueling my willingness to put up with less than the real thing. More than that, producing the pictures opened the door to a career I love. It gives me a great deal of pleasure to help people create a vision that embodies the best of what they want out of life."

"What do you mean?"

Jack's eyebrows lowered to a more pronounced frown. Libby felt her heart sink. He wasn't going to understand. He was going to think she was crazy, a head-in-the-clouds fruitcake. She was accustomed to that reaction, had overcome it before. All she had to do was remain calm and speak logically.

"Well, my more artsy stuff is like the horse you saw running on the clouds," she said. "And actually, it was for a gallery showing of that kind of photo that I came up with the umbrella title of *Dreamscapes*. Then Miriam asked me to help some of her clients see themselves in the life they were working toward. That's why I have all those props and costumes in my basement."

"I see." Jack's nod was stiff, his voice was tight as he went on, "Well, I imagine your dreamscapes must sell well in *this* part of the country. All this New Age visualization stuff must have created quite a market for you and this therapist of yours. But I wonder if it ever occurs to either of you that some people have *real* problems, problems that all the wishful thinking in the world can't help."

Libby sat up straighter, tucking one leg beneath her as she turned to meet the anger in Jack's eyes. "No one is promising that these pictures will *heal* anything. Some of Miriam's patients use them to recreate a happy moment in their past, others ask for pictures that will represent a certain ability they are striving toward. Not everyone is like you, someone who has always known who they are or what they are capable of doing. There are people out there who are accustomed to seeing themselves as losers, who can't imagine themselves as having any value at all."

"Right. So you take a shot of a woman who weighs two hundred pounds, affix her head on the photographic image of a ballerina, and she'll magically lose weight?"

Libby shook her head. "No. I don't promise that sort of thing to anyone and neither does Miriam. I offer people a chance to see themselves as they would like to be. Someone who is afraid of flying might commission a shot of themselves in the cockpit of a biplane, soaring above the clouds. But both Miriam and I make it clear to our clients that dreams are only won by hard work and persistence. Dreamscapes are only meant to show people what is *possible*, not to magically grant some wish."

Jack stared at her a moment, then abruptly stood. Libby blinked at him, then got to her feet, as well, and stood chest-to-chest with him. "You're angry again."

"No, I'm not," he said.

"Okay, you think I'm a nut case, then, a New Age version of a snake oil salesman, that I'm promising people that my pictures will heal all their ills, that I'm bilking my clients and—"

"And if I thought that, I'd take you in on bunko charges right now," Jack interrupted. His lips eased into a lopsided smile. "I'm not thinking any of those things. All this talk of photography reminded me that I never called in about that picture hanging on your wall, the one that looks like me. It's not a call I want to make on the cellular, since it will take quite a bit of explaining, so I'll have to go to a pay phone." His smile widened. "You can state your case further when I get back, if you want. For the moment, though, why don't you stay out here in the warm water while I change. Okay?"

Libby was more than happy to escape the cold air by dropping back into the heated water. Through the beaded curtain, she watched Jack dry himself off in front of the wood stove he'd lit before they entered the tub. The overhead light glanced off the sculpted muscles in his legs, arms and chest as he rubbed the towel along the rugged contours. The contrast of light and dark brought a smile to her face as Libby studied his lean body, one that had certainly not been formed by wishful thinking.

After Jack had disappeared into the bathroom to change into his jeans and sweater, then reappeared to leave by the front door, Libby exited the tub. Locking the glass door behind her, she hurried into the bathroom, where she dried off, then she zipped her oversize navy sweatshirt on over a pair of matching leggings. Not the most seductive outfit she owned, but she told herself that seduction was not likely to be part of the evening's fare.

She wasn't even sure she'd know how to go about it, she thought as she turned out the light and made her way toward the glow coming from the wood stove's glass door. As she sat in the near dark, she considered the fact that she'd had pitifully little experience with men before marrying Dan. Her aunt had kept Libby too busy at home during high school for her to date much. And during the few times she'd been out since Dan's death, the barriers that she'd built to keep Dan-type men away had never been breached.

So what was so different about this man? Libby shook out the ends of her hair, dampened from her stay in the hot tub. Cozying up to the wood stove, she let its heat dry her hair and chase away the chill she'd caught in her race across the deck, and thought about Jack.

It was more than his good looks that drew her to him, she knew, although every time those deep vertical creases bracketed his smiling lips, she grew just the tiniest weak in the knees. And it wasn't his strength, although she had to admit that the most heady sensations swirled through her every time he held her. His mere touch could be intoxicating, for that matter.

So what did that make his kisses? Pure pleasure, that's what.

Libby had never experienced pure pleasure before. Not even the best chocolate possessed the sweetness of Jack's lips on hers, the soothing, stirring sensation of his tongue slipping into her mouth.

Suddenly Libby found that she was far too hot, sitting so close to the stove. Drawing a quick breath, she scooted back to rest against the beanbag chair in the alcove beneath the loft, then watched the flames dance on the other side of the wood stove's glass door.

Fire. Heat. Was that all that drew her to this man? What about the way he looked into her eyes and told her without words that he found her brave and strong, and wasn't threatened by that? What about the fact that although they both had wounds to heal, she believed they could help each other without fearing that either of them would get lost in the process?

What about the fact that she had fallen in love with Jack McDermott?

The sudden acknowledgement of her feelings shook Libby to her very core. She sat very still, listening to the whisper of the fire while she let the truth sink in. She should be afraid. After all, she'd known Jack for a very short time. But she felt no dread, no sense that she was repeating the mistake she'd made with Dan. Instead, she was overcome by a sense that everything was unfolding as it should, giddy with the certainty that she'd been drawn into Jack's life, and he into hers, so that they could complete one another in every way.

The front door opened with a suddenness that made Libby jump, then turn toward the figure standing in the opening as Jack's voice shouted, "Libby!"

"I'm here," she said.

The light came on and Jack stared at her as he shut the door behind him. "What are you doing here in the dark?"

Dreaming of you.

"Just... watching the fire."

"Oh. Well, we have to talk." Jack started toward her as he spoke. Libby didn't like the worried look in his eyes, but she rose to meet it as he crossed the room.

"My call to Semosa comes under the category of perfect timing," Jack said as he stopped in front of her. "They were just about to call me. You were right to be worried about your truck. Earlier today, it was reported as an abandoned vehicle to the Marin County Sheriff's Department. They, of course, have no idea you are in hiding."

Jack paused and put his hands on Libby's shoulders. His fingers were cold, but not as cold as the chilly sensation that swirled in the pit of her stomach as he went on.

"The unit responding to the call found your driver's license. Your picture matched the description that our people had to put out on the body that was supposedly found yesterday." Jack shook his head. "The rest of the story is a long tale full of missed connections, but the upshot is that your mother has been notified of your 'death,' and she wants to identify your body."

Chapter 10

"You don't have to go along with Semosa's plan, you know. Having the medical examiner make you up to look dead, so you can be pulled out of a morgue drawer to be identified is a little extreme."

Jack spoke softly to the figure wrapped in his arms. They sat on the floor in front of the wood stove, where he had lowered Libby after realizing just how badly her legs were shaking. She sat in front of him, her back supported by his chest, where she had remained, unmoving, while he explained the plan that had been outlined to him on the phone. She was perfectly still, the back of her head resting against his shoulder, her eyes reflecting the dying flames in the wood stove as Jack went on.

"Libby. I think everyone will agree that having you lie on a slab wearing body paint and a sheet, just to keep alive the fiction that Matt shot you, is going far beyond the call of duty. I'm sure there are other ways to handle this that wouldn't traumatize your poor mother like this will."

Libby jerked in his arms at this. Sitting up, she turned her head to look into his eyes as she spoke. "Believe me, my mother does not care enough about me to be *traumatized*. A little upset maybe. No one could take a trip to a morgue *lightly*, after all. But she'll get over it."

Her harsh, bitter tone stunned Jack. "Libby, this is your mother. I gather you've had your differences, but—"

"But nothing." Her voice caught. Jack heard the pain beneath her anger as she went on, "Look, this is not like the resentment you feel toward your father. My mother didn't just disapprove of my choice of careers. Good Lord, if she'd shown any interest in it one way or the other, I would have been thrilled. Jack, *the woman gave me up.*"

A frown drew his eyebrows together. "I thought you said she was part of the original photo taken on your grandfather's house."

"She was." The words came out soft, almost wistful. "That was in the good days, when she and I and Granddad lived in his big old house. He was sick some of the time, but Mother and I took care of him and he gave us a home in return. He loved us, accepted us, even if the rest of the family *was* scandalized by my illegitimacy."

Libby stopped speaking and turned her head to stare at the fire again.

"And then he died," Jack prompted.

Libby nodded. "I guess that was when my mother realized how my coming along when I did, under the circumstances that I did, had screwed up her life. She hadn't finished high school, you see. They made unwed mothers leave school back then."

A short pause followed these words. When Libby went on, her wistful tone became hard, flat. "Granddad's will stipulated that all his assets were to be divided between Mother and her older sister, Susan. The house brought in quite a bit, but I guess not much was left after the bills for his long hospital stay were settled. So, Mother and I were left with no home, and she had no way of supporting us."

Within Jack's loose grasp he felt Libby's chest rise and fall in a shaky breath before she spoke again. "My mother decided she needed to complete her education in order to support herself. I was thrilled. In my seven-year-old mind I pictured us sitting at some table, doing our homework together, working side by side as we had when we cleaned Granddad's house. Apparently, though, she felt I would be in the way. So, she handed me over to my Aunt Susan and her husband, Carl. They, in turn, treated me like a servant, one whose moral fiber was questionable, but apparently passable enough to be utilized as a built-in baby-sitter for my younger cousins."

A turn of her head brought Libby's eyes back to Jack's. "Other than receiving a present from her at Christmas that first year, I haven't heard a thing from my mother since. I'm sure the only reason she was traced is that I refuse to list my aunt as next of kin on any form I'm made to fill out, so I always put my mother's name. That's all we are to each other, names on forms."

As Jack felt a shudder ripple through Libby's slender body, he tightened his arms gently around her. "Okay, you've convinced me that the woman is not worth worrying about. But what about you? This isn't going to be a picnic. Do you think you can be shut up in a drawer, then lie still while she looks at you?"

Libby broke Jack's grasp, then turned to kneel in front of him and level determined eyes on his. "If it will preserve the illusion that Matt actually shot me, and keep him safe, I can get through it. As long as there's a chance that someone in the police department might be involved with the man Matt is after, we can't take any chances. You *can* trust the medical examiner, I take it?"

"Yes, Dr. Bloomenfeld is the only one outside of the lieutenant, the captain, Sergeant Semosa and the three local officers working this thing who knows that the body bag brought in that day was filled with rocks and dirt. So far, Matt's cover is safe."

"Then we have to keep it that way."

"Libby, we *can* let your mother in on this. We can figure out a way to see that no one gets to her. We can—''

"No!"

Libby leaped to her feet. Hands on her hips, she glared at Jack as she said, "You *can't!* How can you consider entrusting Matt's life to a woman who abandoned the child that she'd once hugged and tickled and sang lullabies to? How can you imagine that such a woman would... would..."

Jack had gotten to his feet as she spoke. He gazed down at Libby, watching her eyes well up with tears as she struggled to continue speaking. His heart twisted as she tried to blink back the moisture and gasp back the sob. Sliding his arms around her, he pulled her forward to cover her trembling lips with his.

Jack felt Libby relax into him, felt her lips soften under the tender pressure his mouth was delivering. He savored the taste of salt and sweetness with his tongue. His arms began to pull her even closer, but her hands suddenly tightened on his shoulders.

Libby noted the strength of the muscles beneath her palms, even as she pushed back from Jack, reluctantly but determinedly drawing her mouth from the kiss that was filling her with slow warmth. Her chest rose and fell quickly as she fought the anger, the sadness, the overwhelming sorrow that had risen to the surface as she discussed her mother. She looked Jack in the eye and tried to speak past the emotion that clogged her throat.

"I don't want you... to do this... just because you feel... sorry for me..."

Her shaky voice trailed off. She was aware of the way Jack gazed at her. His eyes, dark green in the shadow of his frown, seemed to see directly into her soul. Libby felt some of her anguish ease as she watched that scowl lift and saw tiny crinkles form at the corners of his eyes as his mouth curved into a small smile. He lifted a hand to cup her cheek.

"Libby," he said softly, "I'm not going to tell you that your story hasn't moved me. But believe me, I'm not kissing you because I pity you, or admire your strength, or because I want to make up for what happened in your past. I'm kissing you because ever since I first held you in my arms and you brushed your lips over mine, I've wanted more. More of your touch, more of your lips, more of your body next to mine."

A strange calm washed over Libby. As Jack's voice grew deeper, more husky, sudden heat spread downward, banishing the cold emotions that had only moments before made her gasp for control. When Jack pulled her toward him again, Libby lifted her hands to his shoulders. She glided toward him until her breasts were pressing against his chest and her lips were once more parting beneath his.

Soon, it wasn't enough to be joined at the lips and at the chest. Soon, she and Jack had lowered themselves to lie side by side on the shag carpet, their bodies touching from shoulder to toes. Their legs intertwined as they twisted together.

Libby, a voice warned, *you barely know this man*.

The feel of Jack's lips on hers, the heat of his body pulsing against her, were heady drugs that shushed the admonishing whisper. Besides, she *did* know her heart, knew it belonged to this man. It didn't matter that he didn't understand what she did for a living, or that the dangerous career he loved frightened her. Deep down they were very much alike, souls that had been battered and bruised and had survived to love another day. Jagged puzzle pieces that were meant to fit.

These thoughts, pleasant as they were, fled as Jack's hands slid beneath Libby's sweatshirt, cupped her bottom and lifted her against him. She gasped against his lips as she felt his desire throbbing against her belly. She arched slightly, increasing the contact and eliciting a deep groan from the man who held her so tightly.

Jack relaxed his fingers, splaying them over her warm flesh. Her skin was like satin beneath his touch. Her waist curved beneath his hand as he slid his fingers up, skimming her ribs. Biting back another growl, he let the tip of her naked breast tease his palm.

She was so soft, so tender, so much of everything he wanted. He was aware of voices whispering in his mind, warning against the irresponsibility of becoming involved with someone he was supposed to be protecting, but they were drowned out by the roar of pulsing blood in his ears. He had responsibilities to himself, to his sanity, which demanded that he taste of this woman deeply and completely if it was to be maintained at all.

He needed more of Libby, wanted her naked, all silken skin sliding over his. As he began to unzip her sweatshirt, he lifted his head from hers. Libby's eyes opened to gaze into his. As the zipper reached the bottom of its track, those eyes widened and filled with an emotion that appeared to be doubt, or fear.

"What is it, Libby?"

She took a deep breath. Jack braced himself. She was going to tell him to stop. He would have to respect her wishes, would somehow have to turn off the desire that tortured him with promised pleasure. It would take more than a cold shower, he knew. It would—

"The front window," she breathed.

Jack's forehead puckered with lack of comprehension.

"The light is on," she said. "Someone could look in and see us."

That was all?

Jack was on his feet in moments, across the room and had the heavy mustard-colored drapes pulled shut in one quick swish. The light. He'd turn that off, too, just in case Libby was feeling suddenly shy. Darkness fell with a flick of the switch, then Libby spoke again, her voice soft, uncertain.

"Jack, while you're up, why don't you rescue one of those items you stuffed in the medicine cabinet, behind the bottle of antacid?"

A grin stole over Jack's lips as he turned toward the bathroom. She must have found the condoms. And she wanted him to bring one over to her. Yes, life was good.

Libby heard the mirrored cabinet drawer squeak open, listened to the sounds of ripping cellophane echo in the dark. A shiver trembled through her. An attack of nerves? Perhaps. But she wanted this. If years of therapy hadn't been enough, recent events had shown her that life moved quickly, and not always the way mere mortals would decree.

He who hesitates is lost.

She was not going to hesitate, to risk losing this moment, this perfect space in time where she could test her dreams, trust her belief that this man did embody all the traits she'd tried to infuse in the photographic image that looked so much like him.

In seconds, Libby managed to slip the tight leggings off, then shrug out of the sweatshirt. It was a brazen act, something that had never occurred to her to do before, even when married. But she wanted Jack to have no question about her willingness to share herself with him.

But then, as she lay stretched out on the rug, dressed only in tiny black bikini panties, listening to Jack stumble back toward her, she drew in a quick, frightened breath. It was too late to cover herself, too late to do anything but hope that he would find her actions seductive, not silly, or so forward as to turn him off.

Once Jack was close enough for her to examine his features, it became clear that he was not at all dismayed by her actions. He stood above her for several moments, his eyes traveling every inch of her body with such thoroughness that she could almost feel a caress follow.

When his hands reached for the hem of his sweater, Libby shook her head. "No. Let me, please."

She got to her feet then, grasped the knitted fabric in both hands, then tugged upward. All went well until the material reached just above Jack's head, when his height defeated her.

"Help," she whispered and seconds later his hands took over, sweeping the sweater up, then tossing it to the floor.

Libby smiled up at the eyes gazing down to hers. She placed her hands on his chest, sighing at the feel of the soft, springy curls that covered the hard curves. When his arms reached for her, she went willingly, gasping with pleasure as her breasts felt the heat of his chest, moaning slightly as his lips took hers with an urgency that matched her own.

She let Jack get himself out of his jeans, figuring he could manage the process more quickly than she could. The pressing need she felt, her impatience to be in his arms with her body touching his once more, surprised her. The intensity of her longing frightened her a little. But she willed the fear away, and answered Jack kiss for kiss and caress for caress as he took her with him to the floor, where she didn't have to waste any effort on silly things like keeping her knees from buckling beneath her.

Libby knew she was probably blushing when it came time to help Jack slip the rubber sheath on, but the rest of her was so flushed, so pleasantly heated with desire that her face felt no warmer than any other part of her body. She welcomed him to her, then, with a soft sigh that quivered slightly as it passed her lips. She smiled at the look of concern in the eyes gazing so deeply into hers before lifting her hips to let him know how desperately he was wanted.

Jack was more than pleased to respond to Libby's unspoken request, moving slowly at first, then more and more quickly as she rocked with him in the ancient rhythm that felt oddly new and fresh with this woman. He watched her face closely, saw the look of urgency fill her suddenly wide eyes, gave her a smile and arched more deeply and more rapidly until her body began to pulse around him and he was free to join her in complete fulfillment.

* * *

Libby relaxed against Jack's chest. Darkness surrounded her, yet she felt safe, secure in his bed high above the ground. It was a special place, made even more so by the second session of lovemaking they had shared before burrowing under the covers.

They had spoken very little between the time they spent on the floor, breathing in ragged unison in front of the fire, and the moment when he began to teasingly coax her into the loft, promising chocolate and other delights. Alas, there had been no chocolate, but the other delights had far surpassed her anticipation.

And now he slept. Libby stared at the ceiling, alternately wondering where this thing with Jack was going to lead, and telling herself to simply enjoy the moment. She'd had precious few like this in her life. When it came right down to it, she had never experienced *any*thing like the passion and emotion she had experienced in Jack's arms this night.

The closest she could remember was falling asleep in her granddad's arms each Christmas Eve, waiting for Santa to come down the chimney. But that jolly old elf had never once brought her anything that came anywhere near to giving her the joy, the goodwill toward humankind that the afterglow of Jack's love had left her with.

Love? a voice asked. There was no question in her mind that she was deeply in love. Libby was aware that Jack had made no declaration of his feelings, but she refused to allow any doubts to cast even the tiniest shadow into the glow warming her heart right now.

There was already a small, dark corner of her soul where thoughts about tomorrow's trip to the morgue huddled like a monster in a child's closet. Libby tried to ignore the dread lurking there as she turned on her side and snuggled next to Jack's warmth. The ordeal would be over in moments, she told herself, and Jack would be nearby the whole time.

As if in response to her thoughts, Jack shifted toward her. His arms curved around Libby, drawing her close, anchoring her so securely that the tension eased from her muscles, letting sleep come at last.

It was dark in the drawer. The stainless steel was cold against Libby's back. She was naked, except for a white sheet and the body paint, tinted a gruesome shade of palest blue-green, that covered her from head to toe.

The coroner, a round man with very little hair and tiny wire-framed glasses, had sent Libby into a small lavatory with instructions to spread the thick concoction all over her body. Dr. Bloomenfeld had told her not to worry about the places on her back she couldn't reach. He'd been quite considerate of her, covering her nakedness with a sheet, telling corny jokes while he worked on her face, then holding up a mirror so she could see the realistic-looking "corpse" that his artistry had achieved.

Once word came down that Libby's mother had arrived, he'd helped Libby into the drawer and administered a shot. The medication would relax Libby completely in a matter of moments, he promised. As he slid the drawer into the wall, he assured her that the drug, a derivative of the curare used by natives on poisoned darts, would wear off quickly, as well.

The doctor knew his business. When voices suddenly echoed into Libby's cubicle, she expected her arms and legs to stiffen in a startled response. They didn't so much as twitch. When the drawer began to slide forward, she told her eyelids to close, only to find that they already lay shut, blocking out everything but a slight glow from the overhead light, which told her that the drawer was now fully open.

"Are you ladies both sure you want to do this?" she heard Dr. Bloomenfeld ask. "One will be sufficient."

Ladies? Libby thought. Who—

"Cathy, you heard the man," a high-pitched voice whined. "Only one of us needs to do this."

Oh, God. Aunt Susan. As if her mother's presence in the room wasn't enough.

Libby was very grateful for the drug that held her imprisoned, for if she'd been able to move, she had no doubt she'd have sat straight up, tossed the sheet aside and spit in her aunt's face.

Chapter 11

"Susan, if either of us is going to leave the room, it is going to be you. You've kept my daughter from me for years. Now the least you can do is leave me to deal with this."

Libby decided her mother's voice was coming from the right side of the drawer.

"And *this* is exactly the reason we took custody of Elizabeth," Susan replied. "We were afraid she would come to a bad end, since it was obvious that *you* were incapable of caring for her after Father died. And don't forget, Cathy, you were the one who asked for help. We hardly forced it on you."

This voice echoed from Libby's left. If she'd been able to cringe at the superior attitude in her aunt's voice, she would have done so. But she was helpless to do anything but lie between the two voices as the battle raged on.

"I asked you to watch her while I went to school. I didn't ask you to adopt her. To take her from me."

"Well, you signed the papers."

"I signed what I thought was a medical waiver, to grant permission for any treatment Libby might need in an emergency. The next thing I knew, you had me under a restraining order, blocking my every attempt to see my daughter, finally turning her against me, so she would never answer my letters."

"Ladies, please."

Dr. Bloomenfeld's voice sounded as though it came from somewhere near Libby's feet. She couldn't be sure, however, because her thoughts were occupied with her mother's last words. Letters? There were never any letters. From the age of eight on, Libby hadn't even received as much as a Christmas card from her mother.

A package had come after she married Dan, though, months after the marriage had taken place. It had been the cause of their first argument. He'd opened the card before she'd unwrapped the gift. The moment he told her it was from her mother, she had stuffed the box, still covered in shimmering white paper, back into the packing container and ordered Dan to have it returned to the sender.

"You have just made a perfect case for allowing me to be the one to identify the girl, Cathy. You haven't seen her in years."

"That's not true. She may not have seen *me,* but I've seen her many times. Concealed in my car, I watched her play in the schoolyard, at least once a week when she was little. When she went to high school, I tried to find her at football and basketball games, but she rarely showed up, so I had to be content with watching her arrive each morning. Once she'd graduated and gone to work, I took to sitting on the bus-stop bench across from that photo studio. And more recently, I managed to slip into her first gallery showing. So you see, I know quite well what my daughter looks like."

Libby could hardly believe her ears. It couldn't be possible. It was all too bizarre. She felt as if she were listening to an old-time radio soap. Any minute she expected Dr.

Bloomenfeld to intone, "Next week, tune in once more to *One Life to Lose*." Instead, Aunt Susan's voice echoed off the walls.

"Look, Cathy, it was for the best. Carl and I gave Elizabeth a decent, Christian upbringing. Living as our daughter, she wasn't forced to reveal the stigma of being illegitimate. She could forge a righteous path without your iniquitous example to lead her astray."

"Ladies."

"I see. So *that's* how she came to marry the first man she met—escaping from your narrow-minded, tight-lipped, tight-*assed* attitude. Listen, Susan, she is not your daughter, she is mine. And her name is *not* Elizabeth. Her name is . . . was . . . Libby."

Libby was stunned by the emotion in her mother's voice, the deep sorrow that underscored that last sentence and quivered on her own name.

"Ladies, I understand you are both upset." Libby concentrated on Dr. Bloomenfeld's soothing tones, willing their sound to ease the combination of pain and hope that filled her chest. "This is a difficult time. You'll feel better when we have completed this unpleasant job. Are you ready?"

Both replies in the affirmative were spoken in restrained voices. Libby heard the echo of hard-soled shoes on the concrete floor, then felt a rush of air as the sheet was lifted from her face and chest. Several moments of silence followed. Aunt Susan broke it first.

"Yes, that is Elizabeth. I would know those wanton, gypsy curls anywhere. I always made her restrain them."

"Ms. Wilkinson?"

Libby heard a soft sound from her mother, followed by the quiet words. "Yes. That's my daughter."

The sheet touched Libby's collarbone, signaling her that the coroner was lowering it again. She waited for the covering to shroud her face, but her mother's whispered, "Wait, please," halted the fall of fabric.

"What is it, Ms. Wilkinson?"

"I . . . I would like to touch her."

Oh, God. That was the last thing Libby had expected. Surely the doctor would refuse this request. The makeup might come off. No, he'd told her it was smudge-proof, that it could only be removed with soap and water.

"Certainly, if you wish."

No, Doctor. She will know. My skin will feel too warm, too—

A gentle touch, the pressure of one finger brushing Libby's skin from the top curve of her cheek down to her chin, stilled her anxious thoughts. The finger felt warm. Most likely, those moments waiting in the refrigerated drawer had cooled her flesh.

The finger retraced its path, then moved down again in a rhythm that brought memories flooding back, memories that were reinforced by the snatches of a soft melody, hummed in a breaking voice, that floated down to Libby's ears. Her throat filled with emotion, with a love almost forgotten, with feelings that came near to breaking her heart as Libby heard her mother's trembling whisper, "Good night, baby mine."

Libby was going to cry. Tears were already filling her eyes. In a matter of seconds, they would seep through her closed lids and all of this would have been—

Suddenly, the warm touch was gone, replaced by the cold caress of the sheet, a sheet that began to soak up Libby's tears even as the drawer creaked into the wall.

Dr. Bloomenfeld's muffled voice floated in to her. "Ms. Wilkinson, we must speak about the arrangements. The officers who traced you found a will at the house. Your daughter had stipulated that her body was to be used to help others, and the rest of her remains were to be cremated. Since she was found too late to make organ donating viable—" a door creaked open and the doctor's voice began to fade "—I have arranged for . . ."

By the time Dr. Bloomenfeld had returned to open Libby's "casket," the muscle-stunning drug he'd administered had begun to wear off. She knew that because her chest had begun to rise and fall rapidly as she sobbed uncontrollably in the little enclosure. The doctor tried to tell her that this was a normal side effect of the medication, but she knew better. It was a reaction to all she'd heard, to the anguish in her mother's voice, to the resurrection of a hope for reuniting that she'd thought long dead.

It took Libby twenty minutes in a hot shower to scrub her body free of the clinging body paint. After drying off, she reached for her clothes and spied a small rectangle sitting atop her jeans. A quick inspection brought a smile to her lips as she stared at the newly minted driver's license bearing the name "Jill Dempsey."

When she and Jack had first arrived at the station that morning, one of his friends had taken a picture of her so they could create a fake ID to protect her cover. The result was an image of a pale, sullen young woman with white, spiky hair and thick liner rimming her eyes. Her own mother would not recognize her.

Her mother.

The thought brought fresh tears to Libby's eyes. She blinked them back. She would not have believed that anything could hurt worse than the years she'd spent believing that her mother had abandoned her, yet somehow, the possibility that the woman had been as miserable as Libby had been all this time was even more painful. But she had to be logical. She really didn't know this woman. For all she knew, her mother's words might have just been a show, a way of punishing the older sister Cathy Wilkinson had never cared for.

And she didn't have the time to think about this, anyway. Jack was waiting.

Stuffing her damp hair atop her head, Libby covered it with the spiked wig, then turned to the full-length mirror hanging on the back of the door. She stared at her pale face before lining her reddened eyes in black and coating her lashes twice with mascara, then stepped back to make sure her disguise was complete.

She almost laughed, in spite of the ache in her chest. Wearing her tight jeans over a long-sleeved navy blue bodysuit and the thigh-high boots Jack had insisted on buying for her on the way to the police station, she looked as if she were trying out for a role in a movie entitled *Biker Vampires from Hell.*

Libby drew a deep breath. A little laughter was just what she needed. She had to stop acting as though the world had come to an end, had to concentrate on getting out of the building without drawing too much attention to herself.

Her instructions were to take the stairs up to the station lobby, then exit through the front door and make her way around to the parking lot where Jack would be waiting for her in the VW. For the time being, she needed to forget what had happened in the morgue and concentrate on finding her way through the maze of underground corridors.

Tucking her new identity into the back pocket of her jeans, Libby took a deep, steadying breath, then stepped into the empty beige hallway. Two left turns and a right later brought her to the stairs. Her boots scuffed lightly over the concrete steps as she hurried up, turned at the landing, then started up the final flight of stairs. Halfway up, she heard a woman's voice call out.

"Jack! What a surprise. What are you doing here?"

Libby hesitated on the step, one foot hovering above the next one, listening for the reply, telling herself that Jack was a common name, that it was probably all right to continue up the stairs.

"Sheila." Jack's voice, *her* Jack's voice, answered in a flat tone. "I work here, remember?"

"Oh. I didn't know you were back on duty. How wonderful. You look great."

"I'm coming along, but I'm not back yet."

"Just can't stay away from the old place, most likely."

This last came from a third party, a well-modulated masculine voice that made Libby think of the full-of-themselves art critics she'd met at various gallery openings.

"Jack, this is Steven Trousedale, my new husband. Steven, this is Jack McDermott."

"Her *old* husband. And yes, we've met."

Jack's voice was heavy with irony. Libby was not going to stay where she was one minute more. She wanted to see the idiotic woman who had cast Jack aside, as well as the gem with which Sheila had replaced him. Tossing her long hair, Libby struck a pose—back straight, chest up—then started up the stairs with a decided swagger, making no attempt to soften the echo of her boots.

She still had five steps to mount, when they came in to view, three people standing in the center of the opposite wall. Jack leaned against the pale blue painted surface, looking ruggedly casual in his denim shirt with his jean-clad legs crossed at the ankle and his fingers tucked loosely into his pockets. He had turned his head toward the two people on his right, and the expression on his face was every bit as mocking as his words had been.

The slender woman gazing up at him, with golden-blond hair curving to the shoulders of her royal blue jacket, fairly oozed money and style. Her matching skirt was just the right length to look professional and still show off her long, slender legs. Her makeup was impeccable, accenting her high-cheeked beauty, but the best paint in the world couldn't hide the tight set of her red lips, or the way her eyes narrowed up at the taunting expression on her ex-husband's face.

The fair-haired man with Sheila was every bit as stylish in his dark brown suit and Italian loafers. Libby supposed that Steven Trousedale would be considered good-looking, with his lean, male-model's features and slim build. But she couldn't help wondering how Sheila could prefer this to the rugged masculinity that Jack wore so well.

Not to mention how Sheila felt about the fact that her new husband was a lech.

Trousedale had turned as Libby reached the top of the stairs. His pale blue eyes held hers for one second, then lowered to scope out every curve beneath her tight sweater and skin-hugging jeans. Libby fought the urge to shudder as her flesh crawled beneath his obscene regard.

She had to move, not only to escape the man's filthy gaze, but so that she could observe the trio without drawing further attention to herself. It was one thing to "hide in plain sight," and another to arouse unnecessary and possibly dangerous interest.

Out of the corner of her eye, Libby noticed a bench located against the wall just inside the double glass doors. With a quick turn on her heel, she started toward it, forcing herself to walk slowly, undulating her hips in the in-your-face attitude she'd seen adopted by those who chose to dress outlandishly. Once seated on the bench, she leaned back and pretended to stare directly ahead.

"Steven?"

Libby fought a smile as the man gave a visible start at the sound of his wife's voice before he turned to Jack.

"Well, Jack and I have never been introduced, exactly," Trousedale said smoothly. "The one time we met, I'd just started working for Sheila's father—I was filling in for Adam during the Forester trial, if you remember. Our contact was limited to the roles of witness and questioner that day, of course. I'm glad to actually meet you at last, McDermott. I've heard a lot about you."

"I'm sure you have." The thought of the names his ex-wife had been known to call him lent a distinct dryness to Jack's tone. "And I'm sure all of it is quite accurate."

Trousedale's smile widened. One eyebrow lifted as he spoke. "Well if you're talking about your reputation as a dedicated detective, I believe it. From what I've heard, I wouldn't be surprised if you were down here today to check into some case, even though you're still on the injured roster."

The man is smooth, Jack thought. So urbane, so polite. He and Sheila were a perfect match. Put her in a white dress and veil, with Trousedale in a black tux, and the two of them would make perfect models for the top of a wedding cake. More power to them.

"You here seeing a client?" Jack asked.

"He is," Sheila replied. "Daddy keeps Steven so very busy that I have to track him down to have lunch. Can't have him forgetting that he has a wife as well as a thriving career."

Sounded familiar. Jack fought back the sarcastic words as he stared into the woman's lavender blue eyes. There was no missing the quiet desperation there. Perhaps Sheila had noticed the way her new husband had eyed Libby as she walked by. Or perhaps she'd just never outgrown her need to own a man heart and soul. It no longer mattered. He was well out of the situation.

"Jack! What are you doing here?"

The jovial voice boomed from the double doors. Jack turned to see Sheila's father striding forward. Although he was the same height as his son-in-law and nearly as thin as Trousedale, Adam Monroe didn't move with the same languid grace. Neither did he dress as well. Lint flecked his charcoal gray suit as he stretched out his arm. Levering himself away from the wall, Jack took his right hand out of his pocket and extended it toward his former father-in-law.

"Hello, Adam. I'm just here to fill out more medical forms. What about you?"

The dark eyes behind the gold frames darted toward Sheila and her husband. "I'm here to see if I can join these two for lunch. I have a couple of cases I need to discuss with Steven."

Jack heard a note of apology in the man's voice and saw Sheila's eyes narrow. So much for your private lunch, he thought. Trying not to grin, Jack took a step toward the door and spoke quickly. "Well, I don't want to keep you from your meal. Nice meeting you," he said to Trousedale. "Adam, good seeing you again. Sheila, you look great."

After a nod at each of them, Jack turned and walked toward the glass doors. He shifted his glance toward the figure slouching indolently on the bench, gazing ahead with a bored expression on her pale face. As the air outside cooled his face, he relinquished control and grinned. Damn that girl. She had missed her calling. Would've made one hell of an actress.

Jack waited in the van, almost laughing out loud as he watched Libby saunter into view and slink her way across the parking lot. He turned to her as she slid into the passenger seat, restraining the desire to reach across and curl his hand around the back of her neck, pull her to him and kiss the studied pout from those full, pale lips.

Not here, he told himself. Not yet.

"How did it go?" he asked.

"Pretty well, don't you think? I feel I gave quite a performance back there. I doubt either Sheila or that jerk she married—"

"Not that. Downstairs."

Libby stared at him a moment. The smile slowly faded from her lips. They began to tremble slightly as she blinked at the moisture filling her eyes. Jack frowned as her blinking eyelids lost their battle and two mascara-stained tears ran down her cheeks.

"Libby." He closed his hand over her shoulder, gave it a quick squeeze. "Hold on. Let's get away from here, find somewhere private."

At her mute nod, Jack turned the key in the ignition, then forced his attention to the road as he maneuvered the van out of the parking lot. Something had happened, something very emotional. He had seen Libby battered, confused, angry and hurt, but never had he seen her look anguished, beaten.

After one heavy, shuddering sigh, Libby was silent in the seat next to him. Jack glanced at her quickly once, to see her dabbing at her eyes with the sleeves of her bodysuit, then concentrated on his driving. After he'd turned onto a road that wound beneath towering eucalyptus trees into the hills above San Rafael, Jack cast a longer look her way.

Libby's hands were clasped tightly in her lap, her head bent forward so that her blond wig hung like a curtain over her features. He could almost feel the effort she was exerting to hold herself together.

Turning his eyes back to the road, Jack pulled onto a private road, then urged the van between two eucalyptus trunks, into a grove hidden behind the curtain of weeping branches that he'd discovered in his patrol car days. When the engine sputtered to a halt, he shifted in his seat to face Libby, then reached across to touch her shoulder.

"All right," he said. "Let's have it."

Libby heard Jack's voice, felt the warmth of his hand, the gentle touch of his fingers on her neck. But it was several moments before she could force her frozen body to move, to turn to him. Her thoughts were a tangle of confused impressions, words and emotions. She wasn't sure she would even be able to explain it all, but once she met Jack's gaze, saw the quiet comfort and support in those dark green eyes, the words just seemed to flow from her without effort.

"So, I guess maybe my mother really didn't abandon me, after all," she ended on a choked-back sob.

Jack nodded. "So it seems. That's good, isn't it?"

Libby stared at him, amazed that he'd been able to follow the twisted tale that had been interrupted more than once as she'd stopped to brush away the tears streaming down her cheeks, or blow her nose on the handkerchief Jack had wordlessly handed to her.

"Except," he went on, "maybe it's no longer a good idea to let your mother continue to think you're dead."

"I don't know." Libby released a shaky sigh. "Has anyone heard from Matt?"

"No. Not for a while now."

At the note of concern in Jack's voice, Libby reached across to touch his hand. "Do you think something is wrong?"

"Not necessarily. The guys down in L.A. still have an eye on him. Our prey is being very, very careful. Matt has been sent from blind alley to blind alley. He managed to convey to one of our undercover guys that he's learned that his mission is to exchange his package for another, clean bills for hot ones presumably. Other than that, I think Matt is being extra cautious himself, afraid to call in for fear he'll tip the guy off."

"Then we can't take any chances here." Libby fought the emotion that made her voice shake, then cleared her throat and went on, "I'll just have to deal with my mother after all this is over and Matt is safe. If I can get past the painful belief I've held all these years that she cast me aside, my mother should be able to deal with thinking I'm dead for a couple more days. It's not like she'll have to go through a funeral, and all that. Dr. Bloomenfeld has arranged for a box of ashes, supposedly all that is left of me, to be delivered to her. Everything is set."

She held her head high as she spoke, suddenly ashamed of her tears, of the naked emotion she'd revealed to this man. The dark green eyes that looked into hers held no pity, however, only a quiet admiration as he slowly leaned toward her.

"Libby Stratton, I love you."

The words were a mere whisper, a rush of warmth across her skin, before Jack's lips touched hers. The kiss was tender-soft, soothing the ache in her heart. Jack lifted his lips a moment, then lowered them again to kiss her more deeply, nudging her mouth open with his tongue, then entering it as he gathered her into a fierce embrace.

There was no hint of comfort in this second kiss, just heat and desire that demanded she respond in kind. Libby slipped her arms around Jack, arching toward him in the tight, cramped space as the morning's pain was burned away in the fire ignited by his kisses. All the sensations Jack's caresses had woken in her the night before stirred to life, surging through her like wildfire, whetting her appetite for the delights they had shared.

A moan passed from her mouth to his. Jack's lips left Libby's to trail along her jaw, then his breath rasped in her ear as he whispered, "Let's get in back."

Chapter 12

"**Y**ou know," Jack said as he lowered himself back onto the mattress that all but filled the rear of the bus. "I used to laugh at the hippies that still populate places like the university at Berkeley. I must admit, though, there *is* something to be said for this nostalgia thing."

Libby smiled as Jack's fingers skimmed her bare skin. She cuddled closer to him on the tie-dyed bedspread and smiled at the love beads dangling from the rearview mirror. A very satisfied sigh eased past her lips.

"You okay now?"

Jack's voice was husky with concern and the remains of the passion they'd just shared. Libby lifted her head from the mattress and grinned up at him.

"What do you think?" she asked.

That half smile she loved so well lifted one side of his dark mustache, but his eyes were quietly serious as he replied. "I think that this little interlude was just what we both needed. But as much as I'd like to spend the rest of the day making love to you, I know I have to get back out there and do what I can to help Matt.''

"You're absolutely right.''

Libby sat up and began feeling around for her wig and the clothes that had been peeled off and tossed every which way in their heated rush to answer the call of desire. She wanted to ask Jack about those three magic words he'd uttered before the kiss that had brought on the storm, but now was not the proper moment. That discussion would require the right timing. It was not something she wanted to delve into while Jack was concerned about police work. Or when she was thinking ahead to the moment she could reclaim her life and confront the mother she'd spent years trying to hate.

"I know a woman who owns an art gallery in Mill Valley,'' she said as she slipped into her panties.

"And?''

"And she has a yearly showing for emerging artists. The participants range from painters and sculptors to photographers and textile creators. Oh. These are your jeans. Here. Hand me mine, would you?'' Libby paused as they exchanged bundles of denim, then went on, "You know, people who work with fabrics to create wonderful scarves and sweaters, and—''

"Ties?''

Jack looked up as he finished buttoning his shirt. Libby nodded.

"Well, you'll have to stay in the van while I speak with her.''

Libby finished squirming into her jeans, then nodded as she adjusted the bodysuit. "Of course. Even with this—'' she plucked the blond wig off the back of the passenger seat "—there's a good chance she might recognize me. Though I can't say we were exactly friends. She's one of those superior types, you know, who spell the word 'art' with a capital A.''

Jack had been in the process of buttoning the fly of his jeans. At her words, he stopped and stared at Libby. "What do you mean?"

"Oh, she just makes way too much of the whole thing, one of those people who think the term 'commercial' should never be connected with 'art.' Some critics are like that, too. They seem to feel that no one should make any money with their work, that an artist is only good as long as he or she is starving in a garret somewhere. A bunch of phonies, if you ask me."

The sudden smile that lit Jack's face puzzled Libby, confusion that was lost in the deep kiss he pulled her into.

Jack found Sybil Whitewood in a small building tucked into a tree-lined side street in Mill Valley. Short, white hair framed a face set in haughty lines and dominated by a long, aristocratic nose. She looked down that nose as she lifted her attention from the tie in her hands to nod at Jack.

"Oh, yes. I *have* seen this work before. Very unusual. Each tie was different, like an individual scene painted on silk. Totally unlike the primitive stylized prints one normally associates with batik. The artist was part of my show last year. Unfortunately, the work has become far too commercial for my taste."

Jack fought a grin. Libby had described this person to a T, and it pleased him no end to know that Libby could so easily see through a woman who would have had Sheila eating out of her patronizing hand.

Brushing away the thought, Jack put on his best official attitude and asked, "Do you think you might be able to help me locate the artist?"

He hadn't identified himself as a policeman, but his abrupt manner had apparently been enough to bring the woman down a peg or two.

"I suppose. If you can wait a moment or two, I should be able to locate the name and address in my files."

The moment or two stretched into a half hour as the woman took two phone calls, then greeted a well-dressed woman who entered the gallery. Jack clenched his jaw, fighting his impatience as he stared at a twisted mass of metal in the center of the room.

"Here it is."

Jack looked up. The multicolored jacket Ms. White-wood wore over a purple turtleneck and matching pants flowed behind her as she crossed the room.

Jack took the white three-by-five card she offered, and examined the business card taped above the handprinted notation, Hand-Dyed, Hand-Stitched Ties. He glanced at the name and address, then pulled a notebook from his rear pocket to jot the data down before returning the card to the woman and thanking her for her time.

"The artist lives in Petaluma," Jack told Libby as he slid behind the wheel. "There was no telephone number on her card, only an address. It'll be dark by the time we could get up there tonight, and if the address is a business, it'll most likely be closed. So, we'll make the trip first thing tomorrow. What do you say we pick up some Chinese food, and head back to the beach?" She nodded her agreement.

At the take-out place, Jack handed Libby a couple of twenty-dollar bills.

"I have to make a few phone calls. Order lots of food, okay? The only thing I like better than cold pizza for breakfast is leftover chow mein."

Libby gave Jack a wide grin that completely destroyed the air of sophistication that had become as much a part of her disguise as the spiky wig. "What happened, did you overdose on Wheaties or something, as a kid?"

Jack shrugged. "No. Eggs and bacon. Every morning for more years than I choose to remember."

"Oh. That's too bad. Breakfast is the one meal I actually *like* to fix. I make a killer omelet. Such a shame that you're off eggs. You'll have to miss taking advantage of my one domestic talent."

With an exaggerated sigh, Libby turned and strutted toward the bright red door of Chin Low's Asian Garden Restaurant. As she disappeared into the building, Jack turned to cross the street. A grin that he seemed to have absolutely no control over curved his lips.

She was amazing, this slip of a woman. He could think of very few people he knew who possessed Libby Stratton's resiliency. And he had never met a woman who managed to be so complicated, and yet so simple. So much fun with her wry, quick humor and her outrageous ability to adapt, and yet so damned seductive, with her tiny butt and her soulful eyes and that full mouth that felt so dammed good beneath his.

Or one who could distract him so thoroughly, he thought as he stared at the telephone and tried to remember just who he'd been planning to call and why.

"This is perfect," Libby said. "Heaven is a tummy full of fortune cookies."

She stared at the collection of white cartons sitting at eye level on the trunk in Jack's living room. It had only seemed right to sit on the floor to enjoy the Oriental fare. Now she rested her back against the couch and sighed her satisfaction.

"Yep. And good food always tastes better after good news."

Jack grinned at her from his position on the other side of the trunk, then took a sip of the tea Libby had brewed as he'd laid out the paper plates and opened the cartons. The front curtains were closed, but the muted sound of the waves made for a soothing backdrop.

The news was indeed encouraging. Jack's call had produced word that Matt was on his way back up the coast. As far as they could make out, shortly after Matt had followed a tortuous series of directions to exchange his package for a locked briefcase, he'd managed to make hasty contact with one of the L.A. cops. The plan was for Matt to bring the case back to the mystery man, and hope to hell that something incriminating was inside so Matt could collar him.

"When do you think Matt will get to town?"

The smile that had moments before lit Jack's face faded as he shook his head. "No way of telling. His orders were to take the long way back, up Highway 1, and stop at a series of telephone booths for further instructions. It's going to make things tricky for our guys to tail him without their catching the notice of the other people we assume must be watching Matt."

"Tails tailing tails?"

"Exactly. I have no doubt that our careful mystery man is having someone watch Matt, along with making my cousin bounce around like a pinball. The way I see it, this thing will go one of two ways. Matt might be told to drive directly to some location in our area. In that case, he should get here sometime between the middle of the night and early morning, depending how often he has to stop, and how long he has to wait for the next contact. But then, he could be instructed to stop someplace along the way to spend the night. If that happens, we might not hear from him until sometime late tomorrow. Fortunately, the one cop in L.A. that managed to contact Matt slipped him a small transmitter to use when he gets the final word on where he's to drop the package."

"Won't the cops watching over Matt just follow him to the spot?"

A deep vertical crease formed between Jack's eyebrows. "That's the way it's supposed to work. But things happen, and they could lose sight of him somewhere along the way. It's just always good to have a backup plan."

Libby watched Jack stand up and begin to close the little take-out boxes. She got to her feet and gathered the few that had escaped his grasp and followed him into the kitchen.

"This is the scary part, isn't it?" she asked as she bent to arrange the containers on the refrigerator shelf with the others. She stood up and turned to where Jack leaned against the counter.

"No matter how well you plan these things," he said, "something can always go wrong. And this situation is far from well organized."

"I thought that with the help from the highway patrol and the L.A.P.D., you had things pretty well covered."

Jack's eyes darkened. "There are too many loose ends up here. The two officers borrowed from the L.A.P.D. and working as servers at Foresters are keeping their eyes and ears open. And Nick Forester is under surveillance. But this means that more people in our department know that something is going down and that increases the chances of a leak. I'd feel a whole lot better if we knew who we were after."

"Well, if you knew *that,* you wouldn't need all this other stuff, the money and the tails, would—" Libby broke off. "Oh. It's not enough to *know* someone is guilty, is it? You have to have proof."

Jack placed his arm around Libby and gave her a squeeze. "Elementary, dear Watson."

His words were semilighthearted, but a frown continued to ride low over his eyes as Jack stepped forward, his arm around Libby's waist, and began leading her toward the living room.

Libby knew he was worried. No matter how he tried to hide the fact, it was obvious that Jack feared something would go wrong. And from everything she knew about the man Matt hoped to trap, Jack's anxieties were not unwarranted. It was also clear that Jack was frustrated. He had never said it, but Libby had no doubt that Jack felt he should be the one who was out there, trying to sting the stinger. And beneath the frustration, Libby was certain, lurked the fear that he would never be out there again.

She hated seeing his doubt and his pain, but knew that only time would provide the answer regarding the future of his career, and only Jack could provide the healing if he was forced to leave the work he loved. In the meantime, all she could offer were a few moments of distractions.

Instead of heading to the couch, where Jack seemed to be leading her, Libby turned toward the shelves beneath the loft. Jack stayed by her side, his arm now draped lightly across her shoulders, as she took down a framed photograph from the collection on the middle shelf.

"Your family?" she asked.

She glanced up to see his lips curve as he studied the photograph in her hands. "Yeah, that's us. The McDermott clan on vacation."

Libby turned her attention back to the picture. The scene was a mountain lake, surrounded by pine trees, where children of various ages cavorted in the water. She easily picked out the image of a much younger Jack, twelve or thirteen years old, rowing a boat containing three younger children.

"Who's who?" she asked.

"That's Mike out on the raft in the middle, along with Patty, the oldest girl. Mary's the one climbing the ladder. In the boat with me are Shawn and his twin, Sharon, along with Katie."

Libby heard Jack's voice soften. Gazing closely at the image of the tiny girl with a cap of bright red curls sitting in the bow of the rowboat, Libby observed, "She's a lot younger than the twins."

Jack drew the picture from Libby's hands, and continued to stare at it it. "Yeah. Most of us are only a year and a half or two years apart. I think my parents figured they'd finished building their family, then along came our little princess."

Libby glanced up quickly. "Princess?"

Jack gave her a small smile. "Yeah, that was her nickname. Since she was so young, so tiny, she remained outside all the various sibling rivalries. She was everyone's favorite. Still is, for that matter."

"How old is she now?"

The smile widened. "Twenty-six."

"Oh. Like me."

Libby stared up to Jack's eyes, watched the corners crinkle as he spoke. "You're alike in other ways, too. Even at her most vulnerable, Kate displays an inner strength of will. The way you went from being unconscious, to fighting to stand reminded me of something Kate would do. That's why I called you Princess, until I learned your name. However—" he lifted one brow and regarded her with an expression that could only be called a leer "—I want you to know that my feelings toward you are not at all brotherly."

Heat rose to Libby's cheeks. She thought about their wildly abandoned session of lovemaking in the back of the VW and found herself smiling shyly.

"I bet you were a good big brother, though."

"I was, actually. The three older kids were very close in age. I never seemed to fit in with them. Besides, I *liked* watching over the three little ones, playing the kid games I'd been shut out of."

His words made Libby frown and her heart twist in surprised empathy. She'd always assumed that the loneliness she'd felt as a child had been due, in part, to her lack of brothers and sisters. It had never occurred to her that being part of a large crowd could be just as lonely.

"You never wanted children of your own?"

Jack gave her a quick glance. "Yes, I did. But Sheila convinced me that life would be more enjoyable if we had our freedom to do adult things, like going to the theater and out to dinner. And naive and madly-in-love fellow that I was, I went along with this, figuring that I would eventually learn to enjoy the pastimes she seemed so hot on."

A wry smile twisted Jack's lips. He placed the photo back on the top shelf, and continued to stare at it as he spoke again.

"Once I'd learned that things like wine-tasting parties bored me to distraction, I approached the subject again, explaining to Sheila that we seemed to be growing apart. I suggested that perhaps raising children would give us something we could enjoy together. This time my wife convinced me that it would not be fair to have children when I was in such a dangerous occupation. But I knew that truth of the matter is that she would have never agreed to be a mother. She was just using this veiled promise to coerce me into becoming the lawyer she'd always dreamed of marrying."

The room seemed to echo with an unspoken tale of the arguments that had built in intensity, the divorce that had been inevitable. Libby remembered the battles that had raged between her and Dan once she had started to develop her own interests, recalled the sadness that had enveloped her when she'd realized that his refusal to consider any changes in his life's plan was irrevocably breaking them apart.

"Divorce, ugly as it can be, is sometimes the best move for both partners," Libby mused aloud.

"Funny, that's just what Adam told me."

Libby glanced up at him. "Adam? Your father-in-law?"

"Yes, he was pretty damned decent about the whole thing, especially since the man has practically dedicated his life to his daughter. He's not totally blinded by her faults, of course. Not only does he know that she is incredibly self-centered, he seems to be quite aware that he's partly to blame for Sheila's narcissism. Yet he doesn't seem to mind at all. Some dad, huh?"

"Yeah, some dad. I guess there are all kinds. Not that I'd know."

As she finished speaking, Libby closed her eyes against the sudden rush of longing, tried not to remember all the sleepless nights spent trying to conjure up the man who had fathered her.

"Have you ever tried to locate him?"

Jack's soft question brought her eyes open again to gaze up to his. "Other than in my dreams? No. I don't have anything to go by, really. From what I've managed to piece together, my mom was only with him twice. The second time, Aunt Susan caught them and sent him packing, most likely with a promise of the fire and brimstone that he would face in the afterlife. I know my mother received that lecture more than once from her oh-so-righteous and unforgiving sister."

Libby turned to stare at the photos on the shelves as she went on, "So, I learned not to ask about my father. My questions seemed to mortify my mother and they would invariably start Aunt Susan off on a sermon about the evils of the flesh. The only way I knew to get close to him was with a camera in my hand, and that will have to do. Even if I knew how to start looking for him, I'm not sure I could bring myself to confront a man who would most likely only be embarrassed to learn of my existence."

"Hey." Jack placed his large hand alongside her cheek and tilted her face up again to smile sadly into her eyes. "Remember, I told you that it wasn't Walton's Mountain at my place, either. Photos like these always record the happy times, the vacations, the holidays. No one seems to think of snapping a shot when a father and son are standing toe-to-toe, screaming at each other."

Libby watched pain darken the green of Jack's eyes. She had no doubt it twisted in his heart in an echo of her own pain, like different sides of very similar coins.

"At least there's an explanation for your not knowing your father," Jack said quietly. "I grew up in the same house with my dad, and in many ways he's still a stranger to me. He played with us kids, gave us endless rides on his back and read countless bedtime stories, but it's only recently that I realized he never spoke about himself, always held back a large part of himself."

Libby watched Jack's gaze shift back to a framed image of a smiling woman with short red hair next to a tall man who looked strikingly like his middle son, saw the mixture of anger and sadness tighten the muscles in Jack's jaw. She didn't want to end the night on this note, on regrets about their pasts. She wanted to focus on the future, on possibilities.

A row of books caught her eye, a collection of stories that made her recall a comment Matt had made the night he came to the cabin. "So tell me," she said in a breezy tone as she pointed to the books, "did you become a fan of Arthur Conan Doyle's before or after they nicknamed you Sherlock down at the station?"

Jack turned to her with a puzzled frown, as if she had pulled his thoughts back from some faraway place, and he wasn't quite sure what she'd said. Slowly, awareness opened his eyes and curved his lips into a smile.

"Long before," he replied. "I started reading the Hardy Boys mysteries as a kid, moved on to Doyle, then Agatha Christie. I even read Perry Mason, before people began hounding me to consider a career as a lawyer. The collection just keeps on growing. These books here represent only a fraction of the ones lining the shelves in my apartment."

Libby glanced at the book spines, noted titles by Tony Hillerman, Dorothy L. Sayers and Dick Francis, to mention only a few. An idea leapt to her mind and before she could consider it fully, she turned to Jack.

"Matt mentioned you've been talking about writing a book. Have you considered making a career out of that? With all the things you've encountered working homicide, you'd certainly have plenty of material to draw from."

Jack stared at her a long moment. "I think that writing a book might be much easier said than done," he replied dryly. "Besides, Joseph Wambaugh has the cop-turned-writer market pretty well cornered."

"Don't be silly. Look at all the lawyers-turned-writers."

"Yeah. Well, better to have them writing than getting criminals off and returning them to the street, unpunished." Jack gave Libby a lopsided grin. "I don't think writing would ever be my thing, anyway. I have that allergic reaction to sitting behind a desk, remember?"

Libby nodded. So far, so good. She'd made a suggestion about an alternative career and he hadn't bitten off her head.

"Okay," she braved, "writing about a detective would bore you stiff and sitting at a desk would make you fat. Have you ever thought about *being* a detective? Working for yourself, I mean."

The expression in Jack's eyes sharpened a little. Libby held her breath, waiting for him to bristle and remove the arm that felt so good around her shoulders.

"Become a private detective?" he asked at last. His lips curved slightly. "As a matter of fact, I *have* thought about that. Matt and I used to sit around and joke about going to work together. We thought about calling our agency Magnum and Wesson, P.I."

"Oh, really? Which one of you would be Magnum?"

Jack lifted one eyebrow as he looked into her eyes. "The one with the biggest gun, of course."

Libby fought a smile. "And that would be?"

"You'll never get the chance to find out," Jack growled, then lowered his lips to Libby's, capturing them in a possessive, hungry kiss. The kiss deepened instantly, became a joining of need and desire and joy. Libby wound her arms around Jack's neck and stood on tiptoe to arch forward so that she could feel every inch of him touching her.

Jack's harsh groan shattered the silence, increasing Libby's greed, urging her to draw her fingers back from where they'd entwined themselves in his hair, to reach for the top button on his shirt. Growing passion made her fingers clumsy as she began unfastening each button. When she reached the bottom one and moved on to the waistband of his jeans, Jack began providing the same service for her.

Each time his fingers brushed her skin, Libby squirmed, longing for more concentrated, more purposeful contact. After hurried fumbling, which included retrieving a condom from his wallet, Libby was once more in his arms, her skin hot against his, Jack's hands caressing her, loving every inch of her. But she was not satisfied. The swirling twisting need deep inside her spiraled upward, to be released as a soft, needy moan against his warm lips.

Jack felt as well as heard the soft sound. He felt it in every fiber of his being, a match to the need he felt for this slender, incredibly strong woman. Wrapping his arms around her waist, he drew her up to his chest, pulling her feet off the ground as he had the first time he'd held her, what, only four nights earlier? She had been a stranger then, rescuing her had been almost an act of desperation, a way of proving to himself that he hadn't lost his ability to perform the job he loved.

Tonight he felt a different kind of desperation. Tonight, he was possessed with the need to yield himself to the magic of her lips, to lose himself in her arms. Tonight he didn't have a hill to traverse, only a few feet, to the nearby couch.

Once there, Jack slipped one hand slowly down over her round bottom to her thighs. Never taking his lips from her mouth, he cradled her in his embrace for a long moment, then slowly lowered her to the cushions.

Her body felt so slight beneath his. Slight and eager, arching up in a silent plea, a plea that Jack was more than happy to grant. Entering her was like coming home after a long, cold absence, all warmth and closeness and a pleasure that was bone deep and far more than physical. Libby's response to him, her eagerness, made the act of lovemaking something new, something in which souls mingled, and loved, and healed.

Chapter 13

"You're very good, you know."

Jack felt Libby's head lift sharply from where it rested on his shoulder. Shifting on the couch so that he could look into the shocked expression of her midnight blue eyes, he smiled.

"I didn't mean that the way it sounded," he said.

What it had sounded like was a sleazy line from one of those movies shown on late-night cable. There was nothing sleazy about Libby. Sexy, yes. Damn sexy, with her skin soft beneath the fingers of one hand, her silky hair wildly twining in the other one, and the muffled moans that had mingled with his as they fulfilled each other's needs.

But what they had just shared had gone beyond the physical. He wanted to tell her that, yearned to let her know how deeply she touched him. He wanted to repeat the three words that had slipped out of his mouth earlier that day.

But those words carried so much weight, promised so very much. And although there wasn't one doubt in his mind that Libby would never ask of him what Sheila had, to surrender completely, to give up the essence of what made him "Jack," he knew he needed to promise her something. Until he knew exactly what he could offer, he had to keep from saying those words again.

"Well, just what *did* you mean?"

Jack smiled at the slightly hurt note that colored Libby's question. Before answering, he lowered his lips to hers, kissing her long and deep, hoping his actions would leave little doubt in her mind about how very much she pleased him. Lifting his head, to see the satisfaction in her eyes, he smiled.

"I was talking about your little helpful hints earlier, the ones about my becoming a writer or a detective," he said. "Very subtle. I hardly knew I was being nudged."

A worried look shadowed her eyes. "Jack, I hope—"

"Don't." He placed a finger on her mouth. "It didn't upset me. I know you're only trying to make it easier for me to face what might happen if—"

This time it was *her* finger on *his* lips that interrupted the flow of words as Libby rose to lean on one elbow and gaze into his eyes.

"No. I am *not* trying to 'make things easier.' How could it be easy for you to face giving up the job you love? It wasn't *easy* for me to lose the life I had with Dan, to give up my dream of a large family when it became obvious that he had too many problems of his own to be considered good father material. I was only offering options to you."

"Options?"

"Yes. Options. I always felt that what drove Dan to self-destruct was that he had developed such a narrow view of life. He refused to see that it might be possible to take elements of a failed dream and from them create a new one. He seemed to feel that if he didn't succeed in the area he'd chosen, and do it the exact *way* he'd originally planned, that he was a complete and utter failure, and so, he might as well end it all."

Jack regarded her with a somber expression. "And you think I've been doing the same thing?"

"I don't know about that," Libby said. "I . . . I've only known you for a few days."

Libby had almost said, "I hardly know you," but that would have been wildly inaccurate. She knew this man very well, knew his intelligence, his wit, his tenderness, understood his pain and his dreams. What she didn't know was how he would deal with a broken dream that could not be returned to its original state.

This last thought made a shiver race down Libby's spine. Forcing a smile to her lips, she went on, "I do know that if I were to create a dreamscape for you, I'd never suggest dressing you in a three-piece suit and Italian loafers, posing you in front of a courthouse."

"Bright girl." Jack grinned at her widely as he reached over to brush a curl back from her cheek. "A dreamscape of me, huh? Interesting concept."

"Got any ideas?"

"A few," he said as he tugged gently on the curl, urging her face closer to his as his eyes darkened. "Right now, though, they're all x-rated."

Libby woke early the next morning, before there was any light to seep through the loft's curtained window. But even though she closed her eyes and snuggled up against Jack's warm back, she couldn't return to sleep.

In fact, she could hardly lie still. Last night's lovemaking had left her wonderfully sated, sleepy with pleasure. But after a few hours of rest, the joy and hope that had underscored their physical coupling surged through her anew, filling her with an energy that demanded action.

After slipping softly from the bed, Libby descended the ladder to dress in jeans and her thick hooded sweatshirt. Grabbing her backpack, she loaded new film into her camera, then shifted the pouch containing lenses and extra film onto her shoulder.

Quietly opening and closing the front door, she hesitated a moment while she drew her hood up over her hair, then started down the steps. In the dark gray light, she hurried across to the sand, quickly finding a spot where she could shoot the sun as it rose over the hill behind Jack's place.

An hour later, she had used all of that roll and most of another, alternately taking pictures of the rising sun, then turning to capture its effect on the waves curling toward the shore. She'd just clicked the shutter over a foaming wave that shimmered with pink highlights as it curved forward, when a deep cough made her jump and turn to find Jack, dressed in a denim jacket over a blue chambray shirt and jeans, standing three feet behind her.

"Well, I can see you're not serious about cooking me breakfast," Jack said. "So, if I want to eat, I guess I'll just have to take you out."

Libby blinked. "What about the Chinese food?"

"I want something hot. And, since one of my favorite breakfast places is up in Petaluma, and we need to go there, anyway, I figured we'd kill two birds with one stone. That is, unless you're suffering from starvation and can't wait to eat until we get there."

"Nope," Libby replied as she slung her pack over her shoulder and walked toward the road with Jack. "I can wait. It'll only take me a minute to shower, squeeze into my jeans and slip my wig on. But before I do that, I want to take one more picture."

She tugged on his arm and hurried him toward the cabin. "I'd like one of you on the porch," she said. "It suddenly struck me that after all this is over, I might have a hard time convincing myself this wasn't a dream, unless I have some concrete proof."

Jack turned to her as they reached the top step. His eyes narrowed down at hers as his arms came around her. Before she could do more than gasp, he'd pulled her into a deep kiss, then lifted his head to ask, "Did *that* feel unreal?"

"No." Libby grinned. "But I still want a picture. They say it lasts longer."

Jack agreed to posing, but only if she would be in the shot, too. Libby found a spot on the roof of the van that would hold the camera at the proper level, set the delay on the shutter release, then hurried to join Jack on the porch, turning in the circle of his arms just in time to smile before the shutter clicked.

"Oh, by the way," Jack said as they pulled into Petaluma an hour later, "your Harley should be ready in a couple of days."

The startled, confused look on Libby's face made Jack grin and hurry on to explain, "Officer Terri Hauge donned a blond wig and took a limping cycle into the shop up the street from my place after the team learned about our little radio act the other day, just in case someone might come in and try to verify what they'd overheard."

"Thorough group you work with," Libby noted as she tossed a blond lock over the shoulder of the sleeveless blue shirt she wore with her jeans and boots.

"Yeah. I just wish they could come up with something on who hired those clowns in the first place, but nothing has come in on the tap they set up."

And, he wanted to say, he really doubted that he'd be able to turn up anything on this tie business, either. It was a long shot at best. At the worst, it was something to make himself feel useful, to kid himself that he was more involved in this case than just playing baby-sitter.

Well, as far as that went, things had gone *way* past babysitting.

Jack grinned as he followed Libby into the small café on Petaluma's main street. The black-and-white linoleum, the jukebox in the corner and the red vinyl booths echoed loudly of the 1950s.

"Tell me," Libby said as she slid into one of the booths. "Do you hang out anyplace that was built and decorated *recently?*"

Jack laughed out loud at that. "Yes, as a matter of fact, I do. I'll have you know, I don't come here for the atmosphere. This place happens to serve the best chili omelet north of the Golden Gate."

"Oh. High-octane fuel, huh? If you don't mind, I think I'll try the pancake sandwich."

Jack checked his watch. It was closing in on eight-thirty. By the time they finished eating, it would be a fair time to go knocking on B.J. Dolan's door. With any luck, he'd learn the names of the shops she dealt with, and leave plenty of time to visit several of them before the day was over.

Breakfast was as delicious as he'd expected. No surprises there. But B.J. Dolan turned out to be a he, not a she. Tall and thin with sparse locks of pale blond hair falling over his high forehead, B.J. seemed rather surprised to find a detective at his door at nine-thirty in the morning.

He was most willing to cooperate, however, ushering Jack into his workroom, then leading him past lengths of patterned fabrics festooned on wooden racks. The artist stopped at a desk where pots of wax, various-size paintbrushes and bottles of dye surrounded a basic computer setup. A few keystrokes urged the printer to cough up a list of retail stores, a list that B.J. complained was far too short for his taste.

"I have to tell you, I've sold the majority of these things at craft fairs. I do have a list of some of the people who have purchased from me directly, at least the ones who used credit cards or checks. The shops give me the same information on the customers who've purchased from them. I've been planning to compile a mailing list for when I expand my product line."

Jack didn't bother to ask what other wild bit of wearing apparel the man was preparing to create. That didn't interest him, but names and addresses did. In a matter of moments, he held a much longer roster in his hands, was thanking the soft-spoken artist and hurrying out to the van to share the information with Libby.

"The names might get us nowhere," he said, "but you never know. I'll drop them off at the station later, and Pete can run them through the computer. We'll start with the shops on the other list. Here, look at it and tell me where they are."

The catalog of shops was short. Six stores altogether. Two were in San Francisco, one in Berkeley and another in Oakland. Two of them, however, were on this side of the bay, and Libby was familiar with both of them.

"This first one is a gift shop in Larkspur Landing," she told Jack.

The small upscale shopping area was located just off the freeway near the community of San Anselmo. Jack seemed worried, extra watchful, so she didn't argue when he insisted that Libby stay in the van when he went in. She didn't really mind. She hadn't slept much the night before, so she took the opportunity to rest.

Sunlight streamed in through the front window, warming her as she slumped in the seat, coaxing her eyes shut. She was surprisingly relaxed, she admonished herself silently, for someone whose entire life had been picked up and set on end. She should be wondering how her cats, Barnum and Ripley, were doing, or how her friends were dealing with the news of her "death," or what it was going to be like when she could finally talk to her mother.

These were all major big deals. Well, all except for the cats, perhaps. They had been fed again, Jack had informed her, by the overworked team watching out for her and Matt. The other things had far more serious implications. She had no doubt that Barry and Grace had been devastated to learn of her demise. They would be relieved to learn that Libby was alive and well, but once that emotion wore off, they might be just the littlest bit angry at her for worrying them so. It might take a lot of talking to convince them that circumstances had left her with no other choice.

Her mother was another story altogether. If Libby had to do some explaining there, her mother had an equal amount of talking to do in order to make Libby understand how the woman had allowed herself to be shut out of her daughter's life all this time. She knew that her Uncle Carl was well-off, that he kept a powerful lawyer under retainer, but she also knew that the rights of a natural mother stood for quite a lot in the state of California.

But as important as these matters were to her, those confrontations were too far in the future to get worked up over right now. Now she was warm, she was safe, she was in the company of a man who challenged her mind, who did wonderful things to her body and who filled her soul with joy.

"Well, no luck here." Libby glanced over as Jack slipped into the driver's seat. He switched on the engine, then turned to her. "You said the other place was in Sausilito? We'll head on down there, but we aren't going to try any of the other places today."

He didn't explain why, just turned to face forward, and concentrated on merging with traffic as they moved back onto the freeway headed south. His frown and the tight set to his mouth made Libby ask quietly, "Did you call in again?"

"Yeah. From the pay phone. No word from Matt yet. Worse than no word. They've lost him."

Libby didn't ask for any details. Jack had explained this was tricky work, that Matt would only use the transmitter when he received a final destination, and that the closer this came, the cagier the guy pulling the strings might become.

The drive was completed in tense silence. The bright sun filled the van with heat, urging Libby to roll down her window to draw in cool, salt-scented air. Jack slowed as they approached the main shopping area in downtown

Sausilito, a collection of charming two-story buildings crammed together facing the water of Richardson's Bay. When Libby gave him the name and address of the remaining shop, Jack nodded.

"Interesting. I was going to check this place out the other day, before I got the call telling me to meet Matt."

The shop was on the opposite side of the street, backing up to the water. They drove by slowly, engrossed in the search for the elusive, practically mythical thing known as a parking space in that tourist-crowded town. Libby noted a car pulling out just down from the store in question, but it was on the other side of the street. And before she could say anything, she noticed something even more interesting.

"Jack, look. Isn't that your ex-wife going into that shop?"

Jack slowed to a near stop as he glanced in the direction Libby was pointing, then nodded. The sound of a horn honking behind him drew Jack's attention back to his driving.

"Well, this makes our search for a parking space a little less pressing," he said. "I'd better wait until Sheila clears out of there before I walk in to check on that tie. It might prove to be a rather awkward moment."

He spoke these last words slowly, with an undertone of speculation that made Libby turn to him sharply. "You don't think *she* bought it?"

"Libby, her father represented Forester."

"I thought you said you trusted her father."

"I do. However, there is another person to consider. Steven."

"Sheila's current husband?"

"Exactly. I find it very interesting, now that I think about it, that Steven Trousedale so suddenly left his prestigious Century City practice in Southern California to show up here just in time to work on the Forester trial. I accepted Adam's explanation that Sheila had encouraged him to take advantage of the media coverage on this case to introduce his new partner, and her new love interest, so I didn't question the fact that Trousedale filled in for Adam on the day I took the stand.''

Jack paused as he squinted at the traffic ahead. His next words were spoken in a slow, speculative tone. "I wasn't happy about the way the guy had cross-examined me, found myself wondering if perhaps Trousedale had worded the questions differently, the judge might have allowed us to introduce some of the evidence that would indicate Forester had been framed. But at the time, I just figured that was the breaks and—damn.''

Jack pulled the beeping pager off of his waistband and stared at the number. "Well, at least I can use the cellular to make this call. The odds of finding a parking spot *and* a pay phone in any kind of proximity to each other in this burg are astronomical. Here, read that number to me while I dial,'' he said, handing her the pager.

Seconds later, as they stopped behind a white Mercedes that was waiting to take the spot being vacated by a bright red Porsche, Jack spoke into the cellular telephone.

"It's me. What have you got?... What?... You're sure. Yeah, as a matter of fact, I can be there in fifteen minutes, ten maybe. Yeah, get backup there as soon as you can... Damn.''

This last was said as he slammed the phone back in the carrier sitting on the floor between the two seats. Libby grabbed the window frame as the van jerked suddenly to the left, onto the wrong side of the street, then sped past both the Mercedes and the Porsche, pulling back onto the right side of the road just in time to miss a head-on crash with a tour bus.

"Something's up," she said quietly.

"Yeah. Twenty minutes ago, Matt's car was spotted in the heart of San Francisco. All units assigned to him are either in the city, or in the middle of the Golden Gate Bridge, headed south. Five minutes ago, a message came in from Matt's transmitter. They made him switch cars. He's up ahead, at the bunkers. Not far from where they took you that night.''

''And we're his only backup?''

Jack finished negotiating a sharp uphill curve, then glanced at her before turning back to the next curve looming in front of them.

''No, Libby. *I'm* his only backup, at least until one of the local black and white's makes it.'' Jack was silent for a moment before he spoke again. ''Oh, remember Metzker, master bugger? Pete mentioned that he was playing with the man's bank records on the computer this morning. He found a transfer of funds to Metzker's account from one listed to the firm of Monroe and Trousedale.''

Libby held on to the doorframe as they squealed around another curve. When they were on a straight stretch, headed down a long hill, she tried to block her fear by continuing the conversation. ''So, you might find that Sheila bought that tie, after all.''

''Yep, and since she knows of no way to purchase things other than by using her credit card, we should be able to trace that tie right back to her husband. Poor Sheila, never did quite get the knack of gift giving. Someday, I'll have to tell you the story of the powder blue cashmere sweater that she insisted was absolutely *me*.''

Someday, maybe, when they weren't going seventy miles an hour up a twisting road posted twenty-five, in a vehicle that protested every push of the accelerator, and that ominously rocked to one side at each curve. Libby thought she remembered hearing that VW buses had a narrow wheel base, which caused them to tip easily. Perhaps if she leaned in the opposite direction—

''We'll be there in about three minutes.'' Jack's voice broke into Libby's thoughts. ''I imagine the meeting is set on the other side of the tunnel. I'm going to find Matt. You are to stay in the car, do you understand? On the floor. Under no circumstances are you to leave the vehicle.''

"Yes, sir."

It seemed like the proper response to an officer of the law, which is exactly what Jack sounded like. The thought both reassured and terrified Libby. He knew what he was doing, she told herself as she watched him loosen the gun in the shoulder holster he had donned beneath his denim jacket after their brief cuddle on the porch that morning.

But the fact that Jack was about to go out and do the job he was trained for also frightened her. He'd been shot once in the line of duty. His gun hand was still in the process of healing, and there was no telling what danger he might stumble on as he searched for Matt.

As Jack pulled the VW into the wide dirt turnout, Libby's attention was drawn to two cars, one silver-blue, the other a deep green. Two cars. One must be Matt's. The other could belong to anyone, a history buff who'd come to see the old Nike battlements, a hiker searching for a picturesque hill to climb. Or someone capable of cold bloodedly ordering the murder of Marie Forester, as well as her own.

As Jack parked against the rise on the right side of the tunnel, Libby stared at the opening she recalled seeing the night she was abducted. The huge archway had loomed, evil, dark and gaping in the moonlit hill. She had been illogically relieved when she'd been pulled up the hill to the left of it instead of being drawn into that hungry-looking mouth.

And now Jack was going in there, alone, with no idea of what waited for him on the other side.

Jack exited the van without even a glance at Libby. As the door slammed shut, she watched him move forward slowly, gun in hand, pointed at the sky. Remembering his orders, she slipped from the passenger seat to the floor, whispering a prayer that they had not returned to the spot where Jack had found her, only for her to lose him forever.

Chapter 14

J ack stood to one side of the tunnel's entrance, his back against the hill, listening. Overhead, two gulls wheeled, calling plaintively to each other. A glance at the van in front of him revealed that Libby had followed his instructions to conceal herself.

From beyond the road came the muffled sound of waves crashing onto the rocks at the bottom of the cliff, but from the tunnel he heard only the whisper of the wind. Jack turned, eased himself inside and stared down the passageway that stretched some two hundred feet in front of him. Two hundred feet of shadows. But the pools of black weren't the cause of Jack's loudly pounding heart as he stepped forward. The arching concrete walls were too smooth to conceal anyone. It was the uncertainty of what waited for him on the other side that made his skin tighten and his eyes narrow.

His footsteps echoed softly on the ground. Jack stepped as lightly as possible as he made his way quickly toward the opening at the other end. Here, in the tunnel, he was exposed. Once he was on the other side, he could find some cover, a place from which he could determine whether Matt and the person his cousin was to meet had arrived already, or if someone might still be coming down the dark passageway he was traversing.

The end of the tunnel was now five feet away. Jack slowed his steps as he approached the fog that tinted the trees beyond the archway a dull shade of gray. A memory tugged the corner of his mouth into a grim smile. It looked exactly as it had the first time he and Matt had discovered this spot, the summer they were ten. Entering the tunnel on their bikes, the sun had shone brightly. Two hundred feet of darkness later, the world they'd entered had been shrouded in mist, the perfect stimulus for young imaginations.

They'd learned later that the concrete enclosures tucked into the grassy hillsides had once housed missiles. But that day, the bunkers had made perfect forts as the two boys darted back and forth between the trees, planning battles, imagining a "bad guy" behind every rock and tree.

Today, the possibility that any of those rocks or trees might conceal a murderer was all too real. Jack leaned against the wall of the tunnel, just inside the exit, his eyes searching. The mist was less thick than it had been that long-ago day, more of a fine veil that blurred rather than obscured.

But it might as well have been pea-soup thick, for all the good it did Jack to look around. Nothing moved except a branch of the nearest tree as a bird leapt from one twig to another. Several sounds reached his ears, all soft, muffled. They could be made by any number of small animals scurrying about their business, or a man, making his furtive way through the tall grass.

Damn. He had to move. He couldn't just stand there, waiting for something to happen, something that would be too late for him to prevent once he heard voices. Or shots.

Think. What would Matt be doing if he were already there. Where would he be doing it?

The answer came in a flash. Jack could almost see Matt, climbing the pile of boulders on the other side of the trees to his right, the place they used to call their Impenetrable Fortress. That was the spot his cousin would choose to wait, sitting on that money, certain that he'd be able to spot the enemy as he approached.

Jack moved across the ground with all the stealth and speed he could manage, then slipped from tree trunk to tree trunk until he could see the clearing at the foot of the tower of rocks. A man stood on the grass, a man dressed in a gray three-piece suit that almost blended with the surrounding fog. A man who looked at his watch, glanced around, then finally called out.

"Hey, Minetti. Are you here yet?"

The answer came like a soft echo. "Yeah. I'm here. Who wants to know?"

The half smile on Jack's lips widened at the sound of the familiar voice and the cocky note of defiance in it. But his eyes never left the figure in the suit, watching as Steven Trousedale's head jerked around, searching for the source of that voice.

So far, the man's hands had not left his side, hadn't moved toward any pocket that might harbor a weapon. Not that this surprised Jack. The man they were dealing with was too careful, too smart, to make his move before he was sure that everything was perfect.

"You know damn well who wants to know. You've got the goods and I have your pay. Get out here and let's make the exchange."

Trousedale's voice had lost the smooth, urbane tone of the courtroom. It had an edge to it, a hint of nervousness, that made Jack suddenly tense. There was something about the way the guy glanced over his shoulder, at the trees across the clearing from where Jack stood, that made Jack wary.

Shifting his gaze from Trousedale, Jack studied the veiled shadows. He saw nothing, nothing but unmoving shapes that could be anything from a rock to a bush to a man crouching between the shadowed trunks.

A sound caught Jack's attention, the scraping of pebbles falling over rocks. He turned his head to see Matt standing atop the boulders, dapperly casual with his red suspenders slashing the white of his dress shirt as he smiled down at the man on the ground. Trousedale was staring up at Matt, or rather, at the gun held in his cousin's hand.

Jack told himself to relax. It was over. They had their man. But the twisting sensation in his stomach told him not to trust what he saw. It was all too easy.

"Matt, get down!" The warning seemed to leap from Jack's mouth of their own accord. "I think there might be—"

Before Jack could finish speaking, before Matt could do more than move to one side, a shot rang out. Matt lurched sideways. Jack heard the ping of a bullet striking rock behind his cousin even as he turned to search out the gunman beneath the trees opposite him.

A shadow moved in the dark grove. Jack fired. He heard the report echo across the clearing. A second later, he realized what that echo had been. The bullet from the gunman's nearly simultaneous shot crashed into Jack's right shoulder with a fiery impact that threw him back against the tree he'd been crouched next to.

Sagging against the bark, Jack opened narrowed eyes to study the shadows beneath the trees. Nothing moved. Pressing his left hand over his burning shoulder, Jack bit back a groan as he levered away from the tree and turned toward the towering rocks.

His cousin was getting to his feet slowly, rising from the spot on the ledge where he'd fallen to escape the first shot, staring down at Steven Trousedale who now held a gun, pointed directly at Matt. Jack forced screaming muscles to lift his weapon even as he shouted, "Trousedale, drop it or I'll shoot."

The lawyer didn't even flinch. Having performed as duty required and having received no response, Jack steadied his aim and squeezed the trigger.

Nothing happened.

A shot did ring out, though. Trousedale's weapon discharged, exploding with a loud crack that made Matt jerk sharply to one side, like a fish pulled on an unseen line toward the edge of the rock pile, where he leaned out at an impossible angle, suspended over the precipice for what seemed like an eternity.

At the moment that Matt began to fall, Jack's trigger finger convulsed and his gun kicked to life. The impact of that bullet tossed Trousedale into a wild, spread-eagle leap before the man crashed to the ground. Jack stared at the motionless form for one second, then charged forward, pain shooting through his shoulder with each step.

Ignoring the burning sensation, Jack used his left hand to steady the gun in his right as he approached Trousedale. He came to a stop in front of the man, and when he saw the sightless gaze in the eyes staring up into the fog, he took the gun into his left hand and shoved it awkwardly into the holster beneath his left armpit.

Four feet away, Matt lay crumpled on his side, his left leg twisted, blood staining the back of his white shirt where the bullet had exited. Gritting his teeth against his own pain, Jack stepped over to him, then bent down to close his left hand over his cousin's shoulder.

"Matt."

His throat constricted over the single syllable. Then those thick lashes that Matt loved to bat at women fluttered, and Jack held his breath.

"Fortress not impenetrable, after all, I guess." The voice was tight with pain. But it was strong. Even stronger when it asked, "Did you get the bastards?"

"Yeah," Jack replied hoarsely. "And now I'm going to get some medical help for you. Don't move."

"No problem."

The humor was still there, but the voice was weaker. Jack stood, turned and started up the hillside, aware that his right arm now hung uselessly at his side. He couldn't think about his pain. He had to get out, call for help.

Damn it, help should be on the way. Sirens should be wailing. All he should have to do was stumble out of the tunnel and tell them where to find Matt and the two—

Two bodies.

Jack came to an abrupt stop at the mouth of the passageway as he recalled the shadow beneath the trees. Jerking around, he sprinted across the clearing toward the spot where he'd seen the concealed gunman fall.

The spot was empty. Jack knew he'd hit the shadowy target, but whoever had been there had fled, leaving behind a puddle of blood and a pattern of red splotches that stained the grass in a thin path that led back toward the tunnel.

Even as Jack turned in that direction, a scream split the air, a scream that spoke of terror and pain and lent speed to legs that were shaky with spent adrenaline. Libby. Libby was on the other side of that long tunnel, in the direct path of the gunman.

Jack felt as if he were in some demented nightmare, where everything happens in slow motion. The darkness under the archway seemed to be a physical force that made his feet heavy as lead. When he finally neared the highway end of the tunnel, he realized that the ringing in his ears had muffled the sounds of the sirens. They were loud, close and coming closer every second. But he was afraid they were too late, afraid *he* was too late, afraid that the person who had wounded him had found Libby, had completed the job that Trousedale had ordered Matt to do five nights earlier.

But he was wrong.

Jack stumbled into the light to see that Libby was fine, or at least appeared to be as she got out of the driver's door of the Volkswagen. The van wasn't where he'd left it, though. It was on the other side of the turnout, and the front passenger side of the vehicle was crumpled into the side of the rocky wall.

Two black and whites screamed into the dirt cove as Jack rushed toward Libby. She looked up at him, her face the same shade of white as her wig, then pointed a shaky finger toward the passenger seat. It was then that Jack saw that a figure sat there, slumped forward, head pressing against the center of the spiderweb pattern of cracks on the windshield. It was another minute before he realized that he was looking at his former father-in-law, Adam Monroe.

"How is he, Jack?"

The gruff voice brought Libby's head up to stare at the man who had just entered the hospital waiting room. He was so obviously an older version of Jack, with auburn hair fading to gray at the temples and the same lines bracketing his eyes and mouth that Libby found so attractive on Jack, that there was no doubt in her mind that this was his father.

Libby glanced at Jack. He looked pale, drawn. Blood spattered the front of his chambray shirt. The right sleeve had been torn away to facilitate its removal when he'd arrived for treatment.

Jack lifted his head to gaze at the man who'd spoken, lifted the arm supported by a sling in what might have been a gesture of greeting, but didn't move from the wall he'd been leaning against for most of the long night and equally long morning. That is, when he wasn't pacing. Libby had managed to catch some sleep on the narrow couch, but she doubted if Jack had even sat down.

"They haven't let me see Matt since he came out of surgery," Jack replied slowly. "They had to do some fancy stitching in the lung area, but they say he's in no danger of losing that organ.''

The flat, dead note in Jack's voice made Libby want to cross the room, wrap her arms around his waist and hold him tight. She knew she could hardly do that. It was enough that he had to deal with the forbidding frown on his father's face without having to explain who she was and how she was connected to him.

And she *was* connected to him. She could feel Jack's pain, his frustration, his every worry. She had heard all of it in his voice as he'd answered the questions the other officers put to him when they'd all arrived at the hospital, after one set of doctors had taken charge of Matt's still, white form. A second team had stitched and bandaged Jack's shoulder, congratulating him on the fact that the bullet had passed through him without doing more serious damage.

Then Libby had told her story, explaining how the sound of shots had pulled her into the driver's seat of the van, where she'd clutched the wheel as she listened, watched the mouth of the tunnel, and worried. Adam Monroe had come running out of that opening, his left arm stretching across his chest, bloodstained fingers clutching his right arm. A gun dangled from that hand, a gun the lawyer had lifted with obvious pain as he came toward the van, ordering Libby to start the engine as he got into the passenger seat.

The fingers of Jack's left hand had been warm around hers as she'd described how, as she'd started to turn the vehicle toward the road, a cold fury had settled over her, shutting out the fear that had originally made her respond to the man's orders. Turning sharply, she had jammed one foot against the angled floorboard and pressed the other to the accelerator, angling the passenger side of the van toward the rock wall, ignoring the man's screams to stop, bracing herself against the collision that sent him flying into the windshield.

"And Matt's leg?"

The question pulled Libby's attention back to the men by the door as Jack replied, "Broken in at least three places. They say his knee is a mess."

Libby heard more than just Jack's words. She heard self-condemnation. She had listened to Jack report all that had transpired on the other side of that tunnel, was well aware of the events behind the series of pops that had echoed through the opening.

Jack had stated clearly that his trigger finger had frozen as he aimed at Trousedale. He'd shouldered the blame for Matt's injuries without hesitation. When Pete Semosa had reminded Jack that he'd done the best he could, considering he'd just been shot himself, Jack had shrugged the words away.

She saw Jack make the same motion now, watched the sling that supported his wounded arm rise and fall as his father asked, "What about you? How are you doing?"

"I'll live."

The words seemed to ignite a slow fire between the two men. Libby watched Jack's father take a step back and scowl at his son, then shake his head before speaking in a low voice that trembled slightly.

"And for just how long?"

Again Jack shrugged, then winced before replying, "Who knows? Could be quite a while, now. My days on the force are over. I had them take down my resignation after they finished getting my story."

This came as a complete shock to Libby. When had— Of course, it must have been when she'd taken a few moments to purchase a toothbrush and toothpaste from the hospital gift shop, then slipped into the lavatory down the hall to brush her teeth, remove the wig she'd forgotten she was still wearing and the dark makeup that had still rimmed her eyes.

"You must be pleased," Jack's voice went on. "I'm officially off the force now. Of course, I can't promise to keep your sensibilities in mind when I choose my next career. Not that it should matter. One doctor and one lawyer amongst his offspring should make any father happy."

Jack was fully aware of the bitter edge to his words. He watched the frown shadowing his father's eyes grow more fierce as the man glared silently across the narrow space between them. Slowly, his father shook his head.

"Is that why you think I fought your choice of work?" he asked, his voice low. "Do you actually believe I gave one *damn* about the prestige, or lack of it, in your job? There is no one on earth, *no one*, you hear, who has more respect for the work done by police officers than I do. And no one who knows better what it can do to a man."

Patrick McDermott stopped speaking. His jaw worked while he stared at his son. When he spoke again, his voice was tight, rough. "I worked a beat in Boston, many years ago, you see. Yeah, I was a cop. And I loved the job. But one morning my partner and I were called in on a disturbing the peace. What we found was a small child who had been beaten by her father. She died in my arms. My partner, Tommy Alanso, and I had barely finished booking the bastard when we were called in on a possible breaking and entering in a warehouse area."

Again the man paused. Jack's chest tightened as he watched his father take two deep breaths before going on. "I guess the little girl was still on my mind. I thought I was where I was supposed to be, when I was supposed to be there, but somehow I wasn't in the right place when Tommy was shot. My best friend died in my arms that day. I was twenty-two years old. It nearly destroyed me. It sure as hell made it impossible for me to go back out and do the job I'd sworn to do."

Jack tried to draw some air into his tight chest before responding, "You never told me you were a cop."

His father shrugged. "I never told anyone, not even your mother. I had no family, nothing tying me to my past, so I simply closed the book on that part of my life and started a new one. I found that if I didn't think about what had happened, the nightmares came less often.''

Patrick paused. His eyes lost their focused glare, as if he were staring at something just past Jack's shoulder, something that twisted his lined features into a mixture of sadness and dread. When he spoke again, his words came more slowly. "I didn't want a son of mine to face that pain, but I couldn't talk about it, not without remembering. I'm sorry.''

The quiet regret underscoring these last words emphasized the agony Jack saw in his father's eyes, and for the first time in too many years, he really felt he knew this man. He easily recognized Patrick's desire to keep his pain to himself, to hide it like an ugly wart. After only a moment's hesitation, he reached across to touch one of the arms so tightly crossed over his father's chest.

"Dad. It's okay. I would have become a cop even if you *had* told me. I knew all the risks going in.''

His father replied with a frown. "Maybe. But at least you wouldn't have gone all these years thinking I wasn't proud of you.''

Jack fought the bitter laugh that threatened to rise from his chest. Proud? Now he tells me. Now, when I'm least worthy of that pride.

He bit back these words, though. His father deserved better than to have his peace offering slung back into his face by a man wallowing in self-blame and self-pity. Jack knew how much it must have cost Patrick to choke out those words, to silently ask his son to understand and forgive the rift that had grown between them. He'd bite his tongue in half before he'd do or say anything to threaten their fragile, unspoken truce.

"I don't like that.''
Libby turned to stare at the sign wrapped around the telephone pole they'd just passed.
"What don't you like?''

Libby glanced at Jack. After he had introduced her and given a brief explanation of her part in the case, Mr. McDermott had told Jack to use his vehicle to take her home. When his father had made his offer, Libby had tried to assure Jack that she wasn't in any particular hurry to get back to her house, would be happy to wait with him until the doctors let him in to see Matt. But Jack had said that was likely to be a while, and told her they should take the offer of wheels while it still stood, since the van wouldn't be drivable for quite a while, if ever.

Until this moment, the trip from the hospital had been a silent one. Jack had insisted on driving despite his injury and Libby hadn't been able to stop him. It had been obvious that although Jack's eyes were on the road, his thoughts were with Matt, so Libby had remained silent until now.

"I don't like the sign I just saw," she explained. "The one that said Garage Sale."

Jack shrugged. "I thought you told me that you loved garage sales, that you'd furnished most of your house from them."

"I did. But I think the address on that poster was mine."

This finally made Jack glance at her. She saw a spark of something, some small emotion in his shadowed green eyes, and spoke quickly. "Remember Semosa saying how great it was that I'd arranged for everything in the event that I died, like having my organs donated, and stuff? Well, I also stipulated that my belongings were to be sold off and all the proceeds to be given to the local women's shelter."

"It's too soon," Jack said. "It's only been—"

"Three days since my mother...viewed my body. I know. But that's plenty of time to arrange a sale, for her to put an end to the last reminders that she even had a daughter."

Jack's quick glance made Libby shake her head at her last words. "That sounded pretty pathetic, didn't it?" she said. "Force of habit, I suppose. I'm still not sure I believe that I heard right, that she hadn't stayed away all these years on purpose. A part of me insists that my mother had been an adult, and that no matter what happened, she could have found a way to take me back.''

''It seems our parents can sometimes be more frail than we expect.''

Jack's quiet words reached across the space between them like a comforting caress. She thought back to the scene she'd witnessed between father and son. Nothing had really been settled, but what had passed between them had formed a bridge toward a new start. If she wanted to have the same chance with her mother, she was going to have to relax, to calmly sit back until they got to her house and see what was waiting for her at this new turn.

The fact that Jack was speaking now eased her heart greatly, making it easier to face whatever might lie ahead. For a while there, watching him stare at the walls, feeling him blame himself, Libby had come to fear that he would turn inward completely, shut himself off from her and all who loved him.

She didn't think for one moment that it would be smooth sailing ahead for Jack. He had to deal with Matt's injuries as well as his own. But she'd met Matt, knew he wouldn't let Jack blame himself for long.

And Jack's father would help. She'd seen the love and concern in the man's eyes as he'd promised to wait for Jack at the hospital while Jack took her home. The man had been through the same hell Jack faced now. Something told Libby that Patrick McDermott was more than willing to help his son in any way he could, even if it meant reliving his old nightmare a time or two.

''Looks like you were right about that address.''

Libby blinked away her thoughts as she watched a battered blue pickup pull away from the curb and recognized the sofa, chairs and lamps filling the bed of the vehicle. As Jack eased into the spot vacated by the truck, Libby turned to stare at the house she'd once called home.

Several makeshift tables, formed of plywood panels stretched between sawhorses, littered the front yard. A few objects remained on each surface. The cardboard boxes on the ground also appeared to be empty, or nearly so, and only one or two items of clothing remained hanging on a rack formed of pipe fittings.

Gathered around a card table by the front steps, Libby saw Barry, his dark hair falling into his face as usual, and Grace, wearing Libby's blue scarf around her shoulders like an embrace. Seated in the center, counting a handful of bills, was a woman of forty-odd years with dark blond hair waving into a chin-length bob around a thin face.

A chambray-covered arm obscured Libby's view for a moment, then the car door swung open and Jack's voice urged, "Come on, Libby. They're waiting for you."

Libby stood on legs that suddenly felt weak, then forced her shaking limbs to move forward. No one appeared to notice as she opened the gate in the white picket fence. It wasn't until she was three feet from the table that the woman looked up. Her face was lined with weariness. Sapphire eyes, rimmed in red, looked into Libby's, eyes that slowly widened as the woman opened her mouth in a silent, "Oh."

Libby was aware that the other two figures had lifted their heads, but her attention was focused on her mother. When the woman stood, Libby stopped walking. Someone—Grace—cried Libby's name, and in seconds all three people were crowding forward. Arms encircled her, voices babbled.

"It's you. It's really you."

"What happened? Where were you? How—"

"But I saw you. I saw your body."

The anguish in these last words wiped away the watery smile Libby had been exchanging with Grace. She turned to her mother.

"I know. I'm sorry. I—I can explain, but it is a very long story."

Cathy Wilkinson stared at her daughter for several seconds before stepping forward and taking Libby's hands in hers. "I want more than anything in the world to hear your story. And I hope you want to listen to mine."

Libby's eyes filled as she nodded and pulled her mother to her. She wrapped her arms around the woman who had seemed so much taller the last time they'd embraced, a lifetime earlier. Her mother was now the same height as Libby, and her body shook with the same sobs as the ones that racked her own form. They stood that way for several minutes, until Libby finally took a deep breath, then pulled back to stare into her mother's tearstained face.

"Libby," the woman said, "we followed your instructions to sell everything off. People descended like a plague of locusts on the place at 8:00 a.m. By ten o'clock most of it was gone."

"Your camera equipment went first," Barry intoned.

Libby refused to think about that now. There were too many other things to deal with. "That's all right," she said. "It can all be replaced. I just want to get inside and sit down on . . . on the floor, I guess, and exchange stories."

Three sets of hands tugged on hers, pulling her toward the steps, but Libby shook her head and freed her arm. "I have to get someone else to join us."

She smiled at the quick speculative looks that flew past her shoulder, then turned to the man leaning against the car, quiet green eyes meeting hers. After stepping through the front gate, she ran toward him, stopped and tucked her arm in his uninjured one.

"Well, it's all gone," she said, making her voice as light as possible. "Including the gorilla, I assume. It's going to take some doing, but I guess I'll get my life back together again eventually. Come on, survey the damage with me. There must be *something* salvageable."

Jack gave her a small smile. "I'm sure there is. And you are just the person to find it."

He straightened as he spoke, slipping his arm from her light grasp as he did so, then stared down into her eyes. "I have to go now, Libby."

She took a deep breath to ease the sudden tight chill in her chest. "Of course. You need to be with Matt. I'll see you later, and we can—"

Her words caught in her throat as Jack shook his head. "No *we,* Libby. I won't be able to keep up with you."

"What do you mean? We're both at ground zero."

"Yes, but you still have a dream. Mine is dead."

Libby opened her mouth to protest, to tell him she loved him, that she would be there to help him heal. Before she could utter one syllable, he shook his head.

"No. It won't work for me. I can't take broken dreams and form them into something new. It's not bad enough that *my* career is over. Now, because I refused to admit my own weakness, Matt's might be destroyed, too."

Libby stared up at the hard lines framing Jack's mouth, at the ones etched into the corners of his eyes. She wanted to remind Jack that no one else had arrived in time to help Matt, that if Jack hadn't been there, his cousin would probably be dead now instead of just wounded.

But she knew that look. It was the look of a man who had not lived up to his own impossible expectations. It was the look of a man who would rather give up than compromise in any way, a man headed for his own personal hell. Libby knew what that hell was like. She'd almost followed one man into it. She couldn't do it again.

"I love you, Jack."

The words had to be said. When Jack gave her a weak smile and said, "I know, I'm sorry," she lowered her head in a nod.

Turning, Libby made her way blindly up her walkway, climbed the front stairs and stepped into her living room, where emptiness echoed off the bare wooden floors, then turned to the woman who had entered behind her and let the person she'd once called Mommy take her into her arms.

Chapter 15

"I don't ever want to see her again."

Libby's words echoed across the still-bare wooden floor in her living room. She stood at the opposite end of the comfortably worn royal blue sofa that she and her mother had just muscled through the front door.

She didn't want to argue with the woman. They had just spent several thoroughly enjoyable hours at an auction, taking turns bidding on things both practical and whimsical. This side of her mother came as a surprise to Libby, one of many, some pleasant and others not so, that had been uncovered in the last couple of weeks.

"I don't, either, Libby, but Dr. White feels we need closure on this issue."

The joint therapy sessions had been Grace's idea, and Libby had to admit that she and her mother had worked through more issues in a far shorter time in Miriam's office than they would have on their own time. The first of these had been Libby's reluctance to let her mother loan her the money she needed to replace her cameras and other equipment so that she could complete her calendar proposal.

She'd received word yesterday that the proposal had been enthusiastically accepted. The advance money would be enough to repay her mother and get a start on replacing the props she needed to continue her dreamscapes, as well as begin to refurnish her house.

Libby gave her end of the sofa a quick shove with her knee. "Mom, I know this closure business is a big thing these days, and I normally trust Miriam's instincts in these matters, but I can honestly not imagine anything else that I have to say to Aunt Susan."

Stepping back to judge the couch's relationship to the fireplace, her heel encountered something warm and fuzzy. Turning, she smiled down at the two cats crouched at her feet. Upon learning of her "demise," Barry and Grace had taken the two orphans in, only to return Barnum and Ripley to Libby when she came home. They had been ecstatic to see her, and had been reluctant to let her out of sight ever since. Libby bent and rubbed each head lightly before turning to her mother and continuing her protest.

"Look, the last time I spoke with Aunt Susan was after I'd returned from eloping with Dan. I told her at that point just how I felt about the years I'd spent under her thumb. What else is there to say?"

"For you, maybe nothing." Cathy Wilkinson sighed, then frowned as she shoved her hands into the denim pants that lightly hugged her still-slim hips. "But I have a few choice things to say about the strong-arm legal tactics used to keep me from you, not to mention the outright lies she and Carl told both of us. Since you will be the main subject of our 'conversation,' I thought that you might want to be there. Besides, there are still several issues keeping us apart, questions you must still have. I think if you and I are ever going to be a family, we have to lay these old ghosts to rest, together."

Libby glanced away from the sapphire eyes that were the exact color of her own and stared at the large empty bookcase covering the wall that had once been filled with pictures.

Her "family gallery" had hung there, made up of old sepia-toned photographs of unknown people collected from garage sales and flea markets. Her mother had kept the photos Libby had created for herself, but Grace and Barry had urged the woman to get rid of the faded pictures of people who had never been connected to Libby at all. So, they had all been sold, and Libby had no intention of replacing those. No longer could she be content with a make-believe family, not after seeing the true family connection that shone out of the photos of the McDermott clan.

Not that she harbored any illusions that she had a chance of making that family hers. In the last two weeks, she'd left two messages on Jack's answering machine. He hadn't replied, so she had forced herself to the conclusion that the items she'd left at his small cabin were a lost cause.

It was tempting to wallow in self-pity, to tell herself that she'd left her heart there, as well, and that she would never love again. But she refused to allow herself to think that way. In spite of the fact that her heart ached each time she thought of Jack and the pain she'd seen in his eyes as he turned to leave, she realized that knowing him, loving him, had been a turning point for her. Before meeting Jack, a part of her had still not recovered from her past, in spite of all the work she'd done with her therapist.

It had taken "playing dead" to learn to see how much stronger she had become and how much she had to live for. She would always love Jack McDermott, but she would not forgo her dreams of having a family, a real flesh-and-blood husband and children, just because he couldn't be the one to share that dream.

"Libby Stratton?"

The deep voice drew Libby out of her thoughts. She turned to the front door to see a tall figure wearing a gray sport coat over dark pants, filling the screened opening.

"Yes?"

As she stepped forward, Libby took in the white hair above his brown face, and recognized the man who had released her truck from the police impound lot and personally returned it to her a week earlier. He'd also restored to her possession the composite picture that resembled Jack. She'd forgotten that she'd asked Jack to have it removed, and had feared it had somehow disappeared in the garage sale.

Opening the door, she greeted him with a smile. "Hello, Sergeant Semosa."

The man gave her a nod, then lifted the large rectangular packing box he'd been cradling in his arms. "I have some things here that I believe belong to you," he said.

Libby frowned. "To me?"

"Yes. Jack packed the box and brought it to the hospital. I believe it contains some things you left at the beach cabin."

Memories flooded back, images of warm maple paneling, of a cozy fire dancing in the wood stove, the feel of a soft afghan on her knees, of tender lips on hers.

Libby blinked away the memories, then nodded as she stepped back. "Of course. Just put the box on the sofa, would you?"

She couldn't trust herself to take it from the man. The container couldn't be all that heavy, but her arms hung limply at her side, her body awash with sudden weakness.

Jack didn't want to have anything more to do with her. She had been telling herself that, but in some small corner of her mind she had nurtured the hope that he would wake up and realize he did have the courage to dream after all, that he would suddenly come riding up to her front door, sweep in and tell her this.

So much for having cured herself of waiting for a hero.

Shaking her head slightly, Libby followed Semosa into her living room. When he straightened from the couch, his arms now empty, she was able to swallow her disappointment and present the sergeant to her mother.

After the introduction, Semosa turned to Libby. "I'm glad I had an excuse to come out here again," he said. "I realized after I left the last time that you haven't had an official thank-you."

"Thank you?" Libby asked. "For what? When I was in the wrong place at the wrong time, Officer Sullivan was there to save my life. Whatever I did was just payback."

The man stared at her a moment, then shrugged. "If you say so. Then let me express the department's gratitude for your actions up by the tunnel that last day. Your quick thinking prevented Adam Monroe from escaping, though he's still in the hospital prison ward."

Libby couldn't help but smile as she shook her head. "Hey, my quick thinking was based on saving my own skin. I can't accept your thanks for that."

Semosa grinned. "Have it your way. Just know, if you ever need help, you can call on me."

"Well," Libby hesitated before asking, "could you tell me how Matt is doing?"

Semosa's smile faded as he lowered one snowy eyebrow. "Not well. He still hasn't regained consciousness."

His words stunned Libby. "It's been two weeks. What's wrong? Were there complications to his surgery?"

"No. His lung is healing fine. His leg is coming along, too, although his knee was pretty smashed." Semosa's eyebrows tightened. "It's his brain. Matt fell from quite a height after he was shot, and the doctors believe he must have hit his head. He was alert at the time he entered the emergency room, but while he was in surgery to stop the bleeding in his chest and straighten out his leg, a small vessel was leaking in his brain. This didn't become apparent until he failed to come out from the anesthesia. The doctors immediately went in to release the pressure, and they seem to think he'll come around once the brain has had time to heal, but we're all pretty worried about him."

Libby could see that. Semosa's face was etched with concern. And this man was only connected to Matt because they were both police officers, he wasn't his cousin, his best friend.

"How is Jack doing?"

Libby was afraid Semosa hadn't heard her question, so tightly had her throat closed over the words. But he gave her a small smile and replied, "I can't really say. He's in Matt's room constantly, hardly comes out. His father was the one who asked me to bring these things to you."

Libby nodded. The man didn't have to say another word. She knew just how Jack was doing. Sick with worry and self-blame. Shutting everyone else out.

"Let me know if anything is missing," Semosa said. Libby nodded again, then opened the screen door as he approached. She longed to give him a message for Jack. Instead, she watched the detective make his way down the walkway toward the gate in the picket fence, biting back the words she wanted to send with him to Jack, words of encouragement, words of love, words that would most likely only fall on deaf ears.

Turning to her mother, Libby cleared her throat. "Let's go," she said.

"Go where?"

"To Aunt Susan's. I've decided I need some closure, after all. I figure I should take it where I can get it."

"The truck."

The words weren't much more than a soft croak, but Jack heard them. They brought his eyes open with a snap and made his head jerk from the back of the terribly uncomfortable chair he'd folded himself into next to Matt's hospital bed. Leaning forward, he placed his elbows on the mattress and stared into his cousin's half-open eyes.

"Matt?"

"Yeah."

The voice was a little stronger. The eyes opened further, glinting slightly. Jack felt his chest fill with relief-laden air. In the last two weeks, he'd seen those green eyes only when the nurses pried them open. Jack had died a little death each time he saw the blank, empty stare, the lack of response to the light shining in them.

"Well?"

A frown tightened Matt's eyebrows as Jack stared at him. "Well, what?"

"Did you get the license plate of the truck that hit me?"

Jack could only shake his head. How the hell was he supposed to answer? His stomach was still in knots, tight fists of worry that had grown tighter as he sat by his cousin's bedside day and night for the last two weeks. Now that Matt was awake, he wanted to joke. Jack told himself that he should be relieved. Instead, he found himself fighting the almost irresistible urge to put his hands around Matt's neck and throttle him.

"Yeah," Jack finally managed to say. "The truck had a vanity plate—Monroe and Trousedale."

A slow frown lowered over Matt's eyes, then they widened. "Adam Monroe shot me?"

"No, Adam shot *at* you. You dodged the bullet. I wasn't so lucky." Jack shifted the arm still resting in a sling. "Trousedale shot you."

"Yeah, I remember now." Matt lifted his head. "So what happened next? How—"

Matt broke off, his face tightening in pain. Jack placed a hand on his cousin's shoulder, gently pressing him against the pillow.

"Hey, the story will wait," he admonished. "Right now, I know a doctor and a couple of nurses who would like to check you out while you're conscious."

Matt's eyes narrowed at Jack for a moment before the lids fell shut and Matt gave a resigned nod. Jack stepped out to the nurse's station and discovered the second miracle of the day, Matt's doctor immediately available, standing at the counter, making notations on a chart.

"Dr. Burns?"

The gray head lifted. Brown eyes in a narrow, well-lined face sharpened as he recognized Jack. "What is it?"

"Your patient is awake."

The doctor wasted no time asking Jack questions. He turned, shoved the chart he'd been working on into a circular file and grabbed the one marked Sullivan. One of the three nurses, all of whom had turned with great interest at Jack's proclamation, followed Dr. Burns into the room Jack had just left.

"How did he seem?"

Jack turned to the small, dark-haired nurse who had asked the question. "Fine." Jack frowned as he said the word. "Finer than I'd figured he'd be. I sort of thought he'd be more, I don't know, sleepy and confused. After being totally out of it for two weeks, I expected him to regain consciousness more slowly. He talks like he's just waking from a long nap."

The nurse smiled. "That happens sometimes. Your cousin bruised his brain, and it tends to shut down until it's healed. Waking like he did indicates that there was little or no permanent damage."

"Well, that's damn good news."

Jack and the nurse turned at the sound of the deep voice. Patrick McDermott gave his son a wide smile and stepped forward. "Now Jack can let up on himself a bit," he said. "I take it that Matt is awake?"

"Yeah. The doctor is with him now."

"Good. Then I say it's time you took a break and ate a decent meal. The hospital cafeteria has a fair approximation of that. I'll buy."

Jack gave his father a rueful smile as he shook his head. "As soon as the doctor is done, I want to talk to Matt."

"Mr. McDermott." The nurse's soft voice drew Jack's attention down to her upturned face as she went on, "Your cousin is still going to need quite a bit of rest. And if you don't mind my saying so, you look like you could use some, too."

Jack acknowledged her words with a wider smile and a nod. "You're right on both counts. But Matt woke up with a thousand questions. I doubt he'll rest very well until at least some of them are answered. After that, I promise to leave and let him get some sleep."

"That sounds fair enough," Patrick said. "In the meantime, how would you feel about a cup of coffee in the waiting room while the doc does his job?"

"Sure."

Jack followed his father to a small closet of a room that housed an ever-full, always-hot pot of coffee along with disposable cups, sugar and cream. With one hand drawing warmth from the cup his father had poured for him, Jack made his way to the waiting room. Lowering his frame onto one of the tan couches, he eased back against the soft cushion and let his head rest against the wall.

Apparently just in time.

Jack's muscles suddenly had all the strength of an over-cooked noodle. He couldn't remember the last time he'd let himself relax, could not recall when he had felt such a total lack of tension.

Yes, he could.

Libby. That last night with her. They had held each other tightly as they'd brought each other to ecstasy. Afterward, they had clung to each other with what little strength they'd had left. He'd felt drained then, too, but with that feeling had come the sensation of warmth and a joy that had been heavily tinged with hope. Now he just felt drained. And cold. And alone.

"Drink."

His father's order made Jack blink. God, he must be tired. When had his eyes fallen shut? Forcing himself to sit up, Jack took a gulp of the hot coffee, then swallowed it and shook his head once.

"This had better be high-octane stuff."

"How about a candy bar to go with it?"

Jack glanced at his father. He started to shake his head until he saw what the man held in his hand. The bar of Ghiardelli's dark chocolate brought back sharp memories. As if it were yesterday, he could see his father coming home from a long day behind the steering wheel of his truck, after making his deliveries to various grocery stores in San Francisco. It was Friday, treat day. Each kid had his or her favorite, and the confection Patrick held in his hand right now had always been Jack's.

And his father had remembered, after all these years.

Jack swallowed the lump that had risen to his throat. He wasn't ready to deal with all the pain of the intervening years. And the simple, open expression on his father's face told him that the man didn't expect that of him.

"That would be great," Jack said as he reached toward the bar. His father placed it into his hand, then gave him a quick grin.

"Good thing your mother isn't here. She'd yell at me for spoiling your dinner."

Jack returned the grin as he tore off part of the wrapper and broke off a chunk of chocolate. When he offered some to his dad, the man shook his head.

"No, you need it more than I do."

With a nod, Jack washed the first bite down with a swig of coffee. This was followed by another bite and another swallow, then another. Jack came up for air with a laugh.

"God, I'm famished."

"You sound surprised," Patrick responded. "When was the last time you ate?"

Jack shook his head. "I'm not even going to *try* to remember. The nurses have been shoving things at me on and off, though, and Semosa has brought in burgers and stuff. I haven't starved."

"But you haven't really tasted anything, either."

The words were spoken with quiet certainty, edged with pain. Jack let the chocolate melt on his tongue as he stared across the small room at his father, wondering if the man's partner had died instantly all those years ago, or if his father had kept his own bedside vigil, one that had not had a happy ending.

He wanted to ask about that, wanted to tell the man how much it meant to have him here, now, when his coming here could only be opening old, long-closed wounds. But it wasn't the time, or the place. His own sense of guilt was still too strong, too recent.

"Mr. McDermott?"

The soft voice brought both men to their feet, turning to the nurse in the doorway.

"The doctor wants to see you before you speak to Mr. Sullivan."

The doctor's orders were brief. Don't stay in there too long, and when you're done, go home and get some rest.

Jack had barely entered the room before his cousin spoke. "You look like hell."

Matt's voice was a bit stronger. Jack lowered his bottom onto the far-too-familiar seat of the chair and shrugged.

"So I've been told. You've looked better yourself."

"That's not what that pretty blond nurse said. She seemed quite taken with me."

"Oh, God." Jack shook his head. "You're recovering, all right. I guess I can follow doctor's orders and go home and leave you to her tender mercies."

Matt's eyes narrowed. "Not until you bring me up to speed on the case and tell me how Adam oh-so-honorable Monroe got involved in a money-laundering scheme."

"God, it's a long story. The short version is Sheila."

"Sheila knew about this?"

"I don't think so. But she was a very useful pawn in Trousedale's clever little chess game. He met her some time ago, after our divorce. It's my guess that he marked her for easy prey, someone he could charm with his looks and their shared cultured interests. He'd already set up the money-laundering scheme in L.A., where he had several lawyers and cops in his pocket. After he expanded to the Bay area, only to have Marie Forester cause trouble, Trousedale must have decided that his immediate attention was needed up here. He probably took one look at the way Adam doted on Sheila and decided that moving north and locking up the connection with the Monroes would be quite prudent.''

Jack paused to wait for his cousin to digest this information.

"And Adam?" Matt prompted.

"He's adamant that Sheila knew nothing about all this. He insists that he was in the dark, too, until after Trousedale had swept Sheila off her feet. It wasn't until the two of them were married and Trousedale had established himself as Adam's partner that Adam learned about the money-laundering scheme. He went along with it, he claims, to keep Trousedale from being caught, which would ruin Adam's reputation as well as destroy the life of his darling daughter.''

"Oh, I get it. Trying to shoot me and wounding you comes under the heading of protecting his offspring, I suppose.''

Jack shrugged. "Probably. I haven't talked to the guy. Semosa's been filling me in on the case. The sergeant is concerned that Adam will get off far too lightly. He's already agreed to cooperate with the district attorney's case against Robert and Nick Forester, to assure that they go down for their part in the money laundering. The D.A. tried to get Adam to testify against Metzker, the guy who bugged my place and Gary's, but Adam insists he knew nothing about Metzker and pal.''

"Well, your former father-in-law will be able to score enough points for a great plea bargain if he agrees to testify against Trousedale.''

Jack shook his head. "No deal there. Trousedale is dead.''

"You?"

The image of empty blue eyes staring up to the fog sprung to Jack's mind. "Yeah," he replied. "My last official action as a police officer. A split second too late to do *you* much good, though."

Matt's eyes narrowed as he gazed at his cousin. "You quit?"

"Yep?"

"Because of what happened to me?"

"Because of what might happen to the next guy I'm partnered with. You, it seems, are going to recover."

Matt's eyes held Jack's for a moment before shifting to stare at the cast that encased his leg from thigh to ankle. "The doctor gave me the scoop on my knee. Pretty grim. I should walk again, he says, but the annual Bay to Breakers Run will no longer be a part of my life."

A cold hand gripped Jack's heart. He stared at the IV bag above his cousin's head and watched the slow drip, drip, drip of clear liquid. Guilt had unbearably icy fingers, frigid and relentless around his heart.

When warm fingers closed over Jack's hand, with surprising strength, he looked into Matt's eyes. A deep scowl furrowed the pale forehead above the bright green eyes.

"Jack, you aren't going to blame yourself for this. If you do, I'll never speak to you again."

Jack's jaw tightened before he replied, "If my finger had worked any slower, Trousedale would have gotten another shot off, and the result would probably have been a foregone conclusion."

"I'm not kidding, Jack." Matt's eyes held none of the amused glint that always seemed to shine there even in the most serious circumstance. "You're my older cousin, remember? From what the doctor said, I have a long road ahead of me if I'm to get this leg even into limping shape. You've been this route. I could use someone to show me the way."

Jack couldn't move. He felt some of the ice in his chest begin to melt. When something warm and moist began to form in his eyes, he dropped his gaze to his hands, tightly folded on the blue hospital-issue blanket covering the edge of the bed and blinked rapidly.

Matt had no idea what he was asking. Or maybe he did. When Jack had been shot so many months earlier, Matt had been with him through most of his recovery, egging him on, challenging him to master each new level of therapy. Encouraging him with jokes and gibes.

It was payback time.

Jack slowly lifted his eyes to Matt's. "All right, you're on. I'm going home now, to get some much-needed rest. You get some rest, too. You won't be into therapy until that cast comes off, but I'll be back tomorrow for a strategy session with you and your doctors. Don't think for one moment that any of us will be easy on you."

Matt's smile was wide, though the edges seemed to droop slightly, as did the corners of his eyes as he nodded. "That's it, cuz. Don't let up, ya hear?"

The door opened as Matt finished speaking, and a nurse entered. Jack glanced up to see the dark-haired nurse frowning at him.

"I think the doctor gave you orders to keep it short. Time's over."

Jack got to his feet slowly, every muscle protesting the move, urging him to sit back down, or better yet, to make room for his body on the bed next to his cousin and collapse.

"I guess I overstayed. Sorry. How about if I see if I can do better with the second half of his orders."

The nurse nodded. "Your father is waiting to see that you do just that."

"Your *dad?*"

Jack grinned at his cousin's sleepy, but undeniably curious expression. "Yeah. It's been an interesting couple of

weeks. If you promise to be a good little cousin, I'll come
back tomorrow and fill you in."

With that, he turned and left the room. As the nurse had
said, his father was waiting, leaning against the counter at
the nurse's station. He straightened as Jack approached.

"I've decided you need something stronger than the
cafeteria here can provide. Like maybe a thick, juicy steak.
You name the place."

Jack nodded and suggested a restaurant in Mill Valley
located halfway between the hospital in San Anselmo and
the cabin at the beach. He hadn't the time or energy to
move back to his apartment. The way he was feeling now,
that chore would have to wait a bit longer. Weariness
dragged at his body as they rode the elevator to the ground
floor, such a bone-deep tiredness that he was tempted to
forgo the meal and just speed home to his bed.

As if he was likely to rest there.

He'd been back to the beach several times since the
shooting, to shower and change into fresh clothes. Each
time he'd been there for no more than an hour, just long
enough to notice the silence, the emptiness.

Entering his front door, with his mind on his cousin, he
would find that he'd half expect Libby to be curled up on
his sofa, waiting for him. In the bathroom, he'd catch
himself turning quickly, imagining that he'd caught a
glimpse of her pale, slender body bathing in the tub.
Walking past the kitchen, he'd see a shadow out of the
corner of his eye, and think for one moment that he could
walk in, trap Libby's body against the sink and kiss away
the pain he'd caused by leaving her.

Always he'd remind himself that he had nothing to offer
her, only self-pity and a life with no future.

The last time he'd been at the cabin, he'd stared at the
photos of his family, recalling Libby's wistful gaze as she
asked about the rambunctious group he'd grown up with.
One at a time during the last two weeks, his brothers and
sisters had come to the hospital, just to be with him, to let

him feel their silent support for him and their cousin, until he'd found himself longing for the old noisy times, feeling that all that time alone hadn't been as conducive to healing as he thought.

"We'll make it a quick dinner, son." His father's words cut into Jack's thoughts as they neared his car. "Then you can get home and get the sleep you so obviously need."

Jack nodded absently. During his brief visits to the cabin, the bed on the raised platform had called to him, beckoning his tired body. But each time he'd been tempted to climb the ladder and collapse, he'd warned himself that up there Libby's ghost would be its most active, that he would sleep better on the hard chair in Matt's room than he would up in that too-empty loft.

Now he would have no choice. He no longer had an excuse for his bedside vigil. He would be forced to return to the cabin, face the ghost of the woman he had forcibly evicted from his life and see if he could exorcise her memory, as well.

Chapter 16

Libby propped the screen door open as she stepped out the front door. From the rear of her Datsun pickup, she slid a five-foot roll of rug, muscled it into her living room and plopped it onto the oak floor.

A pattern of dark navy blue and cream scrolled across a maroon background as she unrolled it in front of the dark blue velvet settee. After smoothing the tangled cream-colored fringe on the far edge, Libby rose to survey this new addition to her furnishings.

It was perfect. Well, as perfect as a twenty-year-old rug could be. One corner had a faded patch, where it had sat in the sun, most likely. But an end table, or a basket holding magazines would cover that.

A sigh passed Libby's lips as she gazed around the sparsely furnished room. So many of the things she'd loved were still conspicuous by their absence. But the area seemed larger now, with space to breathe. And new things would continue to come into her life, like the overstuffed brown chair she had seen sitting in the window of the secondhand store the other day.

She shouldn't have bought it, of course. It looked far too much like a certain chair in a certain seaside cabin. Her life was not about the past, she'd admonished herself, it was about the future, about getting on with it. But that didn't mean she had to avoid reminders of the good times, even if pain *was* mixed in with those memories.

"Looks like you're getting things back to normal."

The voice made Libby jump. Not just the suddenness of it, coming out of the silence behind her, but the familiar, low notes. She turned, her heart racing, to look into the dark green eyes of the man leaning against the jamb of her front door.

"Jack."

She could barely say his name. Odd, because she had so much she wanted to say to this man, so many questions she wanted to ask. How was he doing? How was Matt coming along? And more important, why had Jack shown up here now, after nearly six weeks of silence, just when she'd finally gotten used to the idea that she would never see him again?

"Looks like you've been busy."

Busy? Libby almost laughed. She hadn't given herself a moment's rest since she'd brought her tears to a shuddering end that Saturday when he'd driven out of her life. She had forced herself to keep moving, pushed herself to reclaim as much of her former life as she could, in order to forget the interlude with Jack, relegate it to the status of bittersweet dream.

She couldn't say that, though. She had to find something else to talk about, something that she could say without revealing the ache twisting through her heart as she stared at the masculine form dressed in denim, leaning against her doorjamb.

"Yes, I've been on the go quite a bit," she managed to say. "I was able to purchase back my camera equipment from the man who bought it at the garage sale. He made a profit, of course, but it meant that I was able to set up shop again. Thanks, by the way, for sending my things to me."

The box Semosa had dropped off had held her duffel full of clothes along with the backpack containing the camera equipment she'd taken with her to the cabin. The roll of film she'd shot that last morning, various views of the sunrise and the picture of her and Jack on the porch had been missing. Just as well, she'd figured. Less things to remind her of her loss.

And now Jack was here, in her living room, in the light of day. It was no dream, no fantasy, no will-o'-the-wisp imaginary vision. And this made no sense at all.

"Will the trial be starting soon?"

Libby knew the answer to this, but it was the first question that had come to mind.

"Three more weeks, I'm told. Adam will probably get off pretty easily, though."

"But he shot you. You're a cop. Well, you were at the time."

Libby held her breath. Jack seemed to pay no attention to her reminder of his lost career as he shrugged.

"What can I tell you? Adam has retained a very competent attorney. He claims that he was blackmailed into helping Trousedale, and Sheila backs her father up, claiming Trousedale used her to control her father. They make quite a pair."

Libby assumed Jack meant father and daughter, since he had spoken in the present. It occurred to her that with Trousedale dead, Adam and Sheila had a good chance of convincing a jury that only such dire circumstances would induce an upstanding citizen like Adam Monroe to become involved in such an unsavory mess.

And she found she really didn't care, except to think that *someone* should have to face punishment for all the lives that had been ruined. But there was nothing she could do about it. She at least had her life back—a life that seemed more empty than she recalled, despite her busy schedule. She got the feeling that Jack didn't care about the outcome of the trial, either. The noncommital expression in his eyes made her wonder if he cared about anything at all anymore.

"How's Matt?"

"How're things with your mother?"

They finished their questions simultaneously, then stared at each other. Silence echoed in the room until Libby swallowed, and forced herself to answer.

"It's been rather odd, something of a roller-coaster ride for both of us. We'll be going along okay, then I find myself getting angry or she becomes defensive, and we both end up bickering, or crying. Or both."

Libby could have said so much more. She could have told Jack how her mother had taken on an accelerated course of study at an out-of-state university, which gave her no time off for visits, even if she'd had the money to travel back to California. During a very acrimonious visit to Aunt Susan, Libby had heard with her own ears proof that her aunt and uncle had purposely kept back the letters that Cathy had sent to her daughter.

When Cathy returned for her daughter, teaching degree in hand, Susan had convinced Cathy that Libby hated her mother for "abandoning" her, and that ripping Libby away from the "happy" family they provided would not only be cruel, but would most likely leave a permanent scar on her daughter's tender psyche.

But Libby couldn't tell these things to Jack because she was never sure from moment to moment how she felt about all of this. Her reaction to the story still ran from acceptance to doubt-filled rage.

She believed her mother. The pain, the anguish and the contrition that the woman felt shone clearly in Cathy Wilkinson's eyes and echoed softly in the woman's voice each time she tried to explain how she had come to believe that Libby wanted nothing to do with her. Libby didn't doubt that her aunt and uncle had painted a picture of a cozy family life. They had a picture-perfect house, and Libby *had* always been provided with the nicest of clothes.

No one knew about the hours that Libby had been forced to spend cleaning that house so her uncle could entertain important clients, the dances and sporting events Libby had missed attending because she was needed to watch her younger cousins while her aunt and uncle went out on "business" dinners.

The worst of it, though, had been the way these two people had constantly reminded Libby that they had "rescued" her from poverty, that she'd sprung from the womb of a sinner, and that it was imperative that Libby be evervigilant, lest she fall into her mother's evil ways.

The scars from years of feeling unworthy and unwanted had formed a deep chasm between Libby and her mother. However, somewhere between Libby's anger that the woman hadn't fought harder against her sister, and her mother's feelings of guilt, lay a shared sorrow for the years they'd missed. That middle ground had become a healing space, where the two of them had begun to build a relationship based on a shared love of beauty and art, where old pains faded as they discovered that neither of them could read a map, and they were both addicted to Häagen Dazs Deep Chocolate Peanut Butter Ice Cream.

But this was not a story she wanted to burden Jack with.

"So," she said. "Tell me about Matt." *And you,* she wanted to add.

Libby longed to ask Jack about his life. Had he returned to therapy for the new wound to his arm? Had he given any more thought to a different career? But she was afraid. His features were set, his eyes dark beneath a slight frown. Whatever emotion he was feeling was very close to the surface, and he was fighting to keep it hidden. To coax it forth might send him out of her house in the blink of an eye. As torturous as it was to be so close to him and not run to his arms, not pull his solid body to hers, it would hurt far more to have him turn and walk away again.

"Matt's had a rough time of it," he said at last.

"I'm sorry. Sergeant Semosa told me about the complication with the blow to his head. I called the hospital several times, but they wouldn't tell me anything. I finally called Semosa again, and he told me that Matt had regained consciousness and was on the road to recovery."

Jack gave her a brief nod. "He's in therapy for his leg now. His knee snapped completely when he fell."

"Oh. I'm sorry. The papers didn't mention . . ."

She let her voice trail off as Jack shook his head. "The hospital helped us keep his condition quiet. Matt was upset with the high-profile attention that's been given to his injuries. He wants to be left alone while he heals."

Just like someone else Libby knew.

Libby stilled as a shiver chilled her arms. Here it was. The heart of the pain she saw hidden in Jack's eyes, the pain that had made him walk out of her life six weeks earlier. She couldn't tell whether the wound had begun to heal, or if it was still too tender for her to touch. But she couldn't just stand there and let the echo of it make the gulf between them larger.

"That must be hard for him to deal with."

A tight smile lifted one corner of Jack's mouth. "There's at least a dozen pins in the bones, but he's got his cast off and is working with a therapist several times a day."

"I see. Well, they do a great job with that sort of thing these days. He'll be walking again soon, I'm sure."

"Yeah. He'll be in good enough shape to do most of the things he likes. As long as it doesn't require much in the way of speed."

Like chasing bad guys.

The words didn't have to be spoken for Libby to hear them. Loud and clear. Matt, too, would be facing a life behind a desk if he chose to stay on the police force. She knew without asking that Matt felt the same as his cousin about that prospect. And just looking at the scowl shadowing Jack's eyes told her how badly he felt about that.

"Well," she began, "at least Matt had you. You know, to—"

"To what?" The anger Libby had been fearing surfaced in a heartbeat. Jack shoved his shoulder from the doorjamb and stood filling the opening, eyes bright, features set, mouth pulled into a tight, straight line beneath his mustache.

"To help him deal with the fact that he'll never be quite right again?" He went on. "Some help *I've* been. I was still so busy wallowing in my own pain and self-blame that I failed to see that Matt was sinking. He's better at masking his feelings than I am, you see. Matt hides behind humor. I thought he was doing fine, that is, until he developed a staph infection. He didn't respond well to the antibiotics and it wasn't until he almost died that I realized he was giving up, that he was just going to let this take him out."

Jack clenched his jaw over his words, then stood silent, hands in his pockets, staring at the small window near the fireplace for several moments. Libby crossed her arms tightly, her heart twisting as she watched him blink several times. Finally, his eyes shifted to hers.

"I wasn't going to let the bastard die. If I couldn't get out that way, neither could he. Besides, I once knew someone who insisted that new dreams could be found just the other side of a nightmare. I decided it was worth a try. So I practically lived in Matt's room. I fought with him, cajoled, teased him unmercifully, until he had no choice but to come back and defend himself."

A strange, warm light came into Jack's eyes as he finished speaking. Libby met his bright gaze, her heart full of hope, her throat heavy with words, her body shaking with fear that this was all that Jack had come to say.

"I thought you should know," he said at last. "I also wanted to bring you these."

From the inner pocket of his denim jacket, Jack drew a thick envelope. When Libby opened it, she saw the developed prints of the pictures she'd shot at the beach before they'd left that safe haven for the last time.

She barely glanced at the first picture, a shot of the sun's rays haloing the hillside behind his cabin, before closing the flap. She couldn't look at the rest. Not now. Not with Jack watching her.

"Thanks," she said.

It sounded so final, that word. And why not? The reason behind his visit was now quite obvious. He'd come to tell her about Matt, to give her these pictures, to tie up the last of the loose ends before going on with his life.

"I've...uh...taken some pictures myself," he said slowly. "Would you like to see them?"

The soft, tentative note in Jack's voice brought Libby's head up quickly. He held another print in his hand. She took it, then frowned as she realized that the tall white Victorian building in the center of the picture was her house. On one side of the front yard, a piece of white paper had been cut in the shape of a sign and glued to the lawn section. The lettering on the sign said: DREAMSCAPES by Libby Stratton. On the other side of the walkway, a similar square stated: MAGNUM AND WESSON, Private Investigators.

"You're going into business together?" Libby asked as she lifted her eyes to Jack's. "You and Matt?"

He nodded. "It took a lot of arguing and battling, but we both came to the conclusion that neither of us had really wanted to play cops and robbers forever, that the thrill of gun battles hadn't been what drew us into law enforcement, anyway. We had wanted to catch the bad guys, to put them away."

Jack paused, took a deep breath, then went on, "Doing that takes more than chasing them down, it takes hard evidence. The police departments are all overworked and underbudgeted. Many cases that could be solved have to be dropped in favor of other more easily prosecuted ones. Matt and I can take up the slack. We have the investigating skills, the street sense and a wider latitude, now that we aren't tied into the force. The fact that we each limp a little might slow us down, but it won't keep us from doing what we love."

Libby managed a smile. *This* was what he'd come to tell her. It was wonderful, of course. She shouldn't feel sad, shouldn't wish that he had come on an errand with a more personal slant.

"That's great," she said softly. "I'm sure the two of you will be very successful. But about renting from me..." She glanced down at the photo, to the sign glued to her front lawn. "I'm not sure that local zoning laws will—"

"No."

Libby lifted her head to see Jack give his head a sharp shake before going on. "This wasn't meant as a request to rent office space from you. We've found a place in the city. I only made that picture to show you that I finally got the point of what you do with your dreamscapes."

Libby nodded, tried to smile. When she felt her lips begin to tremble, she dropped her gaze to the photo again and fought the blurring tears. That was it, just as she'd suspected. He wanted to thank her, then to move on.

"I have one more picture, however, that I would like you to look at and tell me if you think it has any possibilities."

Before Libby could raise her head to question these words, another picture was placed in her hands, covering the first one. Again, a photo of her house stared up at her. This time, two people stood on the porch, wrapped in a loose embrace, and smiling at the camera, her and Jack, images that had been cut from the photo she had taken of them on the cabin steps their last morning together.

Three more figures had been glued to the lawn in front of the house, three children. The first was a baby in a play-pen, the second a toddler bending over to pluck a flower and the third looked to be about age five, swinging from a tire that hung from the branches of the tree.

On the white picket fence, the shape of a mailbox had been affixed. Painted on its side were the words, The McDermotts.

Libby's hand shook as she stared at those two words, her heart gave two thuds and then began to race. She lifted her eyes to Jack's again and saw uncertainty, along with an openness to pain she'd never seen there before.

"My dreamscape is a little rough," he said. "I don't quite have the technique down right, but I was wondering if you—"

He stopped. Libby started to open her mouth, to tell him yes, whatever he was going to ask, yes. But she kept her mouth shut. She wanted to hear the words.

"If you would consider taking me under your wing," he went on at last, "as a full time apprentice of sorts. If you...would marry me."

The tears welled up again, filling Libby's eyes as emotion welled up within her chest. The words she wanted to say couldn't get past the love lodged in her throat. She saw fear and hope in Jack's eyes, knew that her silence must be prolonging his agony. So she nodded once. Before she could nod again, Jack had her in his arms, crushing her to him.

"I love you, Libby." Jack's gruff voice whispered before their lips met in a hungry, frantic kiss.

The kiss ended just before Libby ran out of breath. Tucking her head beneath Jack's chin, she rested her ear on his chest and hugged him to her. She could hear his heart beating, feel the rush of joy that matched her own. She smiled at the sound even as she raised her eyes to his once more, parting her lips as his mouth captured hers, and sighed her love into their kiss.

* * * * *

COMING NEXT MONTH

#643 ANOTHER MAN'S WIFE—Dallas Schulze
Heartbreakers/A Family Circle

Gage Walker knew the value of friendship—enough to have taken responsibility for his best buddy's widow and young son. But his sense of duty had *never* included marriage—or fatherhood. Then he learned that Kelsey had a baby on the way—*his!*

#644 IAIN ROSS'S WOMAN—Emilie Richards
The Men of Midnight

Iain Ross had no idea that the woman he'd saved from drowning was the embodiment of his own destruction. Feisty Billie Harper seemed harmless—and charming—enough, but an age-old curse had rendered her his sworn enemy. But Iain was powerless to resist her—and their destiny....

#645 THE WEDDING VENTURE—Nikki Benjamin

Laura Burke would never give up her son. Timmy was hers, and no mob kingpin would take him away—even if he was the child's grandfather. Desperate, she turned to Devlin Gray, a man shrouded in mystery. Then she learned that Devlin's idea of protection involved trading danger for wedding vows.

#646 THE ONLY WAY OUT—Susan Mallery

Andie Cochran was on the run, struggling to bring herself and her young son to safety. Yet Jeff Markum was the only man she could trust—and the one man who had every reason to hate her.

#647 NOT WITHOUT RISK—Suzanne Brockmann

Emily Marshall had never dreamed of seeing police detective Jim Keegan ever again. He'd dumped her years earlier without warning—or explanation—and now he was masquerading as her "brother" to catch a drug smuggler. But the feelings that stirred between them were anything but familial.

#648 FOR MERCY'S SAKE—Nancy Gideon

Sheriff Spencer Halloway knew a person in hiding when he saw one, and Mercy Pomeroy was one woman who didn't want to be found. He couldn't figure out what a classy lady and her cute daughter could possibly fear, but he would move the heavens to find out....

Kathleen Creighton's

RITA Award-winning author Kathleen Creighton brings Midwest charm to the Intimate Moments lineup in her ongoing miniseries, "Into the Heartland." A WANTED MAN, IM #547, introduced Lucy Brown to readers in February 1994. Now meet Lucy's brother, Wood Brown, in ONE GOOD MAN, IM #639, coming your way in May 1995.

Wood Brown had been to hell and back. And no one knew his pain better than physical therapist Christine Thurmond. But as she healed his battered body and soul, she yearned for some loving all her own. And only one good man would do....

The Browns—one sister, two brothers. Tragedy changed their family forever, but never their spirit—or their love for the heartland. Look for Rhett Brown's story in 1996 and venture once again "Into the Heartland"—*because sometimes there's no place like home*—only in

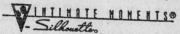

Silhouette celebrates motherhood in May with...

Debbie Macomber
Jill Marie Landis
Gina Ferris Wilkins

in

Three Mothers & a Cradle

Join three award-winning authors in this beautiful collection you'll treasure forever. The same antique, hand-crafted cradle connects these three heartwarming romances, which celebrate the joys and excitement of motherhood. Makes the perfect gift for yourself or a loved one!

A special celebration of love,

Only from

Silhouette®

—where passion lives.

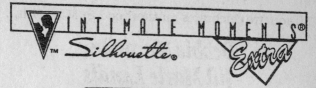

INTIMATE MOMENTS ®
™ Silhouette ® *Extra*

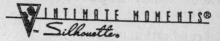

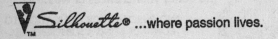

ANNOUNCING THE

FLYAWAY VACATION SWEEPSTAKES!

This month's destination:

Beautiful SAN FRANCISCO!

This month, as a special surprise, we're offering an exciting FREE VACATION!

Think how much fun it would be to visit San Francisco "on us"! You could ride cable cars, visit Chinatown, see the Golden Gate Bridge and dine in some of the finest restaurants in America!

The facing page contains two Entry Coupons (as does every book you received this shipment). Complete and return *all* the entry coupons; **the more times you enter, the better your chances of winning!**

Then keep your fingers crossed, because you'll find out by June 15, 1995 if you're the winner! If you are, here's what you'll get:

- Round-trip airfare for two to beautiful San Francisco!
- 4 days/3 nights at a first-class hotel!
- $500.00 pocket money for meals and sightseeing!

Remember: The more times you enter, the better your chances of winning!*

*NO PURCHASE OR OBLIGATION TO CONTINUE BEING A SUBSCRIBER NECESSARY TO ENTER. SEE REVERSE SIDE OR ANY ENTRY COUPON FOR ALTERNATIVE MEANS OF ENTRY.

VSF KAL

FLYAWAY VACATION
SWEEPSTAKES

OFFICIAL ENTRY COUPON

This entry must be received by: MAY 30, 1995
This month's winner will be notified by: JUNE 15, 1995
Trip must be taken between: JULY 30, 1995-JULY 30, 1996

YES, I want to win the San Francisco vacation for two. I understand the prize includes round-trip airfare, first-class hotel and $500.00 spending money. Please let me know if I'm the winner!

Name_____

Address _____ Apt. _____

City   State/Prov.   Zip/Postal Code

Account #_____

Return entry with invoice in reply envelope.

© 1995 HARLEQUIN ENTERPRISES LTD.   CSF KAL

OFFICIAL RULES

FLYAWAY VACATION SWEEPSTAKES 3449

NO PURCHASE OR OBLIGATION NECESSARY

Three Harlequin Reader Service 1995 shipments will contain respectively, coupons for entry into three different prize drawings, one for a trip for two to San Francisco, another for a trip for two to Las Vegas and the third for a trip for two to Orlando, Florida. To enter any drawing using an Entry Coupon, simply complete and mail according to directions.

There is no obligation to continue using the Reader Service to enter and be eligible for any prize drawing. You may also enter any drawing by hand printing the words "Flyaway Vacation," your name and address on a 3"x5" card and the destination of the prize you wish that entry to be considered for (i.e., San Francisco trip, Las Vegas trip or Orlando trip). Send your 3"x5" entries via first-class mail (limit: one entry per envelope) to: Flyaway Vacation Sweepstakes 3449, c/o Prize Destination you wish that entry to be considered for, P.O. Box 1315, Buffalo, NY 14269-1315, USA or P.O. Box 610, Fort Erie, Ontario L2A 5X3, Canada.

To be eligible for the San Francisco trip, entries must be received by 5/30/95; for the Las Vegas trip, 7/30/95; and for the Orlando trip, 9/30/95.

Winners will be determined in random drawings conducted under the supervision of D.L. Blair, Inc., an independent judging organization whose decisions are final, from among all eligible entries received for that drawing. San Francisco trip prize includes round-trip airfare for two, 4-day/3-night weekend accommodations at a first-class hotel, and $500 in cash (trip must be taken between 7/30/95—7/30/96, approximate prize value—$3,500); Las Vegas trip prize includes round-trip airfare for two, 4-day/3-night weekend accommodations at a first-class hotel, and $500 in cash (trip must be taken between 9/30/95—9/30/96, approximate prize value—$3,500); Orlando trip includes round-trip airfare for two, 4-day/3-night weekend accommodations at a first-class hotel, and $500 in cash (trip must be taken between 11/30/95—11/30/96, approximate prize value—$3,500). All travelers must sign and return a Release of Liability prior to travel. Hotel accommodations and flights are subject to accommodation and schedule availability. Sweepstakes open to residents of the U.S. (except Puerto Rico) and Canada, 18 years of age or older. Employees and immediate family members of Harlequin Enterprises, Ltd., D.L. Blair, Inc., their affiliates, subsidiaries and all other agencies, entities and persons connected with the use, marketing or conduct of this sweepstakes are not eligible. Odds of winning a prize are dependent upon the number of eligible entries received for that drawing. Prize drawing and winner notification for each drawing will occur no later than 15 days after deadline for entry eligibility for that drawing. Limit: one prize to an individual, family or organization. All applicable laws and regulations apply. Sweepstakes offer void wherever prohibited by law. Any litigation within the province of Quebec respecting the conduct and awarding of the prizes in this sweepstakes must be submitted to the Regies des loteries et Courses du Quebec. In order to win a prize, residents of Canada will be required to correctly answer a time-limited arithmetical skill-testing question. Value of prizes are in U.S. currency.

Winners will be obligated to sign and return an Affidavit of Eligibility within 30 days of notification. In the event of noncompliance within this time period, prize may not be awarded. If any prize or prize notification is returned as undeliverable, that prize will not be awarded. By acceptance of a prize, winner consents to use of his/her name, photograph or other likeness for purposes of advertising, trade and promotion on behalf of Harlequin Enterprises, Ltd., without further compensation, unless prohibited by law.

For the names of prizewinners (available after 12/31/95), send a self-addressed, stamped envelope to: Flyaway Vacation Sweepstakes 3449 Winners, P.O. Box 4200, Blair, NE 68009.

RVC KAL